FIXED ON YOU

FIXED TRILOGY #1

LAURELIN
PAIGE

This is a work of fiction. Names, characters, places and incidents
either are the product of the author's imagination or are used
fictitiously. Any resemblance to actual persons, living or dead, events
or locales is entirely coincidental.

First edition May 2013. ISBN: 978-1-942835-56-1

The following story contains mature themes, strong language, and
sexual situations. It is intended for adult readers.

FIXED ON YOU

FIXED TRILOGY #1

CHAPTER ONE

I felt alive.

The alternating flashes of dark and soft lights, the throbbing pulse from an Ellie Goulding club mix, the movement of sweaty bodies dancing, grinding, enjoying each other—The Sky Launch Nightclub got into my blood and turned me on in a way that I hadn't let anyone or anything else do in quite some time. When I was there—working the bar, assisting the wait staff, attending to the DJs—I felt more free than at any other time of my day. The club held magic.

And, for me, healing.

For all its vibrancy and life, the club was a safe haven for me. It was a place I could attach myself without worry of going overboard. No one was going to sue me for focusing too hard or long on my job. But rumor was The Sky Launch, which had been up for sale for quite some time, was about to be sold. A new owner could change everything.

"Laynie." Sasha, the waitress working the upper floor, pulled me from my thoughts and back to my job. "I need a vodka tonic, a White Russian, and two Butterballs."

"Got it." I pulled the vodka from the shelf behind me.

"I can't believe how busy we are for a Thursday," she said as I worked on her order.

"It's the summer crowd. Give it a week, and the place will explode." I couldn't wait. Summer at the club was a total blast.

"That's when things around here get fun." David Lindt, the club manager, joined our conversation, a sparkle showing in his eyes as the bright white light that lit the bar illuminated his face.

"Real fun." I gave David a wide smile and winked while I placed the drinks on Sasha's tray, my stomach tensing with a flicker of desire.

He answered my wink with one of his own, stirring the flicker in my belly to a low flame.

David wasn't the love of my life—not even the love of the moment—but his shared passion for the club sparked something in me. My interest in learning more and moving up from bartending had seemed to interest him as well. More than one late night of showing me the ropes had ended in heavy make-out sessions. Though I hadn't been instantly attracted to him, his small stature, curly blonde hair and blue eyes had grown on me. Also, his keen business sense and exceptional management style were qualities I required in a man. And, truthfully, the lack of effect he had on my emotions provided half the draw. We had decent chemistry, but he didn't have me freaking out all over him like I had over other guys. He was safe and solid and that was my definition of the perfect man.

I rang up Sasha's order while David filled shot glasses—Todd's order, I suspected, another waiter standing next to Sasha. David rarely stepped behind the bar anymore, but we were short-staffed for the night and I welcomed his help. Especially with the way we were picking up. A regular and his friends had leaned against the bar waiting for my attention, and out of the corner of my eye, I saw a suit taking a spot at the far end of the counter.

I handed Sasha her ticket, but David stopped her before she could take off. "Hold on. While there's at least a few of us here, I think we should toast to Laynie." He passed around the shots he'd been filling. Tequila—my liquor of choice.

I peered at him suspiciously. While it wasn't unusual to have a shot or two while working a shift, it was always kept on the down-low, never in front of our manager and certainly not at his encouragement.

"No worries," David said, bumping my shoulder with his. "It's a special occasion."

With a shrug, I smiled and took the shot he offered me. "You're the boss."

"We're too busy for a proper toast, so let's just say this is to Laynie. We're proud of you, girl."

I blushed and clinked glasses as everyone around, including the regular customer and his friends, shouted out "hear, hear" and "cheers".

"Woo hoo!" I screamed my own excitement. I'd worked hard to get my degree. I was proud of myself too. I slammed the shot back, enjoying the burn as it lined my throat and spread through my veins. "Goddamn, that's nice!"

Aware that the crowd was getting antsy, Sasha took off with her order while David filled Todd's. I turned my attention first to the regular, a guy whose name deserted me. He leaned in to give me a hug, which I returned. I might not remember him, but I knew how to earn my tips.

"Four of whatever's on tap," he said, raising his voice over the music which seemed to have gotten louder in the last few minutes. "Where's Liesl?"

I handed him his first two mugs and began work on the next two. "Since she's covering all my shifts next week she has tonight off." That's right—this was the guy that usually flirted with Liesl, another bartender.

"That's cool. So what are you doing on your vacation?" With Liesl not around, Regular turned his charm on me. His eyes travelled to my breasts that were admittedly hard to miss. Especially with my low-cut neckline. I had some nice girls, who could blame me for showing them off?

"Absolutely nothing." I hoped my delivery sounded like I was looking forward to my vacation. Truth was I'd taken the time off so I could go home and spend time with my older brother. But only that morning, Brian had called the trip off, saying that he was too swamped with work. He wouldn't even be able to make it to my graduation.

I swallowed the emotions that threatened to show on my face. On top of being disappointed, I was terrified. Me with nothing to occupy my time was not an attractive me. I'd almost told David several times to go ahead and put me on the schedule, but every time I started, I felt like a total loser. Maybe a week off would be good for me. I could handle it. Right?

Now wasn't the time to fret about the week to come. I finished the transaction with Regular and slid down the bar to take care of the suit at the end of the counter.

"Now what can I get...you...?" My words trailed off as my eyes met the suit's, the air leaving my lungs, suddenly sucked out by the sight that met me. The man...he was...*gorgeous.*

Incredibly gorgeous.

I couldn't look away, his appearance magnetizing. Which meant he was exactly the type of man I should avoid.

After the numerous heartaches that had dotted my past, I'd discovered that I could divide the men I was attracted to into two categories. The first category could be described as fuck and forget. These were the men that got me going in the bedroom, but were easy to leave behind if necessary. It was the only group I bothered with anymore. They were the safe ones. David fell into this category.

Then there were the men that were anything but safe. They weren't fuck and forget—they were, "Oh, fuck!" They drew me to them so intensely that I became consumed by them, absolutely focused on everything they did, said, and were. I ran from these men, far and fast.

Two seconds after locking eyes with this man, I knew I should be running.

He seemed familiar—he must have been in the club before. But if he had been, I couldn't imagine that I'd have forgotten. He was the most breathtaking man on the planet—his chiseled cheekbones and strong jaw sat beneath perfectly floppy brown hair and the most intense gray eyes I'd ever seen. His five o'clock shadow made my skin itch, yearning to feel the burn of it against my face—against my inner thighs. From what I could see, his expensive three-piece navy suit was fitted and of excellent taste. And his smell—a distinct fragrance of unscented soap and aftershave and pure male goodness—nearly had me sniffing at the air in front of him like a dog in heat.

But it wasn't just his incomparable beauty and exquisite display of male sex that had me burning between my legs and searching for the nearest exit. It was how he looked at me, in a way that no man had ever looked at me, a hungry possessiveness present in his stare as if he not only had undressed me in his mind, but had claimed me to be sated by no one ever again except him.

I wanted him instantly, a prickle of fixation taking root in my belly—an old familiar feeling. But that I desired him didn't matter. The expression on his face said that he would have me whether I wanted it or not, that it was as inevitable as if it had already happened.

It scared the hell out of me. The hair on my skin stood up as witness to my fear.

Or perhaps it rose in delight.

Oh, fuck.

"Single-malt Scotch. Neat, please."

I'd almost forgotten I was supposed to be serving him. And the idea of serving him seemed so sexy, that when he reminded me of my job, I nearly fell over myself to get his drink. "I have a 12-year-old Macallan."

"Fine." It was all he said, but the delivery in his low, thick voice had my pulse fluttering.

As I handed him his Scotch, his fingers brushed mine and I shivered. Visibly. His eyebrows rose ever so slightly at my reaction, as if he were pleased.

I jerked my hand back, tucking it against the bodice of my sheath dress as if the fabric could erase the warmth that had already traveled from where he'd touched me to the needy core between my legs.

I never brushed fingers with customers—why had I done that?

Because I couldn't *not* touch him. I was so drawn to him, so eager for something I couldn't name that I'd take whatever contact I could get. *Not this again. Not now.*

Not ever.

I moved away from him. Far and fast. Well, as far as I could get, curling into the opposite corner of the bar. David could serve the guy if he wanted anything else. I needed to be nowhere near him.

And then, as if on cue in the bad luck life I led, Sasha returned. "David, that group in Bubble Five is harassing the waitress again."

"On it." He turned to me. "You can handle it for a minute?"

"I so got this." I so didn't have it. Not with Mr. Draw-Laynie-To-Me-Whatever-The-Cost-To-Her-Sanity sitting at the end of the bar.

But my declaration was convincing. David slipped out from behind the counter, leaving me alone with the suit. Even Regular and his friends had joined a group of giggly girls at a nearby table. I scanned the dance floor hoping I could attract customers by glaring at the sea of faces. I needed drink orders. Otherwise, Suit might think I was avoiding him by hiding in my corner, which, of course, I was. But, honestly, the distance between us did nothing to dim the tight ball of desire rolling around in my stomach. It was pointless avoidance.

I sighed and wiped down the counter in front of me, though it didn't seem to need it, just to keep myself occupied. When I braved a glance over at the hottie who had invaded my space, I noticed his Scotch was nearing empty.

I also noticed his eyes pinned on me. His penetrating gaze felt more than the typical stare of a customer trying to attract the bartender, but knowing I had a tendency to exaggerate the meanings of other people's actions, I dismissed the idea. Summoning my courage, I forced myself over to check on him.

Who am I kidding? No forcing was necessary. I glided to him as if he were pulling me with an invisible rope. "Another?"

"No, I'm good." He handed me a hundred. Of course. I'd been hoping he'd give me a credit card so I could glean his name.

No, no, I was not hoping for that. I did not care for his name. Nor did I notice that his left hand was absent of any ring. Or that he was still watching my every move as I took the cash he'd given me and rung his order into the register.

"Special occasion?" he asked.

I furrowed my brow then remembered he'd seen our toast. "Uh, yeah. My graduation. I walk tomorrow for my MBA."

His face lit up in honest admiration. "Congratulations. Here's to your every success." He raised his drink toward me and downed the final swallow.

"Thank you." I was transfixed on his mouth, his tongue darting out to clean the last drop of liquid off his lips. *Yum.*

When he set his glass down, I reached out my hand to give him his change, bracing myself for the thrill of contact that would inevitably happen when he took it from me.

But the contact never came. "Keep it."

"I can't." He'd given me a hundred. For one glass of Scotch. I couldn't take that.

"You can and you will." His commanding tone should have rankled me, but instead it got my juices flowing. "Consider it a graduation gift."

"Okay." His demeanor took away my will to argue. "Thanks." I turned to stuff the money into my tip jar on the back counter, pissed at myself for the effect this stranger had on me.

"Is this also a goodbye party?" His voice called from behind me, drawing me back to face him. "I don't imagine you'll be using your MBA to continue bartending."

Of course that's what a suit would assume. He was probably some business type that shared the opinion of my brother—there were jobs worth having and jobs for other people. Bartending was the latter.

But I loved bartending. More, I loved the club. I'd only started my graduate work because I needed more to do. Something to keep me "occupied" was what Brian had said when he offered to pay for my expenses beyond what my scholarship and financial aid covered.

It was a good decision—the right decision since it essentially stopped my life from spiraling out of control. For the past three years I'd thrown my life into school and the nightclub. Problem was that graduation took most of my preoccupation away. And now bogged down with student loans, I had to figure out how to make ends meet without having to leave The Sky Launch.

But I had a plan. I wanted a promotion. I'd been helping with supervisory duties for the last year, but had been unable to get an official title since managers had to work full-time. Now that school was over, I was available for more hours. David had been grooming me for the position. The only wrinkle in my trajectory could be a new owner. But I wasn't going to worry about that. Yet.

Explaining my intent to strangers was never easy, though. How wise was it to use an MBA from Stern for a career in nightclub management? Probably not wise at all. So I swallowed before answering the suit. "Actually, I'd like to move up here. I love the nightclub scene."

To my surprise, he nodded, his eyes shimmering as he sat forward into the bright white light of the bar. "It makes you alive."

"Exactly." I couldn't keep back my smile. How had he known?

"It shows."

Hot, rich, and in tune with me. He was precisely the kind of man that I could obsess over, and not in the healthy way.

"Laynie!" The shout of the Regular from earlier drew me away from the intense gray eyes of the stranger. "I'm out of here. Wanted to say congrats again and good luck. And, hey, here's my number. Give me a call sometime. I can help you occupy your week off."

"Thanks, uh," I read the name he'd written on the napkin he'd handed me, "Matt." I waited until he'd walked away before tossing it in the trash under the counter, catching the suit's eye as I did so.

"Do you do that with every number you receive?"

I paused. It wasn't like I hadn't hooked up with customers before, but never with regulars. That was a rule. I didn't want to see them again. Too much temptation to go crazy over them.

But I had no interest in having that conversation with the suit. And with his eyes constantly on me, I finally believed that my attraction to him wasn't one-sided. Not when he'd tipped me so generously. "Are you trying to figure out if I'd throw away your number?"

He laughed. "Maybe."

His reaction made me smile and made the moisture between my thighs thicken. He was fun to flirt with. Too bad I had to end it. I placed my hands on the counter and leaned toward him so he could hear me better over the music, trying not to delight in the searing look he gave my bosom as I did so. "I wouldn't throw yours away. I wouldn't take yours at all."

His eyes narrowed, but the laughter from earlier still danced in them. "Not your type?"

"Not necessarily." Pretending I wasn't attracted to him was futile. He had to be aware of my reaction to him.

"Why then?"

"Because you're looking for something temporary. Something fun to play with." I leaned even closer to deliver my punch line—the one that would deter even the horniest of men. "And I get attached." I stood back up to my full height so I could take in his reaction. "Now doesn't that just scare you shitless?"

I'd expected to see panic flash through his face. Instead, I saw a flicker of amusement. "You, Alayna Withers, do anything but scare me." But despite his words, he stood, buttoning his suit coat as he did. "Congratulations again. Quite an accomplishment."

I watched him for far too long as he walked away, more crestfallen about his abrupt departure than I wanted to admit.

It took me a good five minutes after he left to realize I'd never given him my name.

CHAPTER TWO

"Have you met the new owner yet?"

I glanced up from my clipboard at Liesl's backside as she studied the contents of the small fridge behind the bar, her cascading purple hair dancing with her movements. My brow furrowed. I hadn't forgotten about the new owner but had tried not to think about him, knowing I'd obsess.

Irritation at being reminded of him now filled my response. "When would I have met him?" I hadn't been at the nightclub since my graduation more than a week before.

Liesl closed the door to the fridge and shrugged. "I don't know. You could have stopped by or something."

She knew me too well. I'd stopped myself several times that past week from wandering over. It had been a battle, but I'd stayed away. "Nope. Actually, I spent most of the week at a spa near Poughkeepsie."

"Well, la di da!" Liesl raised a studded eyebrow. "Did you win the lotto when I wasn't looking?"

"Hardly. It was a gift from Brian." He hadn't bothered with a card, just an envelope containing the train ticket and voucher for the resort delivered to me by my doorman the morning of my graduation. It was thoughtful. And so very unlike my brother. Maybe it had been his wife's idea.

"How...nice." Liesl detested Brian and never bothered to hide it. One of the few people in my life who knew my history, she was fiercely loyal and always on my side. My brother, not so much. That automatically put them at odds.

"Don't sound so shitty. It *was* nice. I did a bunch of crap I'd never done before—horseback riding, rock climbing. Tons of spa treatments— feel my skin!" I held out my hand for her to feel. "My hands have never been this soft."

"You're not kidding. Baby smooth."

"It was good for me. Really. Exactly what I needed. Relaxing but still kept me preoccupied."

"Wow. Score one for Brian. Maybe he's finally growing up." Her voice lightened. "And how was your time not at the spa?"

Miserable. The five days at the spa had been perfect, but after the trip was over, I had to return to my real life, which meant an empty apartment and a mind that refused to stop working. "I'm glad to be back, if that's what you're asking. And I may have four or five files of new ideas for the club."

She laughed. "Hey, at least that's healthy obsessing."

I smiled sheepishly. "Healthyish." I searched for the Skyy Vodka that my report said should be on the shelf and marked its presence on my paper when I found it. There were benefits to an active mind. I always had perfect inventories and flawless presentations. It was in relating with people—men, to be precise—that obsessing had its disadvantage.

I leaned against the back counter and checked my watch. Fifteen minutes until opening. That meant fifteen more minutes before the lights went down and into club mode. The club with all the lights on made me vulnerable and bare and out-of-place. Even Liesl's sassy gossipy personality was muted as if someone had turned down her volume. We'd never have this conversation in club mode.

My eyes traveled across the bar, lingering on the spot the suit had sat in the last time I'd worked. It wasn't the first time I'd thought of him since that night. He'd known my name. Had he overheard it? Not my last name. He must have asked someone, although I hadn't seen him talking to anyone else. But maybe before I'd taken his order…I hadn't been paying attention to him. Maybe someone had told him then.

"Whatcha thinkin'?" Liesl cut through my thoughts, mimicking my lean against the counter.

I shrugged. She'd freak if I told her some random guy knew my name, assume that my safety was at risk. I, on the other hand, had distinct empathy for people who had the need to gather more information than they should. And I didn't want a lecture on would-be stalkers. I knew all about stalking.

But I could tell her other things about the mysterious stranger. "Last time I worked, this guy—" I paused, remembering how magnetically attractive the suit had been. "This incredibly hot guy, actually—gave me a hundred dollars for three fingers of Macallan. Told me to keep the change."

"And did he expect you to blow him after your shift?"

"No. I thought that was what he was about, but…" What had he wanted? He'd seemed so into me, or had I imagined that, swayed by my own intense desire for him? "I don't know. He left without trying anything." I'd meant to scare him off, but that hadn't seemed to be the reason he left. "It was…odd."

"Midnight masturbation material?"

"I'll never tell."

"Your face says it all."

Over the past week, he *had* entered my thoughts, wearing decidedly less than he had when I'd seen him at the bar. And while sexual fantasies were innocent enough for most people, thinking too much about any guy was never good for me and Liesl knew it. But I didn't need her lecture. As long as I didn't see him again—and chances were slim that I would—I'd be fine.

I moved to straightening things on the counter that didn't need to be straightened and changed the subject. "So the new owner…you've met him? What's he like?"

Liesl shrugged. "He's all right. Younger than you'd imagine. Like, twenty-seven or twenty-eight. Fucking rich. He's insane about clean-up, though. We've been calling him the Bar Nazi. He inspects everything, wiping his finger on the counters to make sure they're clean, like he's got OCD or something. Oh, and talk about masturbation material, he's psychotically hot."

Liesl thought any guy with a fat wallet who still had his hair was hot, so her statement didn't say much. But the Bar Nazi remark made me smile. The staff had been lax on cleaning standards for some time and could do with some tough love. At least, that's what I'd say if I were a manager. It gave me hope that the new owner and I might get along just fine.

I wondered about the man who finally ponied up the unreasonable asking price for the club. Not that The Sky Launch couldn't be worth it, but it needed some serious overhaul to stand out in the sea of New York City clubs. Would the new owner see the place's potential? How hands-on would he be? Would he leave the business under David's control?

"You'll meet him tonight." Liesl ran her barbell across her lower lip.

"I guess he's a big deal in the business world. You've probably heard of him—Houston Piers or something like that."

My jaw dropped. "Do you mean Hudson Pierce?" I waited while she nodded. "Liesl, Hudson Pierce is only the most successful business man under thirty in America. He's like a god in that world." Hudson had been born into wealth with modern day Rockefellers for parents. The eldest son, he'd expanded the Pierce wealth tenfold. As a business student I'd been intrigued with a number of his dealings.

"You know I'm not into all that Who's Who bullshit." Liesl straightened to her full five-foot-ten plus three-inch heels height. "Though I wouldn't be surprised if he's on the Top Ten of, like, every Hottest-slash-Sexiest-slash-Most-Beautiful list in the world."

I bit my lip trying to conjure up an image of him in my head. I'd probably seen a picture of him somewhere, but I couldn't for the life of me remember what he looked like. I generally didn't pay attention to those things. But something tugged at the edges of my brain, something I couldn't quite grasp. A connection my mind was failing to make.

"Anyway," Liesl said, leaning back against the counter, "I think he's around. I saw him go into the offices earlier when you were grabbing napkins from storage."

I nodded, not sure if I was thrilled to meet Hudson Pierce or not. Part of me wanted to fan girl all over one or two of his more famous corporate decisions. And bouncing ideas off of him could be thrilling.

Or terrifying. What if I had nothing to suggest that he hadn't already thought of? Hudson Pierce didn't need my lame ideas to help him make the club thrive.

Unless he wasn't planning to be involved with the business.

But why would he buy the club if he didn't intend on being involved? In which case...

Crap. Before my visions of the future I desired went poof in my overactive imagination, I needed to meet Pierce and feel him out, whether I was intimidated or not.

I took several inconspicuous calming breaths then returned my focus to stocking the bar. Concentrating on my task, I pulsed absentmindedly to the techno strains that streamed over the sound system and let go of all my worries.

The music wasn't on normal business volume—we could talk comfortably without raising our voices—but it was loud enough that I didn't hear the office door open to the left of the bar. That's why I didn't notice Hudson at first. My back was to him and my gaze fixed above me as I reached for the Tequila Gold on the upper bar shelf. Even after I'd retrieved the bottle and turned around, my eyes first found David's. He scanned me from head to toe and I smiled, pleased that my tightly fitted corset hadn't gone unnoticed. He was the reason I'd worn the damn thing. I could barely breathe under its vice-like grip. But for the searing look he gave me, it was worth it, heating me to low simmer in the arousal department.

Then I met Hudson's stare and two things happened simultaneously. First, my arousal went full boil. Second, my brain finally made the connection it had missed before. Hudson Pierce was the suit.

Without meaning to, I scanned his body. The full view of him was even hotter, especially in the better lighting. Again he wore a suit, two-piece this time, a light gray that I'd almost call silver. It fit his lean body in such a sexual way that it felt obscene to look at him.

When my eyes made it to his face—his strong jaw, even more pronounced than I'd remembered, begging to be licked and kissed and nibbled—I found he was checking me out as well. The knowledge of this made my already warm face flush deeper. Though his gaze wasn't as intense as it had been when I'd first met him, his pull was just as strong, and I knew—absolutely unequivocally *knew*—that he desired me as much as I desired him.

David spoke first, his words coming at me through a haze, barely registering. "This is Laynie." I suspected his eyes hadn't left my bosom. "Um, Alayna Withers, I mean." Normally I'd be ecstatic that I had him so mixed-up and that his pants were visibly straining, but I was thrown by the new owner. More precisely, by how insanely he affected me.

"Hudson Pierce." Hudson's smooth, low murmur had me clenching my thighs together, my panties pooling with moisture. And if I thought he'd claimed me with his eyes the night we'd met, the surge that ran through me as he shook my hand deepened his possession. Almost like an invisible handcuff reaching out to bind me to him permanently. "Good to meet you properly, Ms. Withers."

"Alayna," I corrected, surprised at the low ache in my voice. "Or Laynie."

He dropped my hand, but his touch lingered on my skin, in my veins. Pieces began to fit together. That was how he'd known my name.

He'd probably come that night to check out his would-be staff. But that didn't explain his possessive staring. Maybe he was the type to think of women as objects. Maybe he took the definition of *owner* to a whole other level. The thought made my skin pebble in goose bumps.

And underneath that, panic crept into my gut.

I could not be this twisted up over my boss, the head honcho, the guy who would determine my fate at the club. Freaking out over him would end in serious consequences.

I placed a hand loosely over my belly, encouraging a deep diaphragmatic breath to calm my growing anxiety.

Hudson tilted his head and studied me. "I've heard many things about you. And witnessed your work." He paused, moving his gaze up and down my body once more, scorching my skin as he did. "But none of what I heard or saw prepared me to find you wearing this ensemble."

The color drained from my face. I wasn't sure where he was going with his statement, but from his tone, I felt chided. "Excuse me?"

"I would think a graduate of Stern looking for a career in management would be more appropriately dressed."

As quickly as I paled before, now I flushed, equal parts embarrassed and enraged. Sure my top was revealing, but he hadn't seemed to mind when he ogled me only a moment before.

Or maybe his ogling had merely been wishful thinking.

Shit. I'd imagined it all, hadn't I? That whole knowing he desired me—god, how had I so completely misread him?

Even in my error, I couldn't take his criticism without responding. Whether Hudson owned other nightclubs or not, I had no clue, but he was certainly wrong about what acceptable attire was. Eye candy was expected at a club. Hot girls drove in customers. "What I'm wearing is quite appropriate for a club staff."

"Not for someone working toward manager."

"Yes, even managers. Sex sells, Mr. Pierce."

"Not at an elite club. Not at the kind of club I intend to run." His authoritative tone resonated through my head, but then he lowered his volume and the words resonated through my bones. "You must know that women have a difficult time in the business world. You need to work to be taken seriously, Alayna. Dress sexy, not like a floozy."

I clenched my jaw shut. Normally I'm the type to argue well past the point of winning or losing—I'd had several heated debates in more than one of my graduate classes—but now I found myself flustered and at a loss for words. Hudson was right. I had ideas for the club—ideas that required people to trust my business savvy. I'd learned at Stern what it took to impress people and, to my credit, I'd hesitated when I'd purchased the corset, wondering if the open middle that revealed my midriff from the insides of my breasts to my belly button was *too* revealing. His words validated that fear.

Worse, I realized that what I'd thought was desire was something so much different. He wasn't claiming me, he was judging me.

My stomach dropped. There went any chance at promotion. How could I have been so stupid? Dressing for a guy instead of my career? *Stupid, stupid, stupid!*

I looked to David and discovered he was equally petrified at the transaction. "Um, yeah, Laynie," he said, attempting to recover. "Is that new?"

It didn't matter what David said. The glimmer in his eyes told me he appreciated my outfit. But he was with his new boss. He had to keep it professional.

And truthfully, I cared more about Hudson's opinion at the moment than David's. David was a category one attraction, after all. The kind of guy I didn't emotionally invest in. Hudson, on the other hand, was…

No, I wouldn't think about him like that.

I ran my tongue across my dry lips. "It is new." I hoped I didn't sound as ashamed as I felt. "I apologize. I misjudged." I also sort of hated Hudson Pierce. Even though he was in the right. He was an asshole with wandering eyes, just like all the other suits I'd ever met.

"I've got that lace pullover in my locker," Liesl offered. "It should tame you."

"Thanks. I'll take it."

Liesl whispered in my ear as she brushed past me toward the staff break room. "Though, if you ask me, you look damn fine!"

"Now that that's taken care of…" Hudson turned his attention to David. "I've changed my mind about returning this weekend." David visibly relaxed. But Hudson's next statement had him stiffening again. "I'll be back tomorrow. I can't be here until nine. Could you spare time for me then?"

I fiddled with the napkin holders, even though I'd already stocked them, not sure if I was supposed to be part of the conversation or if I should get back to my duties.

"Of course," David said, even though nine was when the club opened and wasn't really a convenient time to have a meeting.

"Good." Hudson turned to me and I froze mid-napkin shuffle. "Alayna, you'll be here as well."

Still ruffled from my disastrous mistake, I was uneager to accept the invitation—the demand, rather. But I'd have to get over my rough start if I expected to continue working with him. Not even sure he expected a response, I gave one anyway. "Yes, sir."

Hudson narrowed his eyes, so I couldn't be certain, but they seemed to have dilated. He scrutinized me as if deciding something—whether to fire me, maybe, or give me another shot. After several painful seconds, he simply nodded. "Tomorrow." Then he turned to leave.

David and I watched in silence as Hudson walked toward the club doors. At least, I watched, too distracted by the hint of tight rear end under the bottom of his suit jacket to notice what David was doing. Damn, Hudson looked just as good from the rear as from the front. If he was going to be in the club a lot I was going to have to start wearing panty liners.

The minute Hudson's gorgeous backside disappeared into the entrance area, David let out a sigh, reminding me of his presence.

I stared at him, wide eyed. "What the fuck?"

David chuckled. "I have no idea. I've only met with Pierce once before today and we haven't gotten much into anything besides me explaining our current business operations. He's certainly odd, though."

"Well, what do you expect, growing up with all that wealth and pressure to succeed?" Why the hell was I defending him? The man made me feel anxious and intimidated and humiliated. And maybe a little bit excited. Oh, and horny as all get out. I wasn't even going to acknowledge the fixation I knew I would have on him if I didn't get myself under control.

I took a deep breath, hoping to release the strange knot in my stomach that thinking about Hudson created. "I don't know what I'm saying. I guess we'll just have to wait and see."

"Don't worry, Laynie."

Remembering he was the one I was almost sort of dating, I met David's blue eyes, straining to recapture the certainty that he was perfect for me.

Misinterpreting my anxiety to be about my job, he continued. "Pierce has too many high profile assets. He won't want to spend too much of his time on the club. I'm sure he'll let things run pretty much as is with maybe some minor finessing. And as long as I have a say in it, you'll have a more significant role."

David grinned, more at my chest than at my face. "Want to stay and help close tonight?"

His playful change of attitude provided the assurance I needed. "I was counting on it."

• • •

At four a.m. the club shut down for the night, and David and I worked quickly and efficiently, splitting the managerial duties between us. When all the drawers had been counted and the money dropped in the safe, he dismissed the rest of the staff and sat behind his desk to finish up the reports. I perched on the desktop and swung my feet as I watched him work.

David glanced over at me and smiled before returning to his monitor. "Thank god you were behind the counter earlier. Who knows what else Hudson would have said about your outfit if he'd seen those pants?"

I glanced down at the black slinky pants that were so tight they gave me camel toe. They made me feel sexy, and for some reason that made me think of Hudson's dark expression when he'd first laid eyes on me. The expression I'd since convinced myself was imagined.

"Great. Now you're telling me I have to throw these out too?"

"Well, just don't wear them while you're working." He stood so he could reach the printer on the corner of the desk behind me. "For the record," he said as his arm brushed my waist. "I don't disapprove of this outfit in the slightest."

I, on the other hand, wanted to burn the whole ensemble. It had caused me nothing but trouble all night—drunk patrons thinking they could touch me and say things to me that they otherwise wouldn't.

But I'd worn it for David—for the moment when we'd be alone. This was it.

I put on a fake pout. "Too bad your opinion isn't the one that matters."

David leaned in close. "My opinion doesn't matter?"

"Actually," I said, grabbing his jacket by the lapels, "your opinion matters very much."

His voice lowered. "Then I think you look sexy as hell."

He covered his mouth with mine, plunging his tongue deep inside. I wrapped my arms around his neck and darted my own tongue between his lips. The arousal that had been ignited by the heated stare of Hudson Pierce hours earlier had remained just at bay throughout the night. Now it returned full force with David's kiss.

I moved my hands along his torso and downward to his pants. But when I began to fumble with his buckle, he pulled away.

I opened my eyes and startled. For a moment I'd expected to see the gray eyes of Hudson staring back at me instead of David's dull blue. What was wrong with me? Man, that Hudson could mess with a girl's mojo.

David caressed my shoulder. "We need to stop this, Laynie."

I blinked. "What do you mean? Why?"

"Look, I like you. I really like you. But…" He appeared to be struggling with himself. He dropped his arm from my shoulder. "If you're serious about getting the management position, do you really think we should be messing around? How would that look? I'm sure that Pierce wouldn't approve."

I hadn't thought about it quite like that. In my fantasies, David Lindt and Alayna Withers-Lindt ran The Sky Launch as a couple, driving the club to new and unbelievable success. The fantasy had never included a part where the rest of the staff and the club owner accused me of sleeping my way to the top.

"We could keep it secret," I said softly, not willing to let go of a vital part of my dream. Not willing to lose my safety net.

"It doesn't have to be forever. But for now, especially when I'm not sure what Pierce's plans are for me or for the club. I think we need to take a break."

"Sure." I forced a smile. I didn't want him to realize the extent of my disappointment. We hadn't even been dating. We'd barely been fooling around. Why did I feel so crushed?

I thought about what had drawn me to David in the first place. He wasn't the smartest guy I knew and not the hottest. I didn't even really know him all that well. And it wasn't as if I didn't have other options. I was an attractive girl working at an elite nightclub—I'd had plenty of opportunities for sex in the city. Yummy opportunities. Not anyone as yummy as Hudson Pierce, but yummy nonetheless.

I shook my head as I hopped off David's desk. Why did my thoughts keep leading back to Hudson? Even in the middle of a sorta-not-at-all break-up, I was thinking of him. And Hudson was exactly the kind of guy I shouldn't be thinking about. At all. Ever. Not if I wanted to maintain the modicum of control I'd managed to acquire in the past few years.

"Are you okay, Laynie?" David's voice brought me back to the present awkwardness.

Damn it. I'd been so sure of a relationship with David that I'd pictured us sending Christmas cards together. Okay, maybe I'd fixated on him more than I wanted to admit, but not so intently that I was going to wig out about ending it. The biggest bitch of the whole situation was that now I didn't have a safe guy to hide behind. Now I was vulnerable to notice other not-so-safe men. Men like Hudson.

Oh, god, was this the beginning of an obsessive episode?

No, I'd be fine. I had to focus on my promotion. I was stronger than this.

"Yeah. I'm fine. If you're almost done, I'm going to get changed."

David nodded. I hurried to the staff break room across the hall. Stripping out of my corset and tight pants, I changed into sweat shorts and a sports bra, stuffing the troublesome outfit into my duffel bag. Since there wasn't a straight subway line from Columbus Circle to my apartment at Lexington and Fiftieth, I usually ran it. Sometimes after a long shift I'd take the bus or cab, but with all the stressors of the night, I needed the cardio to direct my focus.

Fifteen minutes later, I hit the pavement, taking in the fresh morning air with the rest of NYC's early morning joggers. I loved the feeling of unity it gave me, even though most of the other runners were starting their day, not ending it as I was.

Quickly, I got into my groove, running along the south border of Central Park, but the steady rhythm of my body wasn't enough to drown the thoughts of David and my future at The Sky Launch. Wasn't enough to drown my thoughts of the gorgeous new owner who had demanded I meet with him later that night. Worry set in again. Was Hudson planning to fire me? Or did I still have a shot at promotion?

One thing was certain—I'd be a lot more thoughtful about my choice of wardrobe in the future.

CHAPTER THREE

I took a cab to the club that evening, which had been a mistake. Unusual traffic had me arriving at three after nine. I hurried toward the office but was stopped at the upstairs bar by Liesl.

"David and hot owner boy are already in there," she said over the club music, playing with a strand of purple hair. "Hudson told me to have you wait here. He'll let you know when he wants you."

"Dammit! I'm not that late, am I?"

"No, they went in there about ten minutes ago. They have no idea what time you got here."

I relaxed, thankful that my exclusion from the meeting wasn't because I'd been tardy. I hopped onto a bar stool nearest the office and set my computer bag on the floor at my feet.

"Hold on, Laynie," Liesl said coming around the bar. "Let me see you."

I stood up again and turned around, displaying my bodycon dress. I'd picked it because the white tie color had a business style to it, but the tight black skirt said nightclub instead of office secretary.

"Fuck, girl, you look good!" Liesl's validation calmed me more than she could ever know. Or maybe she did know. She was a good friend.

"Thanks. I needed that. Especially after Mr. Disapproval last night."

"He is now known as the Bar and Wardrobe Nazi."

I laughed and hopped back onto my stool. The same stool Hudson had sat on the first time I saw him. "Hey, you know he's the suit I was telling you about, the one who gave me the hundred."

"You're shitting me!"

"I'm not. Do you think he wants me to blow him to get the promotion?"

"Would it be that bad if he did?"

"Yes. It would be utterly, wonderfully, horrible." But mostly it was horrible how not bad that idea sounded.

While trying to empty my mind of Hudson blowjob images, I surveyed the club. The place was slow, even for a Wednesday night. From the bar, I had full view of the ten bubble rooms that circled the perimeter of the upper level. The bubble rooms were The Sky Launch's highlight. Each room, round in shape, featured a glass wall overlooking the dance floor on the lower level, and had private access much like box seats at a stadium. They all had a curved seating area around a table, and fit eight people comfortably. The bubbles provided a relatively quiet and discreet area while still being very much part of the club. When the occupied lights were on, the outer walls of the bubble rooms glowed red. Only two were lit up. A shame. If the club had the kind of notoriety it could have, those rooms would fill within the first ten minutes of being open.

"God, I hope it picks up," Liesl said, draping her torso across the counter next to me. "I can't make it through a full shift at this pace. It's so boring!"

"I hope so, too." We should have been busting with the summer crowd by now. The lack of business made me feel more confident about my ideas for the club. I fidgeted, anxious to get in the office and share them with my bosses.

"What did you do today?" Liesl asked.

"I worked on a PowerPoint presentation all morning. I crashed about two."

Liesl narrowed her eyes. "You need more sleep than that, Laynie."

"Nah. Five hours is plenty." I actually felt pretty good. Gathering the best of my thoughts for The Sky Launch into a presentation had been very therapeutic, easing my concerns about my future at the club. Hudson couldn't fire me after he saw how much time and effort I'd put into the business, could he? Not if my ideas were good, and I knew they were.

I pulled my phone out of my bra cup where I kept it—no pockets in my skin-tight dress—and checked the time. It was almost nine-thirty. How long would they keep me waiting?

They walked out minutes later. I stood the moment I saw them, smoothing my dress down and looked to Hudson, eager for a sign of approval.

But the expression that met me took my breath away—an expression of total male power and dominance. Even in the dark of the club, I could make out his eyes as they perused me—the way he did every time we saw each other. Again I felt claimed by his overwhelming magnetism, my heart racing just at the sight of him. My legs turned to jelly and my knees buckled, tipping me forward.

Into his arms.

He caught me with a graceful ease that contradicted the solid body that held me steady. My hands clenched his dress shirt—how did my hands get under his jacket?—and I resisted the urge to run them across the firm pecs I felt under my grasp.

He mistook my motion, seeming to think I was searching for further stability. "Alayna," his voice flowed over me like liquid sex. "I've got you."

I've got you. Boy, did he.

"Laynie, are you okay?" David peered at me over Hudson's shoulder. Did he have to ask? Couldn't he see that I was drowning in lust?

"Yeah," I managed. "I'm, um, new shoes."

Hudson glanced down at my strappy rhinestone embellished sandals. "They're lovely." His voice came out so deep it rumbled and my belly knotted with the sound.

"Uh, thanks." I was breathless. And embarrassed when I realized I was still in Hudson's arms. I eased my grip and pushed myself into a standing position.

"Sorry we kept you waiting." Hudson's hands lingered on me until I was steady. "I had a few things to discuss with David privately."

"No problem." I still felt the burn of Hudson's hands on my bare skin. For distraction, I dove into business discussions. "I have so many ideas I'd like to share about the club. I put them into a presentation. I brought my laptop."

Hudson's lips curled with a hint of amusement. "How thoughtful. Set up a time with David. I'm sure he's very interested."

How thoughtful. As if I'd done something cute. Something only big boys did. How fucking patronizing.

My heart plummeted. I really shouldn't have been so disappointed. It wasn't as if I'd been asked to prepare anything. That had been my own hyper-focusing. In fact, I hadn't even known why I'd been invited to the meeting. Especially now that it was apparently over and I hadn't even been in on it.

"How about tomorrow, Laynie?" David suggested. "You're opening anyway. Why not come early? Does six-thirty give you enough time to present?"

"Yeah. I'll leave my laptop here if you don't mind." I bent to pick up my bag, but Hudson reached it before I did.

He handed it to David. "David, could you lock this in the office? I need to eat something. Alayna will join me. I've reserved one of the bubbles." His eyes narrowed as he surveyed the empty rooms. "Though it doesn't seem a reservation was required."

I tensed at Hudson's latest demand. Why wasn't David joining us? Did Hudson plan on firing me over pecan-crusted salmon? Was that what they had discussed privately?

Or maybe Hudson's interest in me was less business and more pleasure. The looks he'd given me had suggested it was, and after receiving the same expression on several occasions, I realized I may not have imagined it like I kept trying to convince myself I had.

And that was a scarier thought than being fired. Especially when I'd already felt a tug of fixation. I'd been so stable for the past three years—I couldn't open myself to get all obsessive over my hot boss. That was a disaster waiting to happen. I definitely should say no to the bubble room.

Except I hadn't given up on my promotion. And because there was a slight possibility that Hudson wanted to talk to me about that, I had to say yes to dinner, though my acquiescence hardly seemed necessary since he'd had his hand pressed against the small of my back directing me to one of the more private bubbles before I'd even agreed to join him. My body tensed under his touch, and my stomach twisted in a nervous knot that wasn't exactly unpleasant.

And I was very aware of the eyes that followed us, few as there were in the club, sure that many of them flashed with envy. Alone in a bubble room with Hudson Pierce? All the women in Manhattan should be jealous. Kinky things had been known to happen in those bubbles. I smiled at the possibilities.

Goddammit. What the hell was I thinking? The guy had invited me to dinner, not to his bed. Just because I was all gaga over him, reading sex into his every move, didn't mean he reciprocated. And the gaga needed to stop once and for all, even if he did reciprocate.

Inside the room, I turned on the occupied light out of habit. Usually a hostess would have done that when they seated the customer, but since we'd sort of skipped the whole hostess formality, I took it upon myself. And I had to do something with my nervous energy. Continuing the job, I grabbed a menu from the wall and handed it to Hudson who stood waiting at the edge of the seating.

He took the menu from me and gestured for me to sit. "After you."

It had been quite some time since I'd been in a bubble room off-duty and the reversal in my role combined with the "Fuck Me" aura that surrounded Hudson unbalanced me. I slid onto the plush cushion, gripping the table for support.

Hudson stayed standing, watching me intently for several seconds before he removed his gray suit jacket and hung it on the hook behind him. Damn. He was even hotter in only his fitted gray dress shirt. I bit the inside of my cheek, admiring his hard thighs straining against his pants' fabric as he sat down. God, he was so yummy.

God, I was in trouble.

He tossed the laminated menu on the table without looking at it. "I don't need this. Do you?"

"No, thank you, Mr. Pierce." I had the menu memorized. Besides, there was no way I could eat in his presence.

"Hudson," he corrected.

"No, thank you, *Hudson.*" His eyes widened slightly when I said his name. "I've already eaten."

"A drink then? Though, I know you work at eleven."

I licked my lips, thinking more about the man sitting across from me than of thirst, wondering what he had in store for me. "Maybe an iced tea."

"Good."

Out of habit, I reached to press the button in the middle of the table to summon the waitress, but he beat me to it, our fingers colliding. I moved to pull my hand away, but he was quicker again, taking my hand into his. I inhaled sharply at the sensation of his skin against mine.

"I didn't mean to startle you. I was admiring your soft skin." But his eyes never left mine.

"Oh." I thought about saying I'd been to an amazing spa, but really, did he care? And besides, talking was difficult with that thing he was doing to my skin, burning it so thoroughly with his caress.

His phone rang and he let go of my hand. I pulled it to my lap, needing the warmth of my body once it'd lost the warmth of his.

"Excuse me," he said, taking his phone out of his pants pocket and silencing it without looking at the screen.

"You can take it if you need to." I could use a few minutes to gather my thoughts. Because, what the hell did he want with me? Not only was not knowing killing me, but the more time I spent with Hudson, the easier it was for me to think about him and his amazing gray eyes. And his hard body. And his smooth voice.

"There can't be anything important enough to interrupt this conversation."

And even smoother lines.

I opened my mouth to say something, but was interrupted by the door opening. Sasha entered with a tray of food and drinks. I watched as she set down a plate of sea bass and a glass of Sancerre in front of Hudson and a glass of iced tea in front of me. Hudson must have preordered, but how did he know I'd get iced tea?

He must have sensed my question. "I asked Liesl what you usually drank. If you had said you wanted something different, I wouldn't look quite so cool at this moment."

That earned him a smile. Whatever his game was, he was working for it. "Hmm, cool is not quite the word I'd use for you." Hot, blazing, volcanic. All of those words were much more appropriate.

"What word would you use for me then?"

I blushed and delayed answering by taking a swallow of my tea.

Thankfully, Sasha spoke at that moment. "Anything else, Mr. Pierce?"

I raised my brow. Would he invite her to call him Hudson as well?

"We're good."

Nope. No first name basis for Sasha. Only me. Well, didn't that have liquid pooling between my thighs?

The door had just shut behind Sasha when Hudson asked again. "What word would you use for me, Alayna?"

The way my name sounded in his sensual voice brought goose bumps to my skin. "Controlled," I said, without hesitation.

"Interesting." He took a bite of his bass and I watched, hypnotized by the way his mouth curved around the fork. "Not that controlled isn't an accurate description of me. But I had thought from the look on your face that you would say something else."

I began to ask what he had expected me to say, but I wasn't certain I wanted to walk through that door he'd opened. He didn't press it, spending the next few minutes eating in silence.

Wanting to let him eat, I turned my body to look at the club below me. Even with my eyes averted, I felt Hudson's presence hanging on me like a cloak. I wondered about the man sitting across from me. Why had he bought The Sky Launch? What did he want from me? And the most intriguing question, how did I feel about this domineering male who bossed me and chastised me and made me want to climb on to his lap and rub against him like a kitten? Yeah, he was good-looking, but did I *like* him? Or was he just another rich pompous ass that I was inexplicably drawn to?

"I know why you agreed to dine with me, Alayna."

I turned back to face him and stilled, wondering where he was possibly going. First of all, I hadn't actually agreed to dine with him, if that's what this was. He'd sort of led me there. Secondly, many of the reasons I hadn't fought against coming with him would be embarrassing if he voiced them. They were numerous: to find out his plans for the club, to get a promotion, to make David jealous. To get in Hudson's pants.

No, not to get in his pants. That could not be on my list of reasons. Could. Not.

Hudson took a swallow of his wine, then wiped his perfectly formed lips with his napkin. "I have to be honest with you. I don't intend to help you with your desire to make management."

I fidgeted, not knowing if I should relax or be disappointed. On the one hand, that was probably the least humiliating reason he could have mentioned for me dining with him. On the other hand, there went my promotion.

"That doesn't mean you won't be promoted." Did Hudson have some sort of mind-reading capability? It would explain how he did so well in the business world. "David said you're quite capable, and I'm sure you'll get the position without my help. I may own The Sky Launch, but I am not your boss. David is your boss and will continue to be unless the business no longer thrives under his command."

Well, then. I could live with that. David had all but guaranteed me a place in management. Plan back on track. And it likely meant that Hudson wasn't planning on spending a lot of time around the club. I might have sighed audibly.

Hudson leaned back against the couch, draping his arm across the top. "But I didn't invite you here to discuss the club."

Finally. I swallowed. "Why did you invite me?"

A hint of amusement crossed Hudson's face. "Perhaps I like you."

I shuddered as a thrill traveled up my spine. But I didn't trust that he was merely trying to pick me up. He was taking too long to make his play, and that would never be Hudson's style. There was more.

God, I hoped there was more. If he was just trying to pick me up, what the hell was I going to say?

I took a sip of my iced tea, wishing it were something stronger. When I lowered my glass, I said, "Perhaps I'm seeing someone."

"You aren't. No man would let his woman wear the outfit you wore yesterday. Not in public, anyway."

The mention of the outfit I'd nicknamed trouble and the idea that any man would *let* me do anything ruffled my feathers. "Perhaps I'm not into controlling boyfriends."

His mouth twitched slightly. "Very well, Alayna." He cocked a brow. "Are you seeing anyone?"

Of course I wasn't seeing anyone, damn it. I looked at my lap, my expression telling Hudson all he needed to know. Why did this man make me so flustered? I was a confident, well-spoken woman on a normal day. But not around him.

I sat straighter, attempting to find some semblance of sure footing. "That isn't why you invited me, Hudson. You have an agenda."

"An agenda." Hudson made a sound that I think must have been his version of a chuckle. "Yes, Alayna, I have an agenda."

And then, instead of sharing his agenda, he changed the subject. "I presume you enjoyed your time at my spa last week."

Startled by absolutely everything he was saying, I attempted to follow the topic swing. "Oh, I didn't realize you owned...wait..." And the light went on. "The gift was from you?"

"Yes. Did you have a nice time?"

"No. Way." I'm pretty sure my jaw dropped. Actually, physically, literally dropped.

"No way?"

Realizing my remark hadn't expressed what I meant it to express, I tried again. "I mean, yes, I had a nice time—a wonderful time, in fact—but no way could you have done that. Why did you do that? You shouldn't have done that."

"Why ever not?"

A whole range of reasons ran through my head, number one being because it was creepy and psychotic. But I had been called both of those things many times and would not throw them easily at another person. I grabbed for the next reason. "Because that's big!"

"Not for me."

"But for me it is." How could he not understand? The vastness of it built in me like champagne bubbles in a newly uncorked bottle. "It's huge! And you don't even know me! It's completely inappropriate and unprofessional and unprecedented and inappropriate. And if I'd known it was from you, I never would have accepted it." This couldn't be only about getting in my pants. I could have been won over by much less, as ashamed as I was to admit that to myself.

Hudson took a deep breath, trying to remain patient. "It's not inappropriate at all. It was simply a gift. Think of it as a golden hello."

My voice was tight as I strained to keep myself from screaming in frustration. "But you don't give gifts like that to women who work for you unless you're running an entirely different kind of club."

"You're overreacting, Alayna."

"I'm not!" Finally his previous statement registered. "And what do you mean a golden hello? You mean, like a signing bonus?" Several of my peers had talked about the bonuses they'd been offered when they'd accepted their six-figure positions after grad school. Cars and stuff like that.

"Yes, Alayna." He tossed his hand in the air. "That's my agenda. I would like to hire you."

He couldn't have startled me more if he'd asked me to strip for him. Or maybe that's what he was asking. What exactly did he want to hire me to do? "I already work for you and I'm happy where I am."

"Again, I don't feel that you do work for me. I am not your boss. I own the establishment that you work for. That is all. Is that clear?"

Semantics. But I understood what he was attempting to do, separating himself from me and my job at The Sky Launch, so I nodded.

"This wouldn't affect your employment at the club." He removed his arm from the couch and sat forward. "Maybe hire is not the correct term. I'd like to pay you to help me with a problem. I believe you'd be perfect for the job."

The whole conversation had my head spinning, but he had my attention. "You win. My curiosity is piqued. What's the job?"

"I need you to break up an engagement."

I coughed, wondering if I heard him correctly, knowing I had. "Um, what? Whose?"

Hudson leaned back, his dazzling gray eyes flickering in the strobe lights. "Mine."

Chapter Four

Hudson tapped one long finger on the table in front of him. "Close your mouth, Alayna. Although it's quite adorable to see you flabbergasted, it's also very distracting."

I closed my mouth. A million questions circled through my mind, too quickly for any to take shape. And somewhere behind all that, I registered that he'd called me adorable. I needed a drink, something stronger than iced tea. Hudson scooted his Sancerre toward me and I took it, grateful.

The wine gave me back my voice. "I didn't realize you were engaged." I blushed then, remembering all the dirty thoughts I'd had about Hudson and how I'd believed—okay, *hoped*—he had been flirting with me. I took another swallow of wine.

Hudson glanced out the window, maybe hoping to hide the torment that flashed across his face. "I'm not really." He turned back to me, his expression now reserved and emotionless as usual. "That's the problem. Neither Celia nor I are at all interested in the arrangement."

This relaxed me, for some reason. But it did little to clear anything up. "Then why not just break up with her?"

He sighed. "It's not that simple."

I gave Hudson my best dumb-it-down-for-me-dude expression. Apparently, it worked.

"Her parents have been friends with mine for decades. They have a specific plan for their daughter's life and they do not accept her choice to not marry me. If she broke it off, they'd cut her off emotionally and financially. That's not something I wish for my friend."

His explanation prickled me. Were we living in the early twentieth century with arranged marriages and shit? God, rich people lived such strange lives. I picked my words thoughtfully, careful to not show the extent of my irritation. "Never mind that parents shouldn't be controlling their grown daughter, they don't control you. Do they?"

Hudson's eyes blazed. "No. No one controls me."

His emphatic response had my body turned on. That command and authority, it was so...*hot*. I licked my lips, and then delighted as he zeroed in on the action. I hadn't imagined it. He *was* reacting to me. Maybe not as forcefully as I reacted to him, but the energy between us was real.

I crossed my legs attempting to ease the need between them. "I'm missing something."

He nodded. "I suppose you are." He retrieved the Sancerre from in front of me and finished it off in one quick swallow. Knowing we'd shared the glass sent another tingle to my lower regions.

"Alayna, if there is anyone in the world who has any power over me, it's my mother. My mother knows that I am...*incapable*...of love. She worries that I will...end up alone. A marriage with her best friend's daughter, at least, insures that won't happen." His words were measured and even. And just like every time he spoke, he hypnotized me with his voice.

"It would make my mother very happy to see me marry Celia. If it comes to Celia losing her entire life, then I'll willingly enter into a loveless marriage. However, I'd hate to rob her future of happiness she might find with someone else."

I shook my head, confused, overwhelmed, dazzled. "Where would I come in?"

He raised his brows. "Ah, see, if Celia's parents believed I was in love with another woman—"

"They wouldn't want her to marry a man who was in love with someone else."

"Exactly. And my mother would be so thrilled that I'd found someone I was happy with, she'd stop worrying about my future."

The idea of betraying someone who only wanted Hudson to be happy bothered me. But I was also extremely attracted to the sweetness of this hard, virile man in front of me caring enough about his mother and his friend to go to such extreme measures.

I also saw enormous potential for me to be made the enemy in the scenario. "So I'm supposed to be the floozy you're in love with."

His lips curved at the edges. "No one would ever mistake you as a floozy, Alayna. Even when you dress like one."

That damn trouble outfit again. I was burning it when I got home.

Mention of it made me suddenly cold and defensive. I crossed my arms over my chest and leaned back—away from Hudson Pierce. "Why don't you hire a real floozy to put on your charade?"

He smirked. "My mother would never believe I'd fall for a floozy. You, however, have particular qualities—qualities that would make the story quite believable."

I didn't want to play this game anymore. My answer was no. But I couldn't help myself from asking, "What sort of qualities?"

His eyes darkened, and I was caught up in them. "You are exquisitely beautiful, Alayna, and also extremely intelligent."

"Oh." I dropped my hands to my lap, stunned. It was a good thing the wine was gone. I'd have slammed it, and I still had a shift to work.

Hudson broke the intense eye contact. "And you're a brunette. All three make you 'my type' so to say."

The absence of his heated stare was both chilling and releasing. I could think again, make coherent sentences. But I also wanted it back with a fierceness I couldn't explain.

"I sense your hesitation, Alayna, and I understand. Perhaps this would be a good time to discuss payment." I admired how he could move from moments of magnitude to straight business with such fluid ease. Me, I had whiplash. I didn't even have time to wonder what someone got paid to fake a romance before he continued. "I understand you have a substantial amount of student loans. I'd like to rid you of that debt."

I laughed. "That's way too much, Hudson." He had no idea how much I'd needed to get through school. No idea how heavy of a burden they were on me now.

"Not to me."

"It is for me." I sat forward, challenging him. "It's eighty thousand dollars."

"Eighty four thousand two hundred and six, to be exact."

I froze. How did he know that?

As he often did, he answered my unasked question. "I own the bank that holds your loans. I looked them up today. It would be very easy for me to have them written off. No actual money would exchange hands, if that makes you feel better."

"That's an awfully generous payment." Too generous. And just like I jumped to buy a lottery ticket whenever the pot got particularly high, I wanted to jump on his offer. But nothing that paid that well ended in good.

"It's worth it to me to see this project succeed, Alayna."

My answer was no. I'd already decided. It had to be no. There was too much risk at entering into an arrangement—any arrangement— with him.

But I couldn't help but want to know more of the details. "What exactly would you want me to do?"

"Pretend we're a couple. I'd invite you to several gatherings where my mother would see us together. I'd expect you to hang on my arm and behave as though we're madly in love."

"And that's all?" I couldn't imagine it would be that hard to pretend to be in love with Hudson. And that was the problem with the whole damn thing. Pretending to be in love with someone who already affected me so intensely was a big fat trigger for obsessing.

"That's all." His shoulders had visibly relaxed. He thought I was taking him seriously, that I was considering his ridiculous idea, and I almost wondered if I actually should.

I swallowed. For eighty thousand dollars there had to be more he expected. Since he wouldn't spell it out, I tiptoed around the topic myself. "This pretend relationship—to what extent would I be expected to perform?"

"Don't pussyfoot about it. You're asking about sex." His eyes darkened again. "I never pay for sex, Alayna. When I fuck you, it will be for free."

There it was, the promise that I'd both longed for and feared. His stark declaration had me squirming in my seat. I had never been so aroused and so confused all at once. We were at my work, for Christ's sake! I had to start my shift in less than half an hour, and all I wanted to do was respond to his crude remarks with equally naughty behavior.

Somehow I forced my mouth to speak. "Maybe I should go."

"Do you want to?" It was an invitation to stay.

"I'm n-not sure," I stuttered. "Yes. I think I should." But I didn't move. I couldn't.

Hudson took advantage of my weakness, pressing me to indulge him with reasons. "Because you're uncomfortable with my proposition? Or because I told you that I'm going to fuck you?"

His profession had no less impact the second time. "I'm...yes. That."

He cocked his head, contemplating me with puzzled eyes. "But

I'm certain that's not a surprise to you, Alayna. You feel the electricity between us. Your body language expresses it quite well. I wouldn't be surprised to find you're already wet."

My cheeks heated.

He flashed a wicked grin. "Don't be embarrassed. Don't you know I feel the same?" He shifted in his seat. "If you were to carefully read my body, you'd see the evidence."

I knew then that he was hard. My sex clenched with the knowledge. If my brain hadn't completely turned to mush, I'd be in his lap by now, taking his length into my hands, sucking him off with my mouth.

Hudson seemed to find my misery fascinating. "Let's table my proposition to hire you for a moment and discuss this other thing further. Please understand that they are very separate from each other. I'd never want you to think my sexual desire for you was in any way part of a sham for my parents and their friends."

Ridiculous giddiness flowed through me. *Hudson Pierce desired me.* And I was going to wreck it all with my flabbergasted reaction. I furrowed my brows in concentration. "I'm—I don't know how to react to someone stating they desire me."

He frowned. Even with his lips curled down they begged to be kissed. "Has no man told you that before?"

I fumbled with my glass, caressing the beads of sweat that still accumulated from the pile of remaining ice. "Not in so many words. Actions sometimes. Certainly not so bluntly."

"That's a shame." He reached across the table and stroked a thumb across my hand, his touch making me dizzy. "I plan to tell you every chance I get."

"Oh." I pulled my hand away. It was too much, too fast. Maybe I could end up in Hudson's bed and it would be all right and I wouldn't freak out.

But this wasn't his bed. This was the club. And whether I freaked out or not, mixing work with sex was never a good idea.

Ah. Was that what David had been saying when he broke it off with me? What a moment for understanding to click in.

I put my hands on the edge of the table. "I, uh, I'm feeling a bit overwhelmed. I need to go. You've given me a lot to think about."

I stood and he did too.

"I wish you wouldn't. But if you must..." He sounded needy,

reflecting how I felt.

I couldn't look at him. If I did, I'd stay. "I've got to get to work."

I moved to the door and placed my hand on the knob. But Hudson's palm pressed on the top of the door, holding it closed and trapping me between him and the wall.

He lowered his head to my ear. "Wait, Alayna." His breath tickled and burned simultaneously. I closed my eyes, taking it in, bearing it. "I apologize for overwhelming you. That wasn't my intent. But I want you to know that whether or not you decide to help with my situation, I will continue to seduce you. I'm a man who gets what he wants. And I want you."

Um, holy wow.

Turned on did not begin to describe how his statement made me feel.

Then his mouth was on me, nibbling at my earlobe. I drew in a sharp breath. Involuntarily, I let my head roll to the side, granting him better access.

And, man, did he take what I gave, nipping a trail down my neck, sending ripples of desire through my belly. I moved my hand off the doorknob and grabbed his arm to steady myself. He curled his other arm around me, his hand settling on my breast. I gasped at the contact, leaning in to his touch.

He kneaded my breast as he nuzzled his face in my hair. "I should have told you earlier," he said softly. "You look absolutely beautiful tonight. I can't keep my eyes off you. Serious and sexy wrapped into one package." He pressed against me and I could feel his erection at my lower back. "Kiss me, Alayna."

It was so hot how he used my name freely. As if it was his to use. And in many ways it was. Almost no one called me anything but Laynie. He'd claimed my name when he claimed me.

All that was left was for me to accept it.

His mouth was waiting as I turned my head. Instantly, he captured mine with his own and I whimpered. He slipped his tongue in possessively and skillfully, urging mine to come out and play. His kiss was just as demanding and confident as he was, his firm lips driving the tempo, stealing my breath and sending a firm buzz to my lady parts. *God, imagine his lips down there…*

I shifted my body, needing more contact, and instinctively, he turned too so we were face to face. Wrapping my hands around his neck, I pulled him deeper, wanting to feel him in every part of my mouth. He knew what I needed, licking and stroking into me, as his hands slid down to clutch my ass.

I wanted all of him. Screw my shift and any other excuse I'd made to myself during the course of the conversation. Even if it led to obsessing, I needed him inside me, and not only with his tongue. I rolled my hips against his, begging for him to touch me there, to ease the ache at my core.

Hudson responded, moving his hands from my behind to my shoulders. Then he gently pushed me away, breaking our kiss, but leaving his hands on my shoulders as if trying to hold me at that distance.

My mouth felt empty and cold as I struggled to calm my breathing. Hudson's breaths were equally ragged, and he panted in rhythm with me. As my brain returned from a state of blissful haze, I became uneasy, unable to understand his sudden retreat.

Recognizing my concern, Hudson moved his hand to brush my cheek. "Not here, precious. Not like this." His other hand wrapped around my neck and he pressed his forehead against mine. "I will have you beneath me. In a bed. Where I can adore you properly."

His statement was a promise. A sensual threat that had me itching to make it come to pass.

But I had to get to work. And he was right. A fast fuck in the bubble room would not nearly be enough for what I wanted with Hudson. No, *needed*. Hudson was far from what I wanted. But I'd gone beyond that now. I had to have him, bad for me though he may be.

I closed my eyes as Hudson trailed a hand down to my bosom and reached inside. My eyes startled open when, instead of feeling his fingers on my breast, I felt my phone being removed.

He unlocked the screen and dialed a number. A moment later I heard his phone ring. "Now we have each other's numbers. I expect you to use it." He replaced my phone inside my bra cup, his eyes lingering on my cleavage before pulling me in to brush his lips across mine. "Call me when you're ready. Tomorrow."

He kissed me swiftly and then was gone, leaving me to wonder if I'd be "ready" to call him as soon as tomorrow. And if I could wait that long.

Chapter Five

I woke up right before noon the next morning when I heard my phone buzz an incoming text. It was plugged in on the nightstand next to me, but I wasn't ready to wake up, having gotten to bed after six.

Lying with my eyes closed, I grinned into my pillow and recalled the events of the night before. The things Hudson had said to me, the way he'd kissed me, touched me—my heart sped up at the memory. Had all of that really happened? My obsessive relationship disorder made it really easy for me to imagine that things happened between me and others that actually hadn't. It had been several years since I had fallen into those old habits. Now, was I doing it again?

No, I wasn't making it up. I couldn't make up a kiss like that. It had happened. And I had wanted more to happen. But in the morning with distance and fresh eyes, I could see so much better how it shouldn't happen. As much as I wanted him, I was already thinking about him way more than was healthy.

I went through the steps of recognizing unnatural fixation in my mind:

Did I think about Hudson to the point that it affected my work or daily life? I'd certainly thought about him a lot after he'd left the club, but I'd managed to work my shift without a problem.

Did I think he was the only one for me? No way. In fact, I suspected I shouldn't be mixed up with him at all.

Did I believe I would never be happy if I didn't see him again? I'd be disappointed, but not devastated. Well, probably not devastated. All right, I'd be devastated.

Did I call him or visit him obsessively to the point of stalking? I didn't know where he lived or worked. If I was fixating, I'd have figured that out before I'd gone to bed that morning. I didn't even have his number.

Oh, wait, I did. But I hadn't used it. I was fine. For the moment.

Still, I couldn't help but wonder why he wanted to be with me. Hudson Pierce held celebrity status. He could date supermodels and pedigreed women—why would he want *me*? The lack of an answer kept me doubting what had really occurred between him and me.

And then there was his ridiculous offer to pay off my student loans in exchange for hanging on him like arm candy. How on earth did I qualify for that? If I were another type of girl, one with dollar signs in the eyes, I'd be all over his—what did he call it?—*proposition*. Fortunately, money didn't speak to me beyond what I needed for survival. The only temptation was the opportunity to spend more time with that delicious specimen of a man. But I'd already been through this—it was not a good idea.

Besides, if I'd understood him correctly, the option to spend time with him stood with or without accepting his job.

Not an option, Laynie!

It was a confusing idea anyway. Sleep with him without a relationship but pretend to have a relationship. Why not just have a relationship?

And there I was, already trying to make his offer more than it was.

I sighed and stretched my arms above my head. Clearly I wasn't going back to sleep and Hudson was too much to contemplate without coffee. I turned over and grabbed my phone to read my text, secretly hoping it was from him.

It was from my brother. *"Be there in twenty."*

I sat up, panicked. Did I forget a visit from Brian?

Scrolling through my texts I saw he'd sent one at seven in the morning. *"Court cancelled. Taking a fast train to NYC. We need to have lunch."*

I threw my phone onto the bed next to me and groaned. As my only living relative, I loved Brian with extreme depth and neediness. But his role in my life had transformed from sibling to caretaker when I was sixteen after the death of my parents, and in an effort to compensate for all he knew I'd lost, he'd alienated me in many ways.

He'd also saved me, and I'd be eternally grateful.

Plus he paid the rent for my apartment. So when Brian trekked out from Boston on a weekday to have lunch, I better be ready and waiting. Even though I knew a surprise visit couldn't mean anything good.

I took a deep breath and jumped out of bed. I didn't have time for a shower. Brian and the patrons of whatever swank place he took me to would have to settle for the smelly version of me. I pulled on a pair of taupe dress slacks and a cream blouse and sprayed myself with a generous amount of Pear Blossom Body Spray before throwing my long brown hair into a messy bun. I'd just located my keys and purse when my phone rang.

I pulled the door closed behind me and stepped toward the elevator as I answered.

"I'm outside your building," Brian said.

"Hello to you, too." Never any small talk for Brian. I hit the elevator call button and waited.

"Whatever, sassafrass. We have reservations in fifteen minutes at The Peacock Alley. Are you ready?"

I rolled my eyes at his restaurant choice. How unoriginal of him to pick the Waldorf. "Already on my way down. You know, you could have used the apartment buzzer instead of calling."

"But then you couldn't walk and talk like you are."

"And I'm about to lose you now as I get in the elevator. See you in a sec." I wasn't certain that the elevator would cause our call to drop, but I was facing a whole lunch hour with Brian. I needed the fifty-second reprieve.

"There she is," Brian said to no one when I walked out of the front door of my apartment building. The apartment had been Brian's pick since he was footing the bill, and I was sure that its proximity to the Waldorf had been half of the reason he'd chosen it. No one could mistake the place as classy, but the location was killer. My only gripe was the lack of a subway to the west side, but that only became a problem in bad weather.

"Hey, Bri," I said throwing my arms around him. "It's good to see you."

"You too." He pulled away and looked me up and down. "You look terrible, Laynie. Like you need more sleep."

"Gee, thanks." We started toward the restaurant. "I didn't get off work until five. Yeah, I'm a bit tired."

"Isn't it time you started working a more normal job? Something nine to five like?"

"I work nine to five. Just not the same nine to five you work." As if Brian worked nine to five. He was a workaholic, often burning the midnight oil working on his latest case. If his paralegal hadn't been his type, he never would have gotten married. The man had no social life. I'd be surprised to learn he had a sex life, even with a new wife. "You know what I mean."

We'd only been together five minutes and he was already picking. If that was an indicator of how lunch was going to go, I'd rather skip the meal and get right to whatever bug was up his ass. "What brings you out here, Brian?"

He studied me, deciding whether to show his cards yet or not. He chose not. "Can't a brother come visit his only sister on a whim? I still feel bad for missing your graduation."

I hid my eye roll. He could have made my graduation if he'd wanted to, and we both knew it. But we had to play the game of happy family. "You're a busy hotshot lawyer. I get it."

"I sense the sarcasm in your voice, Laynie."

My brother excelled at reading people, making him a force to be reckoned with in the courtroom. "Okay, I was pissed you didn't come. Does that make you happy?" Actually, I'd been hurt. He'd had the date for almost nine months. How could I not feel low priority? "I'm over it now, though, so forget it."

We'd reached the hotel, which gave us the perfect chance to drop the subject. At the restaurant, we were seated right away, and I let the new environment transform me from outwardly brooding to introspective.

I deliberated for a long time about my menu choice, annoying Brian who knew what he wanted instantly. When the tempo of his leg bouncing under the table accelerated, I settled on a house salad. God, the man had no patience. He should take a lesson from Hudson.

The thought of Hudson brought warmth to my body and a furrow to my brow. Something was poking at the edge of my thoughts, something I couldn't quite grasp.

Brian chatted with me casually, keeping me from focusing on what perplexed me about Hudson. He briefly told me about a case he was working on and about the renovations he and Monica had done to their brownstone.

When he'd finished a decent portion of his meal, about the same time I thought I'd shoot myself over the banality of our conversation, Brian cleared his throat. "Laynie, I'm not here to catch up. I've been doing a lot of thinking about our situation lately and have realized that you're a grown woman with an excellent education. It's time for you to assume more responsibility for yourself. I'm not doing you a favor by enabling you."

I took a long swallow of my water, contemplating how to react to his sudden statement. Old connotations of the word "enable" stung me. Was he insinuating that I wasn't well? And how was I not responsible for myself? I was living and working in the Big Apple—if that didn't take responsibility, I didn't know what did.

Ever impatient, Brian didn't wait for me to choose my response. "I can't let you throw your life away at a nightclub. You are too vulnerable to work in that type of establishment."

The Sky Launch. Brian had never liked me working there, not from day one. But he'd accepted it because I'd kept out of trouble. Had he now forgotten? "I haven't had any issues since I've worked there."

"You had school to keep you occupied. You need something more challenging to focus on."

Never mind that I'd worried about the exact same thing myself, I was pissed. "Brian, I know how to handle my triggers. And what do you know about it? You never went to any support meetings."

His voice rose uncomfortably high for the serene surroundings. "Because I'm not your parent!"

That was the crux of the whole conversation. Brian had been forced into parenting me and I'd always suspected he resented me for it. Now I knew for sure.

He stared at his near empty plate. When he spoke again it was quieter. "Look, Monica's having a baby."

And everything clicked into understanding. I was being replaced. "Congratulations."

"I need to focus my energy and money on her and the baby. It's time for you to be grown-up." He straightened in his seat, as if to strengthen his position. "I'm not paying for the apartment anymore."

"But I can't afford to pay for the apartment! Not right now with my student loans about to be due." I was painfully aware that I sounded petulant and spoiled, but I had always assumed he'd help me for a while longer. It wasn't like he didn't have the money.

"Then maybe you better look for a better paying job."

"Brian, that's not fair."

"Think about everything I've been through with you and then talk to me about fair."

He couldn't have hurt me more with any other words. "I haven't had any problems in a long time," I whispered.

"You violated a restraining order."

"Over four years ago!"

"I'm sorry, Laynie. I can't support you anymore." His words were final. He'd made his decision; there would be no convincing him otherwise.

I saw what it had done to him, the years of caring for a mentally disturbed sibling. I'd known—I'd always known—but had never wanted to believe that my actions had hurt him so deeply. It stirred an old ache I had buried.

But I was also angry. I might not be fragile anymore, but I certainly wasn't steady on my own. Not financially anyway. I needed his support now as much as ever and as shitty as it was, he was my only family. I had no one else.

I threw my napkin on the table and, not sure if I hoped to sound more sincere or snotty, said, "Thanks, Brian. Thanks for everything." I grabbed my purse from the back of my chair and walked out of The Peacock Alley, careful not to look back. I wanted to appear strong and stoic. Turning back would give my brother a good look at my tears.

I let myself cry until I left the hotel. Once on the street, the city bustle and grit steeled me. I didn't need Brian. I could do it on my own. Sure he'd helped me foot the bill since my crazy antics had ran through all of my inheritance money, but support and responsibility was much more than throwing cash around.

I hurried back to my apartment, aware that Brian didn't try to stop me or call me. I spent the next hour behind my computer, figuring out my bills and expenses, searching for ways to make cuts. With a promotion at the club—which wasn't guaranteed—I could pay for my apartment. But I wouldn't be able to afford my student loans when they went into repayment the next month.

Brian had effectively trapped me. Not a bad strategy. The Laynie from a day before would have to give in to his wishes, taking a job at one of the high paying corporate offices that had pursued me at graduation.

Fortunately, I had another option.

Taking a deep breath, I picked up my cell phone and pushed redial. God, was I really doing this? I was. And if I was honest about it, I was glad for the excuse. Maybe I really should have been thanking Brian.

The number Hudson had called the night before rang only once before he answered. "Alayna." His voice was smooth and sexy. Not sexy like he was coming on to me but like the sex he exuded naturally.

The confidence threw me. "Uh, hi, Hudson."

I paused.

"Is there something I can help you with?" I sensed he enjoyed my uncertainty. Why couldn't I display the same confidence he did? I never had anxiety issues at work or at school.

The thought of school jostled something and I blurted out the question that had niggled at me during lunch. "How did you know I was intelligent?"

I heard a creak and I pictured him leaning back in a leather chair behind an executive desk. "What do you mean?"

"You said I was…" I blushed, glad he couldn't see me. "Beautiful and intelligent—"

He interrupted me. "Exquisitely beautiful and extremely intelligent."

"Yeah, that." Having heard them before made his words no less effective. The matter-of-fact manner of his statement should have felt clinical and cold, but they were anything but. A shiver ran up my spine. I cleared my throat. "But you've barely talked to me. How do you know anything about my intelligence?"

He paused only briefly. "The graduate symposium at Stern. I saw you present."

"Oh." The symposium had been held a month before graduation and had featured the top students from the MBA program. Each of us had presented a new or innovative idea for a panel of experts. My presentation had been called *Print Marketing in a Digital Age*. I hadn't wanted to know who was on the panel, knowing that names would send me into obsessive researching and online stalking. Afterward, the experts and presenters were invited to a wine and cheese soiree, so that students could schmooze and corporate execs could make job offers. I'd presented for the experience. For the honor. I hadn't wanted a job, so I'd skipped the after affair.

Now I wondered what would have happened if I'd gone. Would Hudson have tracked me down? Was it entirely coincidental that he'd made an offer on the club I worked for around the same time as the symposium?

"Is that the only reason you called, Alayna?" His all-business words held a hint of a tease.

"No." I closed my eyes and clutched onto the side of my desk for support. Accepting his offer was harder than it should be. I couldn't help but feel it was too easy of an out—like I was selling my soul to the devil.

But I also felt a surge of excitement, a thick electric wave of freedom. "Your proposition—I'd like to do it. I'm saying yes." Remembering his other proposition to seduce me, I clarified. "Your offer to pay my student loans, I mean."

His chair creaked again and I imagined him standing, his hand thrust in the pocket of an Italian suit. Ah, yum. "I'm very happy to hear that, Alayna."

I shook the vision out of my head and waited for him to say more. When he didn't, I said, "So what happens now?"

"I have time in my schedule at four-thirty. Come to my office at Pierce Industries then and we'll finalize the details."

I'd get to see him in—I looked at my watch—two hours. My heart sped up. "Sounds nice. I mean, good. Sounds good."

He chuckled. "Goodbye, Alayna."

"Bye." I hugged the phone for several seconds after he hung up, mesmerized by this stranger's effect on me, wondering if I'd be able to pull off the scam he'd concocted, hopeful I'd be able to thwart his promised advances.

All right, maybe I didn't hope for that last one, but I wanted to believe I did. For my sanity's sake.

I also thought about the symposium, considering the possibility that Hudson Pierce had gone to greater lengths than he'd let on to set up this facade for his parents.

Maybe the thought should have scared me. But it only intrigued me more.

CHAPTER SIX

Two hours turned out to be barely enough time to prepare for seeing Hudson. I spent a long time in the shower, shaving my legs and underarms and cleaning up my Brazilian, chastising myself as I did since there was no way Hudson was going to see my lady parts.

Then I stood in front of my closet for what felt like hours. I'd be going straight from Hudson's office to the club to meet with David then a full shift of bartending after that. I needed the perfect blend of smart and sexy with a dash of fuck-me-please—for work, of course. Finally, I settled on a belted teal and black shirt dress. It was shorter than I would have liked for the business part of my plans, but still longer than most of the dresses I wore at the club. I pulled my hair into a low ponytail and kept my makeup to mascara and lip gloss. I looked good—fresh and natural.

Having been too distracted to ask Hudson where Pierce Industries was located, I had to Google it. Turned out the offices were near the One Worldwide Plaza, a straight subway shot to the club. From my apartment, I took a cab, not wanting to get sweaty. And, hey, I was getting eighty thousand dollars—I could afford a taxi to the West Side.

I'd been by the beautiful copper-topped granite and brick building many times, but never inside it. Pierce Industries took the top several floors, and I recognized some of the other tenants listed in the lobby as Pierce Industry subsidiaries. I got directions from the security guard and took the elevator to the top floor.

The lengthy ride gave me one more chance for a silent pep talk. *Three years sober, Laynie. You cannot fixate on him. You cannot obsess.*

But as I checked in with the pretty blonde receptionist, I felt an aching stab of envy because she got to work close to Hudson on a daily basis. God, I was already in trouble. He didn't make it into the *Oh, fuck* category of attractive men for nothing.

"Miss Withers," the blonde said after notifying her boss I'd arrived. "He's ready for you."

I checked my watch—four-twenty-two. How long had Hudson been waiting? Did I get the time wrong?

The thick double doors behind the receptionist's desk opened, seemingly by themselves. She must have pushed a button somewhere. "Right through there," she said.

I stepped tentatively into the office. Hudson, who sat behind an expansive modern executive desk, stood when he saw me. "Alayna. Come in."

When I caught a full view of him, I froze. In his well-lit office, I truly saw Hudson Pierce for the first time. And he was gorgeous. He wore a pin-striped three-piece suit with a crisp white dress shirt and a plum and white striped tie. His black thick-framed glasses, which should have screamed nerd alert, had me slipping in my panties. He looked sharp and smart and commanding and...wow.

I swallowed. Twice. "Am I late?"

"Not at all." His sexy voice made my knees buckle and I suddenly regretted my high-heeled Mary Janes. "My last appointment finished earlier than I'd anticipated. Have a seat."

Determined to appear poised and with it, I straightened my stance and strode to the chair he gestured at in front of his desk.

"Hmm," I said, looking around after I was seated. The generous office space continued the modern décor throughout. Behind his desk were floor to ceiling glass windows giving a breathtaking view of Midtown. "Nice place. Not what I'd pictured, but incredible."

Hudson unbuttoned his jacket and sat down, brows raised. "You pictured my office?"

My cheeks grew warm. Now he thought I'd been thinking about him. I had been, but he didn't need to know. "I thought you'd be more traditional. But the modern really suits you."

A small smile crept on his face. "Actually, I have a designer. I have no idea what's modern or contemporary or traditional. She showed me pictures of things she thought I'd like and I nodded."

I grinned, knowing he was attempting to put me at ease, but my stomach bunched into knots. Hudson's office was unfamiliar territory for a nightclub bartender and we were meeting to discuss an unusual business deal. And he was so fucking hot, he dazzled me.

"I hope you don't mind if we get to business first."

"Of course not." If business was first, I wondered what would follow. Nothing. Nothing would follow because when we were finished I would politely thank him and leave his office.

Ha ha, right.

"As I said earlier, I'm very pleased that you've accepted my offer. Before you officially agree, though, I want to make sure you understand exactly what I am asking of you. We tabled this discussion last night..." He paused and I suspected he was recalling the reason the discussion was tabled. At least, that's what I was thinking about. "So I neglected to mention a key point."

Hudson leaned back in his chair, placing his arms on the rests. "I'm a very high profile man, Alayna. Convincing my mother that we are a couple requires putting on a show for the world. That means you will be 'on duty', so to say, at all times. When we are together around other people, we will play the happy couple. When we aren't together, you must still act as though you're mine."

Was it my imagination or had he emphasized the words *you're mine*? Either way, goose bumps travelled down my skin.

"You can't tell anyone that we are not really in a relationship."

I creased my forehead and my mouth suddenly went dry. "I hadn't realized that."

"No, I suspected as much." He narrowed his eyes, gazing my reaction. "Are you still interested?"

I didn't really have a choice. Either accept it or give into Brian's wishes. Besides, whom would I want to tell? Liesl. And David. Was I still thinking about David with tall, hot, and devastatingly handsome sitting in front of me? Yes. Because David had the potential of being real. And frankly, I didn't know that I actually liked Hudson beyond the whole physical thing. I certainly shouldn't.

"How long would we keep up the act?"

"As long as we feel we can without imposing too much on our personal lives. The longer the better, obviously, but if my mother sees that I am capable of falling in love, she won't try to press me into a loveless marriage, even if you and I have 'broken up.'"

"Are you still interested?"

"It's eighty thousand dollars, Hudson. That's a drop in the bucket for you, but for me...I understand if I have to work for it."

He relaxed, nodding. "Good." Hudson pressed a button on his desk.

"Yes, Mr. Pierce?" The sweet timbre of the receptionist's voice filled the room.

"Send him in, please, Patricia." Hudson stood and pressed another button on his desk.

I'd heard her answer the phone as Trish when I'd arrived and I wondered if he was opposed to nicknames for people in general, or if he just knew the weight of using a proper name—the power it held over people.

The doors opened and a dark-haired, muscular man in a black suit walked in. If Hudson hadn't already sent my horny button into overdrive, I was pretty sure this guy would have set it buzzing.

"This is Jordan," Hudson said, crossing around to the front of his desk. Jordan nodded. "He's been assigned to drive you to and from work and anywhere else you may need to go."

Not that I wanted to turn down such a beautiful gift, but one thing I loved about NYC was alternate modes of transportation. My parents died in a car accident. Cars weren't my favorite. "I don't need a driver." Then, so I wouldn't seem ungrateful I added, "I usually get my exercise running home."

"Then he will drive you to work and follow you home when you run to make sure you arrive safely." Before I could argue, Hudson eyed me sternly. "Alayna, my girlfriend would have a driver. She'd also have a bodyguard. I'm willing to forego the bodyguard if you use my driver."

I took a deep breath. "All right."

"He'll be waiting downstairs to take you to the club when we've finished. Thank you, Jordan."

Jordan nodded again and then left the office. Hudson pushed a button and the doors shut behind the driver.

"And Alayna, wipe that look off your face. Jordan's gay. I wouldn't have hired him for you otherwise."

I folded my arms over my chest, embarrassed and chided. Also, I decidedly did not like Hudson. Beyond the sexual appeal, anyway. "Anything else?" I couldn't look at him.

He leaned back to sit on the front edge of his desk, his body close enough to touch without much movement on my part. "My mother is hosting a charity fashion show on Sunday. That will be our first outing as a couple."

"Okay." I crossed my leg over the other, his close proximity making me fidgety. And while I was so affected by him, I realized he'd been nothing but business since I'd arrived. Had his move on me the night before been a way to insure I'd accept his proposition? If so, he was a total ass.

"Your loans will be written off as of nine a.m. Monday morning. A written confirmation will be sent to you."

"Don't you want to wait and see if we pull this whole thing off first?" I hadn't meant to come off snotty. Well, not entirely. I was beginning to feel like a deal he was negotiating. I didn't like it.

"I'm really not worried about it, Alayna." Hudson seemed on edge as well. "But if you prefer, I'll postpone the write-off by one week."

"Fine, whatever. Do I sign some agreement or something?"

"I'd rather there isn't a paper trail on this."

"But if anyone questioned my loans being paid off—"

"I would pay off my girlfriend's loans." Of course he would. "And any other debt. Do you have other debt?"

"No." I had a Visa I'd charged up. He didn't need to know about that. "Is that all?"

Hudson shrugged, the gesture out-of-place for such an assured man. "Unless you have any other questions."

I hesitated to ask, but I had to know. "When we're together, in public, I mean, I can hold your hand and…kiss you?" I peered at him through my mascara thick lashes.

The corner of his lip twitched. "I expect you to. Often." Um, wow. "Anything else?"

Thinking about kissing him, I ran my tongue over my lower lip. "No."

"Then the business portion of this meeting is done." He stood and moved back around to his side of the desk. He removed his suit jacket and hung it on the back of his chair. Fuck—the vest, tight across his torso, showing his lean muscular middle—yeah, it was distracting.

Hudson stood in front of his chair and leaned on his desk, his palms flat in front of him. He stared at me for several seconds, and I itched to know what he was thinking. When he spoke, his tone was low and even. "In about two minutes, Alayna, I'm going to come around this desk and kiss you until you're wet and gasping for air."

Oh, wow.

"But first, let me clear up one thing that I suspect may be an issue.

This charade is mostly about me convincing my mother. I will be saying and doing things—romantic things, perhaps—that are not genuine. I need you to remember that. Out of the public eye, I will seduce you. That will be genuine, but it can never be misconstrued as love."

"Because you're incapable of love." My voice sounded meek and flat.

"Yes."

Curiosity pulled me to lean forward. "Why do you believe that?"

Hudson straightened and removed his glasses, setting them on the desk. "I'm twenty-nine years old and have never had any inclination toward a woman other than to have her in my bed. I don't do romantic relationships. I'm married to my work." He walked slowly around his desk toward me. "That, and casual sex, are what fulfill me."

I sorted through the oddity of the situation in my mind. Hudson Pierce wanted sex. With me. But not a relationship. But he wanted his mother to believe he had a relationship. With me. So that she didn't realize her son was incapable of love. Which he was.

The whole thing had me spinning in a circle.

And the worst part was that I knew that I wasn't capable of the casual relationship he was demanding.

Except…I thought back on the other category two men I'd been involved with in my life—the men that I'd been too attracted to. Joe, Ian, Paul—they'd all wanted a relationship in the beginning. If they hadn't, if they had made a declaration from day one that they didn't want more, would it have made a difference in how attached I became to them later?

I was justifying and I knew it. With Hudson, I was an alcoholic walking into a bar but deciding I could withstand temptation as long as all the bottles were sealed.

It was a lie I decided to try to believe. "No romance? I can do that."

Hudson leaned back on the front of his desk again. He raised a brow, amusement in his eyes. "Are you also incapable of love?"

I met his gaze and ignored the little voice in my head telling me to run. "No, just the opposite. I love too much. Keeping love out of the equation is a very good thing."

"Good. No love."

He stepped forward and leaned toward me, a hand on each of my armrests, caging me. His stare was hungry, and a thrill ran through my body, as I realized I was about to be kissed.

But before that happened, I had to know something. When he

moved closer, I put a hand against his chest. His very strong, rock hard chest. "Wait."

"I can't." But he paused. "What?"

He was inches from my face, and the lips I longed to nibble on kept my focus as I spoke. "Why me? You could have anyone you want."

"Awesome. I want you." He leaned in again, his mouth brushing mine, his breath heating my skin.

"Why?"

He pulled back. Not far, only far enough to look at me. "I don't know. I just do." His words came out a whisper, as if he rarely made statements of uncertainty, and I doubted he did. "From the moment I saw you…" He trailed off as he brushed his fingertips across my forehead, his eyes fixed intently on mine, and I briefly wondered which moment—the night of the graduation symposium or when he'd first seen me in the club?

Whenever he meant, his bewildered possessiveness was sincere, and when and why didn't matter anymore and the little voice screaming in my head was drowned out by the loud whooshing sound of desire pulsing through my veins. I leaned forward.

Hudson didn't hesitate for a second, meeting my mouth with his. As doubtful as his words had been, his lips were confident and firm. He moved a hand behind my neck to direct me, deepening the kiss, stroking my tongue with his own. He sucked and licked into me, sending shivers down my spine and I imagined his wet, hot mouth on other parts of my body. I sighed.

Without his mouth leaving mine, he pulled me to a standing position. This was better. I could press my body into him, feel his lust along my belly, get the contact that I yearned for. I ran my hands through his hair and down along the base of his neck, enjoying the tingles shooting through my limbs as he moaned against my lips.

A sharp buzzer made us both jump and pull away. I put a hand over my chest, my heart beating rapidly from the scare and from the intense kiss.

Hudson grinned. "The intercom," he explained, his voice ragged. He moved behind his desk and pushed a button. "Yes?"

The secretary's voice poured into the room again. "I'm about to leave, Mr. Pierce. Is there anything else you need?"

"No, thank you, Patricia. You may go." He'd gotten control of his voice now. Amazing. I was still reeling.

Hudson put one hand on his hip and stared at me, as if wondering what to do with a problem in front of him. It both heated and chilled me simultaneously, to be looked at so intensely, to be considered so scientifically.

I hugged my arms around myself. "What?"

He shook his head. "Nothing." He grabbed his jacket off the seat chair and extended his hand to me. "Come, Alayna."

My body responded to his command before my brain could decide to. I took his hand, the warmth of it rekindling the fire he'd started in my mouth.

He led me to an elevator in the back corner of his office that I hadn't noticed before. Inside the car, he entered a code into the panel and we traveled what felt like one flight up. The doors opened to a fully furnished loft, styled in the same modern design as his office below. Floor to ceiling windows lined one whole wall. The theme was echoed throughout the sprawling space, glass walls partitioning off a dining room, a sitting area, and peeking behind half-drawn curtains, a bedroom.

I quickly looked away from the bed, scandalized by the wicked thoughts that flashed through my mind at the sight of his personal space, and met Hudson's gaze, aware of the amusement in his eyes. I flushed.

He walked to the kitchen and opened a cupboard pulling out two glasses. "Can I get you some iced tea?"

"Sure." I wondered if he always had iced tea or if he'd stocked it specifically for me. I followed him to the kitchen, climbing up onto a sleek metallic looking barstool. "You live here?"

He opened the freezer and grabbed a handful of ice cubes, dropping half in each of the glasses. "Sometimes I stay here. But I don't consider it my home."

I looked around the loft again, realization setting in. "Hudson! Is this your fuck pad?"

"Sometimes." He poured tea into our glasses and then turned to hand me one across the counter.

I took the glass from him, sipping eagerly, needing the moisture for my suddenly dry mouth. "And you brought me here because…?"

He took a swallow of his tea, and licked his lips. He raised a brow. "Why do you think I brought you here?"

A sudden thrill set in followed by a wave of panic. I wasn't ready for this, was I? I looked at my watch. There was no time. "Um, I have to leave for work in ten minutes."

"Twenty minutes. You have a driver."

I shifted, the inside of my legs feeling sticky and moist. "That's still not a whole lot of time."

Hudson came around the counter, took my tea from my hand and set it down with his. "Not a whole lot of time for what?"

My throat felt like it had closed, but somehow I managed weak words. "Are you going to make me say it?"

He grinned as he swiveled me around, then caged me against the bar. "No. Not now. If you say it, I won't be able to resist you, and, as you said, there's not enough time. So instead, I'll have to settle for a sample."

His mouth sealed over mine, consuming my lips and my tongue with heated frenzy. My hands crawled up his vest, yearning to be on his skin. I could feel the hard, broad muscles of his chest underneath my fingertips. Jesus, this man had to work out, the sculpted definition of his torso evident through two layers of clothing. I wanted to run my nails over his body, aching to discover if he had hair or was bare-chested, desperate to be naked against him.

Hudson didn't let the minor detail of fabric get in the way of his desire. He undid several buttons at my torso so he could slip his hand in and cup my breast. My nipples stood up as he flicked lightly at one with his thumb. Then he squeezed using just the right amount of roughness that I liked, causing me to sigh with pleasure into his mouth.

He placed his other hand on my bare leg and slowly traced up my limb. His touch was fire against my skin and I fidgeted under his caress wanting more of the burn, greedy for the inferno at bay. I opened my thighs for him, coaxing his hand upward with one of my own. He smiled against my lips as I willingly showed him my need—my insane craving for him.

And then his fingers were on me, pushing aside the thin material of my panties, reaching for the sensitive bud at my core. I moaned at his touch, his thumb circling the bundle of nerves with a skilled mixture of deep and gentle pressure. Feather light sweeps followed measured rubs. I was already writhing when he dipped a finger into my hot opening. I gasped, lifting my hips to meet his probe, out of my mind with the desire to come.

He murmured against my mouth. "Christ, Alayna, you're wet. Ah, so wet. You're driving me crazy with your sounds and how wet you are for me." He dragged my juice up and over my clit, then rammed two fingers inside me, luring a series of whimpers from my body. One more brush of my clit and I was over the edge, my orgasm spurring me to convulsions.

But even as I came over his hand, Hudson didn't stop his assault. "God, you come so easily." His voice betrayed his amazement and his own longing. "I have to make you do that again."

He slipped off my panties while I still shuddered. "Lean your elbows back on the counter," he commanded.

I did, grateful for the support it gave me. Then Hudson put his hands on my knees and spread my legs apart, opening me further. Before I realized what was happening, his fingers returned to my hole—three of them now—and his tongue was on my clit.

"Fuck!" I cried, unable to bear another climax, unable to live without it.

His skilled fingers fucked me, plunging in and pulling out in long, steady strokes as he sucked and licked at my cleft. I clutched the end of the counter behind me as I felt the ripple of another orgasm overtake me, all my muscles tightening, my core clenching around his fingers.

Still, he fed on me, lapping up the evidence of my ecstasy, caressing my tender nerves with his tongue with endless devotion. It was so much—too much. A third climax tore through me, right on the heels of the last. I threw my head back, trembling violently and cried out—a curse, maybe, or his name or unintelligible sounds, too mindless to identify the details of my cry.

When my vision cleared and my brain returned, I found Hudson holding me, whispering at my ear, my scent wafting off his lips. "You're so sexy, precious. So fucking sexy and soon I'm going to come with you just like that."

My fingers clutched at tufts of his hair.

"Soon," he promised. "And often."

CHAPTER SEVEN

When I'd recovered enough to sit without support, Hudson left me, returning with a wet washcloth. I watched as he wiped the insides of my legs and my sex, the warmth of the cloth and the intimacy of the action transfixing me.

"Thank you," I said when he met my gaze, my gratitude extending beyond the cleansing.

He kissed me, my taste clinging to his tongue. Though sated, arousal began anew at the touch of his lips and the awareness of the bulge in his suit pants.

Too soon he pulled away. "You're welcome."

I followed him with my eyes as he walked to the bedroom and threw the washcloth in a tall, black laundry basket. When he looked back, he caught me staring and winked.

I blushed. The new familiarity he had with my body made me feel awkward. Scrambling to compose myself, I fumbled with the buttons of my dress. Then I slid off the barstool, found my underwear on the floor and stuffed them into my purse.

He raised a questioning brow as he straightened his tie.

"My panties are, um, soaked." I noted his expression of satisfaction. "I can't wear them."

A frown replaced his smile. "You can't work without them. Your dress is too short."

"I'll be careful. I don't mind."

"I do." Hudson approached me, putting his hands on my upper arms. "Alayna, you not wearing panties is very sexy. When I'm with you. I definitely don't think it's sexy knowing you're bare and surrounded by a bunch of grabby drunk customers." He was stern, as though he were reprimanding a wayward child. "In fact, it makes me very unhappy."

Well, well. Hudson had a jealous streak. Could he be any hotter?

But I couldn't have him infiltrating all aspects of my life. He'd already insisted on a driver. And weighed in on my wardrobe choices. I stood my ground. "I can take care of myself."

He folded his arms over his chest.

I mirrored him. "I'm not putting on soaking wet panties. I'll smell like sex all night and let me tell you what that does to a bunch of grabby drunk customers."

He scowled. "Leave them then. I can at least have them laundered."

I held out my panties for him. "If you wanted a memento all you had to do was ask."

He took them, his expression still tight. "I'm not keeping them. Excuse me a moment and I'll be ready to go." He disappeared into the bathroom, leaving the door open.

"You'll be 'ready to go'?" I hadn't expected him to be going with me. He didn't respond, though, or I didn't hear his answer over the sounds of water running.

"Did you say something?" he asked when he returned. He put on his suit jacket and held his hand out to me.

I took his hand, realizing he no longer smelled like me, his hands washed and his teeth freshly brushed. It was practical, but I deflated as he officially distanced himself from the passionate scene of moments before. "I hadn't realized you were going to the club."

"I am." He pulled me through a main door into a corridor with another elevator. This one, I guessed, led to the main lobby instead of his office. He let go of my hand and pushed the call button. "Is that a problem?"

I shrugged though I wanted to say, *Hell yes, it's a problem. You befuddle and dazzle and distract.* How could I present my ideas with Hudson's hot eyes on me, staring at his incredibly wicked mouth that had recently devoured me with such skill? Especially when his hot eyes and wicked mouth gave no indication that anything out of the ordinary had occurred.

Unwilling to be that honest but unable to let it go, I pushed. "Why did you have me meet you here when you could have met me at the club?"

"Privacy, Alayna. I can't imagine you would want to experience *that* at the club, would you?" The doors opened and he ushered me into the elevator. "Do you regret coming?" The smile in his tone emphasized the double meaning in his words.

"No," I answered quickly as he pushed the L button. "I regret *you* not coming." I couldn't think of a time when a man had let me take all the pleasure without receiving any of his own. It made me feel even more vulnerable in front of him.

"You'll have opportunities to rectify that."

And then thoughts of *rectifying that* raced through my mind, touching Hudson's naked body, his shaft in my hands…

My sex felt swollen and needy. Again.

Damn. Not what I needed at the moment. I had to get my head in the game. Which would be easier without the object of my desire standing next to me, his arm brushing at my shoulder. "Just after all your talk about not being my boss and all that, I didn't think you'd show."

"David may want advice. I should be there." He peered down at me. "Also, I'm curious. Is that going to bother you?"

"I wasn't prepared. That's all."

His eyes lit with understanding. "You're nervous."

"Yes."

He shifted behind me, wrapping me into his arms. "Don't be. You're perfect. You'll be perfect."

I sunk into him. That's what I'd needed—his touch after such an intimate act. I'd felt bereft and exposed. I needed reassurance, not just about the business presentation I was about to give, but about his feelings, or attraction, or whatever it was he had for me.

As we descended, I turned my thoughts to David and the presentation I was about to give. Oh, god, David. A new horror struck me. "Could we…?" I didn't know how to ask what I wanted to ask. "Do we have to, um, do the pretend thing today?"

"You don't want David to give you extra points because he thinks you're dating his boss."

"Right." And since I still might marry David one day, my sham with Hudson required delicacy. Though the idea of marrying David sounded less appealing than it once had.

"We can keep it under wraps for a day or two, if you'd rather."

"Thanks." Anxiety crept into my belly as I wondered how I planned to balance the men in my life and all the facets of my relationships with them: the fake romance with Hudson, the wannabe future with David, the severing of dependence on Brian, the real sex with Hudson, the possible promotion from David. I shivered and pulled Hudson's arms tighter around me.

He misread my anxiety. "You know what they say to do about nervousness," he whispered in my ear. "Imagine your audience naked." I raised my brows. "You and David?"

"No, precious. Just me. That's an order."

Hudson's commanding tone sent a trickle of desire to pool between my thighs. Somehow I didn't think picturing him naked would be any help.

Jordan waited for us on the street in front of the building in a black Maybach 57. I'd never been in a luxury car and my natural reaction would have been to gush and salivate, but I held in my enthusiasm, trying to appear more unaffected than I actually was. I did recline my seat, taking advantage of the footrest, while Hudson attended to some work issues. He typed away on his Blackberry and made several phone calls.

I should have been focusing on my presentation, but listening to him conduct business fascinated me, his commanding tone and demand for respect radiated so naturally in even the simplest directives. Usually when he spoke like that to me, I felt shaken and off-balance. But when I witnessed him speaking that way to others, or perhaps because of what had transpired between us, I felt empowered. As if I could embody those qualities myself through osmosis.

We arrived at the club five minutes before the scheduled meeting. Hudson stayed in the car for a while, allowing me to go in first instead of together. In the office, I found David setting up my laptop.

"Hey," he said in greeting. "Are you ready to show off those brilliant brains of yours?"

I wondered if David knew about Hudson's plan to attend or not. Either way, I didn't want him to know I knew. "Should I start?"

"No, Pierce said he might come. You should give him a few minutes."

Hudson walked in seconds later. "David," he said, shaking his hand. "Alayna." He nodded at me, and I wondered if this was out of consideration to me, knowing that his touch drove me beyond distraction. Or did touching me do the same thing to him? I couldn't imagine that could be true—he compartmentalized so naturally, I had to think his thoughts were sincerely only on the moment at hand.

Beginning my presentation of ideas took the most effort, but with my PowerPoint slides to rely on, I easily fell into the zone, soon forgetting my audience. First, I focused on the operational aspects of The Sky Launch, items that threatened our competitiveness with other clubs, suggesting an increase in hours and days we were open, a retraining of key personnel, and a unified mode of operation between bartenders and wait staff. Then I moved to marketing recommendations, emphasizing a total rebranding with a spotlight on the bubble rooms.

I spoke for nearly an hour and a half. Sometimes David asked questions, and I answered confidently and succinctly. I knew The Sky Launch. I knew business. I knew what would make the club a rockin' place. I felt good.

Except for occasionally asking for clarification, Hudson remained quiet and attentive. When I finished, I looked to him, hoping for feedback or praise or a reaction of some sort.

Instead, he looked at his watch. "David, I have some place I need to be now. You can call me tomorrow if you want to discuss these ideas."

The endorphins of presentation performance weren't enough to shelter me from the defeat of Hudson's lack of acknowledgement. Had I completely sucked shit? Did smart girls turn him off? And where did he have to be at eight o'clock on a Thursday night?

Whatever. If Hudson didn't like it, then tough. He wasn't my boss, as he'd so vehemently pointed out. I didn't need his stupid validation. I'd been top of my class. I knew my stuff. I put my laptop away, fury leaking into my brisk movements.

"Thanks," David said.

"Great. Alayna?"

"What?" I may have snapped.

Hudson waited until I met his eyes to continue. "Walk me out, please."

I bit my lip as I followed him out the office door, knowing my attitude had been less than professional. At least he would chastise me in private.

We walked in silence down the ramp toward the entrance. The club didn't open for another hour and the place was empty except for a few employees preparing for the night.

When we neared the front door, Hudson pulled me into the coat-check room. I squealed in surprise.

"Alayna," Hudson growled, pressing me against the wall with his body, pinning my hands to my sides. His nose traveled along my jaw. "You were brilliant, do you know that?"

"No." My voice squeaked, his unexpected change of temperament throwing me for a loop. "I mean, I thought my ideas were good, but then you didn't say anything…" I trailed off in a moan as he nipped at my earlobe.

"I couldn't. I was too fucking turned on." He pushed his groin against my stomach, emphasizing his point and I fought off another moan. His warmth against me spread tingles throughout my body.

"Then it was good?"

"Oh, precious, do you really have to ask?" He pulled back to look at me. "You think smart—practical and yet outside the box." He leaned his forehead against mine. "And it drives me fucking crazy."

I felt giddy. I generally hooked up with men who were attracted to my body, not my mind. It elated me. I was also now sure that Hudson's attraction to me began at the graduate symposium at Stern. "So Hudson Pierce is into nerdy girls."

He alternated his words with hot kisses at my neck. "I'm into *you*— when you're nerdy, when you're flustered, when you're whimpering under my tongue."

Damn, Hudson knew how to hit my buttons—buttons I wasn't even aware I had. I shivered under his kisses. I longed to touch him, to run my fingers through his hair, to pull his body closer to mine. But he still had my arms pinned so I had to settle with telling him with words. "I'm into you, too."

He crushed my mouth with his, letting go of my arms to let his hands wander under my dress. He grabbed my bare ass squeezing and caressing my tender skin as he kissed me aggressively. My fingers flew to his face, and I cupped his cheeks as his tongue danced with mine.

When he pulled away, we were both panting. His eyes gleamed mischievously. "During your presentation—did you picture me naked?"

Always. I grinned. "I didn't have enough to go on. I haven't seen ya naked."

"I haven't seen you naked and that doesn't stop me from picturing." He scanned my body momentarily and growled. As if he were picturing me naked that very second.

His playful mood made me braver than I had been with him. "So when are we going to remedy all the seeing of naked bits?"

Hudson rubbed his thumb along my cheek. "Ah, now she's eager. After she's sampled the goods."

"I was always eager. Now I'm sure." I turned my mouth to nibble on his thumb and he raised a brow.

"What time do you work tomorrow?"

"Nine."

His eyes widened as my nibbles turned to sucking. "I'll make sure I'm done with work by five," he said hoarsely. "Come by the loft then. Take the main elevator to the penthouse. You'll have to enter the code: Seven-three-two-three. Repeat it for me."

"Seven-three-two-three."

"Good. I'll text it to you so you don't forget. Five o'clock. Don't eat. I'll feed you." He pulled his thumb from my mouth and gave me a swift kiss. "And I'll feed on you." He returned again for a deeper kiss.

He sighed when he pushed away from me. "Tomorrow, precious." He grabbed my hand and held it as long as he could while he walked away. Before he disappeared out of the coatroom he turned back. "Oh, and I assure you, bits is not an appropriate word for my naked parts."

I assumed that already from the outline in his pants.

Less than an hour after Hudson left, Liesl stopped me as I passed the lower bar. "Laynie," she said, nodding to a small bag on the counter. "Hot Stuff left that for you while you were pulling the cash drawers from the office."

I bit my lip. "Hot stuff? You mean Hudson?"

"Yeah." I had no idea what Hudson could have given me, and though I had been on my way to unlock the front doors and open the joint, I changed my direction and headed to the package.

A folded paper was taped to the outside. In neat block print he had written: *I can't let you go without.* I blushed as I peeked inside, suspecting I knew what I'd find. Sure enough, there were my panties—laundered and folded neatly. I didn't even want to think about what member of his staff got the job of cleaning the under things of Hudson's fuck buddies. But the fact he'd made it happen was kind of cute.

"So what the fuck, Laynie?" Liesl said, and I quickly closed the bag.

"It's nothing. I left something when I was at his office earlier." Internally, I smacked myself. Next she'd question why I'd been in Hudson's office.

But that wasn't what she asked. "You left your panties at Hudson's office? Yeah, I looked. What did you expect from me?"

I rubbed a hand over my face. Liesl would find out soon enough. She'd find out the fake story, anyway. This was the perfect opportunity to tell her I was dating the man.

But I didn't. I couldn't. I wasn't ready to share him yet. I wanted to live with the genuine a little longer before I started playing the pretend.

"Liesl, I promise I'll tell you. Just not tonight."

She breathed out an exaggerated puff of air. "Fine, whatever. But you better have juicy details when you're ready to spill."

"Deal," I said. I took the bag and its contents to the bathroom to put them on.

After I did, I caught myself smiling in the mirror. Maybe I'd been wrong about Hudson. He obviously wasn't the pompous asshole I thought he was. In fact, he was turning out to be a pretty decent guy.

Damn it.

CHAPTER EIGHT

I woke up the next day with Hudson on the brain. Again. I'd never scheduled sex and knowing it was on the day's agenda made my belly tight and my pussy throb. But with the constant replay in my head of words he'd said, moves he'd made—my panic flag began to rise. I wondered as I had many times in my life if I was doomed to live either obsessing about my relationships or obsessing whether or not I was obsessing over them.

With three hours before I was set to meet Hudson at the loft, I had to address my anxiety. Otherwise, I'd be too wound up by the time I saw him and I doubted even his magic charm could unwind me.

I decided to take a jog and quickly regretted it. Midday runs were brutal in the summer, especially when I'd become used to running in the cool of the morning. Halfway through my planned course, I gave up and slowed to a walk. None of it helped ease my mind—the heat, the exercise—I still couldn't stop wondering about Hudson, what he was doing and what he would do to me when I saw him.

By coincidence or subconscious effort, I found myself wandering over to the Unity Church where my old Addicts Anonymous group met. I'd discovered it at the height of my obsessive disorder—a place where atypical addicts got together to discuss everything from video gaming addictions to obsessive shopping. I'd moved away from attending on a regular basis since I hadn't had any attacks in several years, but maybe checking in now wouldn't be a bad idea.

I went inside and down to the basement meeting rooms, finding a session led by my favorite facilitator ending. I hung in the back until they'd finished, then made my way toward Lauren.

"Well, there's a sight I haven't seen in a while," Lauren said, throwing her arms around me in a friendly hug, her hair hitting me in dozens of long braids. "Should I be concerned to see you?"

"I don't know yet. Do you have any time to talk?"

"A bit. Wanna grab a cup of coffee at the corner café?"

"Yeah."

As we walked, I caught Lauren up on my graduation and the prospects of promotion at the club, as well as the blow Brian had dealt me with his retraction of financial support. Lauren had counseled me through many of my family issues and knew probably better than anyone about the intricacies of the relationship with my brother.

"Will you be okay without the help from Brian?" Lauren asked when we were seated outside, each with an iced coffee. Her subtext said she was talking about more than the money. Stressful situations led to relapses in mental health disorders, and she wanted to know if I was stable enough to hold up.

"Maybe," I said with a sigh. "I think so. Brian hasn't been much help with any of my crap except financially. And I've gotten the money worked out."

"You have? That's great. I'm sensing a 'but,' though."

"But there's a guy."

"Mm hmm." She sat back, her arms crossed over her chest. "Go on."

I paused, not really sure how to explain my relationship with Hudson, wanting to give details and knowing I couldn't. I tried to pinpoint exactly what concerned me and express it as simply as possible. "We work together. And I can't stop thinking about him."

"Is it David?"

Thinking about David now seemed odd. I'd mentioned David before in the group, when we'd started our occasional make-out sessions. Now he felt distant and in the past though he'd only put a hold on us two days before. "It's someone else."

Lauren cocked her head. "What sort of thoughts are you having about him?"

"Fantasies." I lowered my face to hide my blush. "Sexual fantasies."

"What else?"

"That's it."

Lauren shook her head. "You're not going to get me to say you're having problems because you're thinking kinky about a hot guy."

"But it's all the time. I mean, I wake up thinking about him, I go to sleep thinking about him, I'm tending bar and I'm thinking about him."

"But no stalking or calling him at work or emailing him incessantly?"

"No."

"Only sexual thoughts?"

"No, I replay things he's said to me in my head. I wonder what he's doing and thinking."

"Have you considered you might just like him?"

I took a swallow of my coffee. Up until the night before I had spent a lot of time considering that I didn't like Hudson. Except sexually. I always knew my female parts were drawn to him. But other than that, no, I hadn't considered it. I couldn't.

"Lauren, I can't like him," I groaned. "We...there's no chance with him."

"Are you sure?"

"Yes. We've discussed it."

She looked at me curiously. I searched for something more I could give her. "He doesn't do romance," I conceded.

"Lots of women get the hots for men that are unattainable. It's natural. It doesn't mean you're falling backwards. Stay realistic about the situation. If you feel he's consuming your thoughts to the point that it's affecting your daily routine, then you need to seek some help."

"So would sleeping with him be a bad idea?" If she said yes, I didn't know what I'd do. I didn't think I could cancel on Hudson. I wanted him too badly.

"Have you?"

"Not yet."

Lauren looked at me sternly. "But you're planning on it, right? Now, girl, sex with no intention of a relationship opens up a whole other host of problems that have nothing to do with addiction but certainly can add to it."

"Is it impossible to have meaningless sex?"

"I'm sure it's possible, I just don't know very many people who get away with it. And I don't mean to imply that you're not strong enough to deal with it, but, honey, are you?"

"It might get rid of the fantasies."

"Maybe. It also might make you latch on."

"Not to sound like a slut, Lauren, but I've had quite a few one-night flings in the last few years with no attachment issues."

"Then maybe you'll be fine. But your one-night things work because you don't see the guy every day after. You'll still see this guy after, right?"

My one-night flings worked because those guys were fuck and

forget guys. Hudson, not-so-much. And I would be seeing him after. "Occasionally." Probably more than that. Truthfully, I didn't have any idea how much our little scam would require me to see Hudson. The charade was set to start Sunday, though, and he'd been intent on keeping the sex separate so I imagined that we'd be having a one day affair and then would move on.

Lauren studied me carefully. After a few minutes she shrugged. "I can't tell you what to do, Laynie. And I can't tell you that sleeping with this guy or not sleeping with this guy will make any difference in whether you do or don't fall into obsessive patterns. What I can do is be there for you and suggest that you come back to group for a while for some extra support."

Extra support was a good idea. Before we parted, I agreed to come to a weekly meeting. Then I hurried home to prepare for my evening because I had not agreed to cancel my sex date with Hudson.

• • •

Again I agonized about my wardrobe choice for my night with Hudson, finally settling on a black sequined cowl neck shirt and sequined striped shorts. Jordan dropped me off in front of the Pierce Industries building a few minutes before five. By the time I'd entered the elevator code and ridden up to the penthouse, I was shaking in my strappy three-inch heeled sandals.

It took at least one full minute before I could bring myself to knock on the loft door. Hudson opened it immediately, as if he waited just on the other side, but he had his cell phone to his ear. "Roger, I don't want to hear that we lost this company because my staff wasn't able to foresee the possibility of separation." He held the receiver away from his mouth. "Come in," he whispered to me. Then he returned to his call as he shut the door behind me.

I couldn't decide if his preoccupation with work made me more or less nervous, but I took the opportunity to check him out. He wore tailored black suit pants and a light gray dress shirt with several buttons open at the top, his tie hanging undone around his neck. I fixed on his exposed chest, picturing myself licking the patch of bare skin that I was seeing for the first time. God, if I was this enthralled by a few square inches, what would I do when he was naked?

He returned my stare, his eyes intense and dilated with want. The heat I always felt in his presence turned on full force and the moments he stood there on the phone felt like agonizing hours.

"Take care of it, Roger. I expect this to be resolved before I arrive on Monday." He ended the phone call without saying goodbye, tossing his Blackberry onto the table beside the front door, his gaze never leaving mine.

"Hi," I whispered, unable to handle the acute silence.

His lip curled slowly into a sexy grin.

That was all it took. One smile and I couldn't hold back any longer. I'd imagined the first move would be his, but it was me who moved to him, my mouth crashing against his.

His surprise lasted only a millisecond before he responded in kind. His previous kisses had been deep and passionate, but this one held no restraint as he plunged his tongue into the recesses of my mouth with desperate hunger. I met his eagerness with equal fervor, licking into his mouth, swooping my tongue across his teeth.

Without breaking our kiss, Hudson's hands moved under my shirt to palm my breasts through my bra. I gasped at the wonderful tingles that shot through my body under his gentle squeezing. My own hands fumbled with his shirt buttons, images of me ripping the damn thing off filling my mind.

Just as I'd completely opened his shirt, he pulled away, panting. "Jesus, Alayna. I want you so bad, I'm not behaving."

"Hudson," I said, closing the distance he'd created. "If this is misbehaving, please don't stop." I slid his shirt off his shoulders, letting it fall to the floor, then put my tongue on his chest and licked under his collarbone toward his nipple.

He groaned. "At least let me take you to a bed. If you keep this up, I'm going to fuck you against the door."

"That doesn't sound like the worst thing in the world," I murmured, but I let him lead me toward the partitioned bedroom.

"No, it doesn't." He stopped a few feet from the bed and pulled me into his arms. He nuzzled my neck as he said, "But I won't be able to savor you properly and I'll forever regret it."

He tugged the bottom of my shirt up and over my head then reached behind to undo the clasp of my lacey black demi-cup bra. When it fell off, releasing my tits from their C cup prison, I wanted nothing but to press my skin against his naked chest.

But Hudson wanted to gaze, mesmerized. "I imagined you'd have beautiful breasts, Alayna. But I had no idea..." He broke off, his voice choked. He pushed me back until my legs met his bed and I had to sit. Kneeling in front of me, Hudson flicked one breast with his tongue, cupping it toward his mouth with his hand, his other hand wrapped around my back.

With a growl, his mouth covered my nipple and sucked and tugged with pleasing pressure. I cried out at the jolt that accompanied his ardor, my cunt tightening. I clutched his hair as he feasted thoroughly, leaving me gasping and near orgasm before he turned the same attention to my other breast.

When he'd finished, he kissed his way down my stomach. "You're so responsive. I could spend all day sucking your gorgeous tits." He pushed me back on to the bed. "But there's so much of you to adore."

He gripped his fingers in the waistbands of my shorts and panties and pulled down. I arched my hips to help him. "My shoes," I said when my bottoms reached my ankles.

"I love them." He maneuvered my clothing over my high-heels. "I want them digging into my back when you wrap your legs around me."

I quivered at his sensual instruction. Not a particular lover, I enjoyed the way he told me how things would be, trusting that his way would bring us both pleasure.

"Lean on your elbows." I did and he bent one leg up then the other, anchoring my heels on the edge of the bed, my thighs open. He sighed as he slid his hands up the inside of my legs. "You're so fucking sexy like this. All spread out for me." My sex clenched and he smiled, running his fingers down my slit. "You want me. Look how your pretty pussy throbs."

No one had ever talked to me like that—so raw and crude. It was incredibly hot and savage and combined with the repeated tease of his fingers brushing across my pulsing bud, it wouldn't take much to bring me to convulsions. As soon as his tongue replaced his fingers, grazing me with velvet licks, I unraveled, throwing my head back to let out a ragged cry.

"Again," he demanded gruffly, plunging three fingers deep inside me. My hands curled into the bedspread, not sure I could take another, wanting even more than his fingers. He stroked me, rubbing the inside of my walls as he returned his mouth to suck on my clit. When I'd reached the brink of climax again, shuddering under the building tension, he stretched his other hand up to my breast and tugged at my nipple with his fingers. I came violently, thrashing against the bed, my sex rippling around his digits.

As I lay shaking, I was vaguely aware of Hudson removing his clothing. I heard the drawer of the nightstand open and close and the rip of a condom foil. He shifted me backward on the bed, giving himself space to crawl over me. Then he settled between my legs, his hot staff pressing at my quivering entrance.

"You're ready for me," he said, leaning his weight on his forearms. He aligned his erection with my opening and entered me partway. "Jesus, Alayna," he hissed. "You feel so goddamn good."

I gasped as he invaded me. He was so big. Not sure if he would fit, I tensed, knowing that I had to relax if I had any hope of accommodating him. He adjusted my leg and that's what I needed. I opened to him and he sunk deeper, nestling in my tight channel.

I couldn't remember ever having felt so completely filled, not only because of his girth, but because of the way his eyes pierced mine as he stretched and moved within me. He circled his hips nudging his tip forward. "So good."

He pulled out slowly, almost the entire length of his cock, and I bemoaned the emptiness left behind. Then he flexed his hips and rammed inside me with a fierce stroke.

I cried out and he echoed with a low grumble of desire. He pressed his chest against me and captured my mouth, kissing me roughly with my taste on his lips as he pounded into me.

Even though he'd already taken care of me—twice—I was desperate for him to bring me to another orgasm. I rocked against him, meeting each grinding pulse of his hips, moaning and panting as I took each one of his blunt drives.

"Wrap your legs around me," Hudson grunted as he continued his assault.

I obeyed, having forgotten his earlier wish for me to do so. My heels hit against the back of his thighs, digging into him as he moved in and out of me, adding an additional level of eroticism. Lifting my legs also opened me further, and his cock bore deeper into me, hitting a spot within that ignited at each stroke.

My orgasm built from there, my body tightening and clenching and contracting around Hudson's pummeling thrusts. "I'm going to come," I groaned, already trembling.

"Yes," Hudson cried. "Yes, come, Alayna." My climax crashed through me, brought to a head by his coaxing. Seconds later, his own body tensed and jerked, releasing into me long and hard, my name spilling from his lips.

He fell onto my quaking body, our chests rising and falling in tandem. His head buried into the crook of my neck as I pulled my fingers through his sweat-dampened hair.

"I knew sex with you would be like that," he said, his voice almost a whisper. "Powerful and intense and fucking incredible. I knew it."

I swallowed, forcing down any emotion that threatened to show itself except for satiation. "Me, too."

Chapter Nine

I must have dozed. When I woke, Hudson stood over me, pulling a comforter over my naked body.

"Sleep, precious," he said as I struggled to sit up. He'd put on a pair of sweats, but he still smelled like sex. My belly tightened in response to his scent. Would my lust for Hudson never be satisfied?

He brushed a kiss on my forehead. "I need to order dinner. Chinese okay?"

I stretched. "Sounds delicious."

"I'll call it in."

I watched his gorgeous backside as he left the bedroom, luxuriating in what was left of my post-sex high. God, I felt good. I hadn't been fucked like that in…well, ever. The care and attention Hudson delivered as a lover left little to be desired. Of course, that made me want him. Again.

I tugged the comforter tighter around me, an uneasy feeling creeping over me. I tried to dissect its source. The fact was I felt comfortable—too comfortable. My number one rule in avoiding unhealthy attachments was to avoid attachments in general. Getting comfortable was too close to attached. And there was no way I could get attached to Hudson.

A tenuous ball of anxiety began forming in my belly. I could stay through dinner, I decided, but I needed to be dressed and sitting at a table. And then, after the night was over, Hudson and I had to keep our relationship to business only.

Throwing off the blanket, I began to gather my clothes. I found my panties and slipped them on then reached for my bra.

"You're getting dressed?"

I jumped. Hudson was standing in the doorway, watching me, carrying his shirt and tie that he'd—um, *we'd*—discarded earlier in the main room. Suddenly feeling awkward at my near nakedness, I crossed my arms over my chest.

He tossed his clothes on top of the laundry basket then crossed his own arms. Hudson didn't appear to be hiding as I was, but looked like he meant to scold me. He raised a brow. "Are you in a hurry to leave?" I shivered. His gaze and my lack of clothing made it hard to remember why I'd wanted to go. I looked away. He probably wanted me gone soon anyway, having already gotten what he wanted. We didn't have to pretend otherwise. "Guys don't usually want me to hang around after sex."

"That statement brings up so many issues for discussion that I don't know where to begin." He stepped toward me. "What is wrong with men to not...?" He shook his head. "Alayna, please don't group me with other guys you know. I'd like to think I'm not like most of them. And I don't want to know or think about you having sex with other men. I don't share."

Not meeting his eye, I picked up my shorts from the floor, ignoring the thrill that ran up my spine from his suggestion of possessiveness. "That sounds awfully relationshippy to me. I thought you didn't do relationships."

"I don't do *romantic* relationships. Sexual relationships are another thing entirely. Why are you getting ready to leave?"

Avoiding his question, I dove for my shirt at the foot of the bed, but Hudson beat me to it. "Stop," he said, holding my shirt out of my reach. He put his finger under my chin so that I would look him in the eye. His brow creased in confusion and his tone held sincerity. "I want you to stay. And, if you are so inclined, I'd prefer that you not be dressed."

I wanted to melt under his invitation, but I refused to be affected. "You're dressed," I said, crossing my arms over my chest again, sounding like a pouty child. The knot of anxiety was tightening, and I was grabbing at anything I could to try to stand my ground.

"As soon as the food's here, I'll be happy to lose the clothing. Would that make you feel better?"

"Yes." But that was my hormones talking. My hormones wanted him naked. And hard. And slippery with sweat.

But my brain wasn't sure it was a good idea. "I don't know," I corrected.

Still holding my chin, he brushed my cheek with his other hand. "What's going on inside your head, precious? Are you going to run off every time we have sex?"

He wanted to have sex with me again. My girl parts clenched at the thought. But, as my arousal piqued, so did the terror throbbing in my veins. Usually sex ended any interest I had in a guy. Except for before—when nothing ended my interest in a guy and I obsessed about them endlessly. And now—when every part of my body screamed with the need to have more of the man in front of me. Oh, fucking god, was I falling into old patterns?

I turned away. "I hadn't really thought this would be more than a one-time thing, Hudson."

He grabbed my arm and pulled me to him. "Alayna." He searched my eyes, looking for an answer I knew he wouldn't find because I didn't have the answers myself. "If you don't want to have sex with me again, you need to tell me."

"I do!" His hands on me, and his piercing eyes elicited the truth from my lips. "I do," I said again softly. I threw my arms around him and pressed my face against his chest, nuzzling his hard pecs. He returned my embrace. *So warm.* He felt so warm and safe and strong. Like he could shield me from whatever scared me. Like the reality of him—the reality of what he was to me—might be enough to keep me from needing more.

"What is it?" His voice was light. He stroked my hair, and my panic lowered half a notch. "Tell me."

Tears threatened and I was grateful he couldn't see my face. Was I doomed to live the rest of my life afraid of becoming close to people? To men? "I'm not good at relationships. Of any sort. I have...issues." What the fuck was I doing? Casual sex meant no sharing of inner secrets. But it felt good to say it.

"Like what?" Hudson's hands tangled in my hair, soothing me. "Does this have anything to do with that restraining order?"

The floor dropped from underneath me. I couldn't move. "You know about that?" No one knew about that. At least, very few people. Brian, my support group, Liesl had heard bits and pieces. But I would never have told Hudson. I broke free of his arms and fell onto the bed, burying my face in the blankets. "Oh, god, I'm so embarrassed!"

He laughed and lay on the bed next to me, his head propped on his elbow near mine. He rubbed his hand across my backside, massaging my tense muscles. It felt so good that, had I not been dying of humiliation, I'm sure I would have moaned.

When he spoke, his voice was low and at my ear. "I know intimate things about you, precious—the way you look and the sounds you make when you're about to come—and you're concerned about this?"

I groaned into the bed, half from misery and half from the pleasure I felt from his fingers on my back. I turned my head so he could hear me talk, but away from him so I wouldn't have to see his face. "It was a big deal. The biggest deal. Like my biggest secret. I thought my brother had buried it." I rose up on my elbow and turned to eye him. "And are you saying I should be embarrassed about how I look and sound when… you know?"

"I needed to know anything that might come up about my pretend girlfriend. It wasn't necessarily easy to find, but not incredibly hard. It's been buried now." He cupped my cheek, his eyes growing dark. "And never, never be ashamed of how you look or sound at any time, especially when you're about to come." He circled his nose around mine. "I'm honored to be acquainted with you in that way."

"I'm mortified." I let my head fall back on the bed, but stayed facing him. "About the restraining order, I mean. I don't know how to react to the other."

"Why?"

He ran his hand across my face and through my hair, each stroke setting off an electric charge that sparked in my core. It relaxed me and comforted me and made me feel like Jello. He could have asked me anything right then and I'd have surrendered. "Because it makes me feel all weird and tingly. And turned on."

"Fantastic." He grinned. "But I meant, why are you mortified?"

"Oh." I flushed. What I'd said in error was actually less embarrassing than what he had really asked. But since he was still stroking me with that magic hand of his that had more power than Chinese water torture, I answered him that, too. "Because it's evidence of my crazy. You know, when I said I love too much? The restraining order is part of that, and I like to pretend it never happened."

"Then it never did." He kissed my nose. "We've all done insane things in the past. I'd never hold it against you." He stopped stroking my hair, and looked somewhere beyond me. "Just another reason romantic love holds no interest for me. People get crazy with it."

Then he relaxed and focused back on me. "But going back to the heart of this conversation—why does that have a bearing on a relationship between you and me?"

I sat up, unnerved by how easily he dismissed my past behavior. "I freaked out, Hudson. About a guy." He wasn't taking me seriously and I needed him to understand. "Several guys, actually, but it was the last one that ended not well."

He sat up next to me, our shoulders brushing. "And do you think you're going to 'freak out' about me?"

I focused on my hands in my lap. "I really can't honestly tell you. I've stayed away from any relationships for a while so I wouldn't have to deal with it. Trying to have something now with you—it's uncharted territory for me." Truthfully, as scared as I was of falling into unhealthy patterns, I didn't want to end things with Hudson. And we would be working together. Even if the best course of action was to not sleep with him again, would I be able to resist?

I looked him in the eyes, wondering if I'd scared him off yet. Because as much as I knew he should run, I hoped he wouldn't. "I haven't freaked out so far. With you. And I don't want to not have sex with you again. I mean…" I turned away, blushing for the millionth time.

He wrapped his arms around me and nibbled on my ear. "You're adorable when you're flustered. I don't want to not have sex with you again either. So we won't do that. We'll have tons of incredible sex instead."

I let myself be held in his embrace. "I'm not saying yes, yet." But wasn't I? "I have to take this one day at a time." And what would I do if I woke up one morning completely obsessed with him? As if I could stop things with him at that point.

"Alayna, you might have to take this one day at a time, but I already know there will be tons of fucking between the two of us." He pulled me closer, and I melted at his words, at his touch. "In fact, I'm going to have to be inside you again before you leave for work."

I felt his erection at my bare belly. Instead of being surprised and ashamed that I still wanted him so very much, I decided to relish in it. "Like right now?"

He kissed me, deeply, his tongue taking over my mouth. Then, just as quickly, he broke away. "Not right now, precious. Dinner's almost he—" The intercom buzzed before he'd finished his word. He smiled as he stood. Then he headed to the front room, saying over his shoulder, "But your enthusiasm is super hot."

I smiled to myself, enjoying the residual tingle from our kiss. Fuck. Dinner was here and I wasn't dressed. Putting on my own clothes now would be a statement. Staying naked would be too. I sat up and eyed his shirt on top of the laundry basket. It would have to do as a compromise.

I pulled off my shorts and had barely finished buttoning his shirt when Hudson returned with a bag of food in one hand and two plates in the other. He scanned me up and down, a pleased glint in his eye. "If you have to be dressed, I completely approve."

Suddenly feeling playful, I curtsied. "Well, thank you very much, Mr. Pierce. I don't know what I'd do without your approval."

He grinned, crossing to the bed. "Should I undress? I said I would."

"Not if you want me to actually eat. I'd be much too distracted. And I already have a hard time with chopsticks."

Hudson gestured for me to join him on the bed. "Do you need me to feed you?"

"Hmm. Maybe."

We ate together, eating Mongolian beef and Szechuan chicken spread out over the bed. I struggled with my chopsticks, half of my food not making it to my mouth. Every now and then he fed me, and I let him, enjoying being cared for in a way I hadn't been in a long time, if ever.

"What are you doing tomorrow?" Hudson asked after he'd left and returned with two glasses of iced tea. "Before work, I mean."

I took a swallow, moved that Hudson chose to drink with me when he probably preferred wine. "I'm off work at three tonight. Or tomorrow morning, however you want to look at it. I'll probably sleep a good part of the day. I work at nine tomorrow night. Why?"

He reached over to feed me another bite. "I need to take you shopping. You'll need an outfit for my mother's charity event."

I practically choked on a water chestnut. "Oh my freaking god, one inappropriate outfit and you assume I can't dress myself. Seriously, I should burn it."

"That's not it at all. I happen to love that outfit and would be very disappointed to find you'd burned it. I actually hope to see you wearing it again. In private, of course." His eyes glazed, perhaps picturing me in the tight corset I'd worn that night I officially met him. "And I've adored every other outfit of yours." He tugged at the bottom of my shirt—*his* shirt—that I was wearing. "You have an excellent sense of fashion. But my mother would expect a girl I dated to be dressed..." He paused. "How should I put it?"

I kind of liked watching him struggle with his words for once. But he seemed miserable so I helped him out. "I get it. I need designer clothes." I paused, trying to decide if I was offended. "I guess if you want to take me out and buy me expensive clothes, I'm not going to argue."

His lips curled slightly. "That's a beautiful attitude. I'll pick you up at two. Plan to spend the day with me. And don't look at me like that—there will only be sex if you want there to be."

Of course I'd want there to be. But whether or not I thought it should happen remained to be seen. I let myself consider it. "How do you intend on this working, exactly? Do you text me when you want a booty call?"

"Sure. Or you can text me. Or we can arrange ahead of time like we did tonight." Hudson studied me. "What would you say to no condoms?"

I'd always thought condoms were a drag, but I hadn't ever been in a committed relationship where I could consider not using them. It struck me as odd that after one time I was having this conversation with Hudson. "I suppose if you're clean…I'm on birth control. I get the shot. My last STD test was a month ago and it came back clean."

"I am clean. I'm checked monthly. And I hate condoms."

"Then no more condoms."

He smiled and I caught my mistake.

"If I agree, I mean."

"Mmhmm." He stroked his hand up my bare thigh. Sexual tension hung in the air between us, but my brain screamed at me to be cautious.

I hugged my knees, casually pulling away from his touch. "You said you expected fidelity—can I expect the same from you? Or will you be using this loft with other women?"

Hudson moved our leftover dinner to the floor, clearing the space between us. Then he put a hand on each of my knees, pinning me with his eyes. "I'm not a slut, Alayna. This loft has been used for sex, yes, but I have it so I can be close to my office, not for fucking." He stretched a hand out to brush a strand of hair behind my ear. "I will be as faithful as I expect you to be."

His nearness, his touch, his promise of fidelity—it stirred my arousal, begging me to give in. But it also tugged at something much deeper, something both familiar and unknown, something I couldn't name or identify, and I knew if I tried, it—whatever it was—would come rushing up and consume me.

I scrambled off the bed. "I can't think about this anymore right now." I began gathering my clothing.

"Why are you panicking?" Hudson stood as well.

I turned to him, suddenly angry—with him, with myself, with my stupid compulsion to cling and drive people away, with my parents for dying and pushing me into that behavior. "You know, it's all very good and fine for you to say you want a committed sexual relationship. You'll have no problem remaining unemotionally involved—that's your default. It's not my default. Don't you see what you're asking of me might be impossible for me to deliver?" I rubbed at my eyes, hoping to stop any tears before they dared to fall.

Hudson reached toward me, but I stepped away. "The more we have sex, Hudson, the more I'm likely to latch on, and even if you were into that, you wouldn't be into the level that I latch. So, trust me when I say this has bad idea written all over it. Let's call this a wonderful—oh, my god, such a wonderful evening—and now we need to move on."

His mouth tightened into a straight line. "If that's what you need."

"I do." I hugged myself, embarrassed by my outburst. "And I need a shower. Do you mind?"

"Not at all. In there." He gestured toward the bathroom. "I'll bring you some towels."

He sounded distant, and I immediately regretted pushing him there. Already I missed the warmth of him.

In the bathroom, I threw my clothes on the black granite counter and avoided looking in the mirror, not liking who I'd see staring back at me. I turned the shower on extra hot, hoping the heat would relieve the chill that had settled on me, and climbed under the heavy spray.

In there, alone, water and steam embracing me, the tears came freely. I cried soundlessly, surrendering to the hollow loneliness that I had grown accustomed to before Hudson arrived to show me something new.

Absorbed in my self-pity, I didn't hear him enter the bathroom with the towels, and when he opened the shower door and slid in to join me, instead of cursing his obvious lack of respect for my wishes to withdraw from him, I abandoned myself and pressed my lips to his.

He responded without hesitation, kissing me with gentle aggression. When I pulled away to catch my breath, he reached for the bottle of body wash and poured a small dollop onto his hand. Then he began to wash me. He took his time, running his soapy hands over every inch of my body. At my breasts he lingered longer, squeezing and caressing them both, flicking across my nipples with his thumbs. I sighed into the pleasure.

When he'd thoroughly cleaned the top half of me, he bent to wash my legs, starting with my feet and moving up my long limbs. He moved so slowly, so sensually, massaging the suds into my skin, that by the time his fingers slid through the folds at the base of my belly, I was ready to beg. His thumbs brushed past my clit and I moaned.

He swept through my folds over and over, and I jerked at each teasing pass. "Hudson," I said, my teeth gritted, my pussy clenching with need.

"Is this what you want?" He thrust two fingers inside me, twisting them.

"Yes!" I gasped. "I mean, no. I want you."

His grin was wicked as he continued to grind into me with his fingers. "You'll have to wait. I'm enjoying making you wait."

I wanted to argue, but he added a third finger to his probe and gently squeezed my clit and speech became impossible. I moaned as I rocked back and forth, digging my nails into Hudson's broad shoulders.

Just when I'd reached the brink of orgasm, his fingers left my body. I opened my eyes and found him standing in front of me, holding the bottle of body wash. "I need to be washed too."

My body ached with yearning, but I was eager to explore him. I hadn't even fully taken in his naked body, having been too distracted in the bedroom and now in the shower. Lathering my hands up, I began as he had, at his shoulders, but I was too greedy to move slowly. Soon, I'd cleansed all but his cock. I stared at his giant erection, fascinated by its length and girth. He'd felt big, but I had no idea he was *that* big.

I swallowed. Hard.

"What's the matter, precious?" I sensed he was smiling, unable to move my eyes from the sight in front of me.

"Um, wow," I managed. "I'm a little intimidated."

"But it's already been inside you. You know it fits." His voice grew ragged. "Touch it, Alayna."

His command stirred me to movement. I circled my hands around his shaft and stroked his hot silky skin. He felt so firm, so powerful, so perfect. I moved my fist up and down, once, twice, and the third time, he leapt in my hands.

At the next stroke, he growled and hoisted me up, encouraging me to wrap my legs around him. He pressed my back against the tile wall, his mouth ravaging mine, and in one fierce thrust, he was inside me. I tangled my hands in his hair as he rammed into me, feeling every inch of his cock filling me and fucking me.

I cried as my orgasm shook through me, the tremors of it spreading all the way to my toes. Hudson quickened his pace, clutching tighter to my hips so he could pump through my sex as it spasmed around his steel shaft. Several strokes later he released with his own cry, his cock jerking inside me as he spurted hotly into my sex.

In that moment, I let myself believe we could be together like that, how he wanted, without becoming consumed, even though I was afraid that I already was.

CHAPTER TEN

Anxious for our shopping adventure, I decided to wait for Hudson in front of my building. I'd expected Jordan and the Maybach, so I was surprised when Hudson pulled up driving a Mercedes SL Roadster.

I slipped into the passenger seat. "Nice wheels."

His lips curled up into a sexy grin as he eased the car out into traffic. "Glad you approve."

I didn't know where to look first—at the luxury sports car or at Hudson in his tight dark blue jeans and fitted maroon button down shirt. I hadn't seen him in casual wear, and, as good as he looked in his suits, this new look had my tummy fluttering.

Well, Hudson in general made my tummy flutter.

"So you drove yourself?" Normally, I'm not much into small talk, but the sexual undertone between us needed silencing. Especially because another morning of constantly questioning the healthiness of my Hudson relationship had led me to decide the day needed to be sex free. I needed to counteract any attachment with distance. Hopefully, I wouldn't chicken out when it came to telling him.

He glanced at me over his shoulder before he switched lanes. "Why does my driving surprise you?"

I shrugged, securing my seatbelt. "I figured you always had a driver." Not that he needed one. He navigated city traffic well and watching him handle the wheel was hot.

"What's the fun of having a cool car if you don't get to drive it?"

"Good point."

At the next stoplight, Hudson peeked at me over his Ray Ban Aviator sunglasses. "You look gorgeous, Alayna. As usual."

His voice oozed pure seduction, and I pulled at the hem of my blue shift dress, wondering if it had always been as short as it suddenly seemed. "Are you buttering me up so I'll let you choose what I try on?"

"I'll choose what you try on anyway."

"Of course, you will." He was paying, after all.

We drove in silence for a few minutes, exchanging occasional glances that held the entire weight of our attraction. Under certain circumstances, the flirting and tension would be fun, but not when I felt so off-balance and unsure.

I had to get my declaration over with. "Um, Hudson, could we keep today to shopping only?" I hoped to God he understood what I meant without spelling it out.

He did. A brief flash of disappointment crossed his face—or maybe it was my imagination. His voice seemed stiff when he said, "Whatever you want, Alayna."

Immediately, I regretted saying anything. The fun flirty mood vanished, and Hudson became reserved and withdrawn. I considered taking my words back, but really, how could I do that?

"We're going to Mirabelle's," he said after a few minutes, not looking at me.

"Mirabelle, your sister?" Hudson's sister, Mirabelle owned a popular designer boutique in Greenwich Village. It was the type of place you could only get into with an appointment, but from what I'd seen from window-shopping, the woman had mad fashion skills.

"Yes. Her friends are throwing her a baby shower today and so I'd hoped she wouldn't be at the shop. However, when she learned I was bringing my *girlfriend* in for a fitting, she insisted on being there to meet you. Which means we're officially on the job. Is that a problem?"

"Um, no, of course not." My palms started to sweat. It occurred to me that the hours I spent worrying if I had any impulse to stalk Hudson online should have been spent actually stalking him online. Then I'd maybe have some more info about the supposed love of my life. "What if she asks me things? About you? About us?" And how would we be able to pull off the image of a happy couple when the tension between us was palpable?

"Don't worry about it. I'll be there. Follow my lead." Hudson reached under his glasses and rubbed the bridge of his nose. "Frankly, you're unlikely to get a chance to speak at all. Mirabelle is somewhat of a talker."

"But...what do I *do*?"

"Just be my girlfriend."

• • •

"Oh my god, Hudson, you told me she was gorgeous, but I had no idea!" The perky brunette who stood in front of me was clearly Hudson's relative. They shared many of the same features—chiseled cheekbones and strong jaws and matching hair and skin tones. Where Hudson was broad and muscular, Mirabelle was petite, her small stature accentuated by the round belly that protruded in front of her.

Mirabelle continued talking as she scanned me up and down, circling around me and Hudson, who had held my hand since grabbing it right before ringing the service bell. "She is going to be so much fun to dress. She's got my favorite body type—all boobs and hips and—" She paused as she raised my already short dress. "Fantastic legs, Hudson!"

Hudson's wicked grin appeared as he squeezed my hand. "Yes, I'm well acquainted with Alayna's physical assets."

Heat ran to my face.

Mirabelle hit her brother playfully. "You're such a bad boy." Then she faced me and gasped, covering her mouth with her hand. "Oh my goodness, I'm talking about you in the third person. How could I be so rude! I'm so excited to finally meet you, Alayna! Hudson has told me so much about you!"

She threw her arms around me in a generous hug. I glared at Hudson over her shoulder, wondering what he'd said about me and how I'd let myself walk into this moment so unprepared. He shrugged in response and let go of my hand, no longer giving me an excuse to not embrace her back.

By the time Mirabelle released me, I'd realized I needed to stop fretting and get into character. I swallowed and gave her a wide smile. "Glad to meet you too. But call me Laynie."

"And you can call me Mira. Huds is way too proper." She wrapped her arm around mine, reminding me of the annoying popular girls in high school who walked down the halls with their hands clasped with their girlfriends. Though admittedly, it wasn't as annoying when you were the girl being clasped. "Okay, okay, okay, I can't stay long today which I regret immensely, so let's get started. I already have a million ideas for you."

I hadn't had a chance to look around, having been accosted by Mira at the entryway, but now I surveyed the shop. Though small, Mirabelle's held a wide range of women's clothing and shoes. The walls and furniture were all brilliant white, giving the room an air of elegance while letting the clothing on display pop like art.

"Are we shopping only for Mom's event?" Mira asked, her forehead creased as if pondering where to start.

Hudson kept his hand at the small of my back. Despite knowing that the gesture was part of the show staged for his sister, the electricity that always accompanied his touch ran up my spine. "Specifically for the fashion show, but let's see what else we can find. Whatever Alayna loves, we'll buy." He gazed at me with a look that could only be described as adoration. God, he was good.

Mira's attention was on us so I made sure to return Hudson's stare, fighting to not lose myself in his intense, gray eyes. "Aw, thank you." I added sugar to my usually unsweetened tone. I turned to Mira. "Hudson spoils me. I don't deserve him."

Hudson began to protest but was interrupted by a buzz on his phone. "Excuse me." His eyes narrowed as he read his text.

Mira ignored him and gathered clothing over her arm. "This and this, oh and this will be perfect on you!" She called toward the back of the store. "Stacy, can you start us a room?"

A tall, skinny blonde appeared out of an office in the back. She took the clothing Mira handed her. "Which room do you want to use?" Although she spoke to Mira, Stacy stared longingly toward Hudson. Longingly enough to make me wonder if they had a history or if Stacy wished they had a history.

I snuck my own glance at Hudson. He was still typing things into his cell phone, his brow furrowed and his mouth pulled in a tight line.

"The big dressing room please. Laynie, this is my assistant, Stacy." Mira drew the blonde's attention back to her. "Laynie is Hudson's girlfriend so make sure she gets VIP treatment."

"Certainly," Stacy said with a bright fake smile, her eyes shooting daggers in my direction.

When Stacy had retreated out of earshot, I leaned into Mira. "Your assistant seems not to like me very much." I paused. Should I say more? I decided yes. It was the real me that wanted to know about Stacy and Hudson, but girlfriend me would want to know too. "And she seems to like Hudson an awful lot. Is there something between them?"

Mira hesitated, not looking me in the eye. "Ignore her. Stacy's totally been in love with Huds for forever, even though she's completely not his type. Nothing to worry about. It's actually comical."

She seemed like she may have been holding back, but on the other hand, maybe she was just awkward about talking girl crushes with her brother's girlfriend. I decided on the latter when Mira lowered her voice. "Did you notice how Hudson didn't even give her the time of day?" She giggled.

"I did." I giggled too. For real. I liked Mira.

Mira continued gathering clothing and accessories. "Hudson, what do you think about these?" She held up a pair of strappy heels.

Without looking up, Hudson grunted his response. "Uh huh."

I bit my lip, wondering what had him preoccupied. He'd been determined to pick clothes for me, and I knew he wanted to play up the sham for his sister. Instead, he'd been on his phone since we'd arrived. A small part of me feared he was passively-aggressively dealing with my no sex declaration by avoiding our situation. But then again, Hudson wasn't ever passive about anything.

Mira didn't approve of his lack of attention either. "Huds, it's the weekend. Put your Blackberry away." She nudged him with her elbow. "You finally have a girlfriend. Are you trying to run her off?"

Hudson finished his typing and raised his head. "Hmm?"

I stepped in front of him and put my hands on his biceps— his perfectly sculpted biceps. "Listen to your sister and stop with the working."

He pocketed his phone and wrapped his arms around me. "Are you feeling ignored?" His face had relaxed, but his eyes still showed signs of distress.

"You're going to make me think you have another girl." Maybe he did have another girl. I'd nixed the sex and maybe he was now going through his contact list.

I shoved the idea out of my mind and rubbed my nose against his. Then, because I couldn't help myself, I lowered my voice and asked. "Is everything okay?"

"It's work." He nuzzled his face against mine, but not before he glanced at Mira to make sure she was watching. His phone buzzed in his pocket again. He pulled it out, leaving one arm wrapped loosely around me. His body stiffened under my hands as he read his text. "I'm sorry, baby, I have to make a phone call."

Baby? In my head, I rolled my eyes.

Mira actually did roll her eyes. "Come with me, Laynie. He can make his boring call. Let's go try some of these things on you." She took my arm, ready to lead me to the dressing room.

Hudson paused his dialing. "Hold on a second, I'll join you."

Mira shook her head. "We'll come out and show you her outfits. Don't worry."

"Mirabelle, I'm not leaving Alayna alone with my over-enthusiastic little sister."

I vacillated between gratefulness for Hudson's protection and suspicion that he didn't want me alone with Mira for reasons of his own. I leaned toward suspicion, but that may have been because I'm suspicious by nature.

Mira glared at her brother. "You're not coming in the fitting room. That's just…wrong."

Deciding that I could handle her fine on my own, if that was indeed the reason he meant to keep us apart, I pulled away from Mira's grasp and leaned into Hudson. "I'll be fine, H." I shortened his name partly out of the need for something more familiar to call him and partly to irritate him. "Take care of whatever you need to."

"H?" he questioned so only I could hear.

I whispered in return. "Go with it, *baby.*" I meant to only give him a peck, but when my lips brushed his, he pulled them in for a deeper kiss—a kiss that felt much more involved than necessary if it was only for Mira's sake.

The afternoon went quickly as I tried on nearly every item in the boutique. Mira helped me dress, pairing each outfit with appropriate shoes and accessories. I had always loved trying on new clothes, but I'd never looked or felt as good as I did wearing Mira's choices. I felt like a model.

At each outfit change, she'd parade me out for Hudson who smiled and nodded in between talking on the phone. Occasionally he'd shake his head in disapproval, usually when an outfit was slightly risqué. And a few times I saw the glint of desire in his eyes—the one that had claimed me on the night I met him. Those outfits were the ones I set aside as my favorites.

When we'd already selected a dress for the fashion show, plus a stack of additional outfits, Mira held up a long black evening gown with a corset bodice. "We've saved the best for last," she said.

Though the idea of wearing a corset around Hudson had me slightly anxious because of my first encounter with him, I'd never seen anything so exquisite as the gown Mira held, and I knew before I'd even put it on that it would be gorgeous.

Mira helped me remove my bra then lifted the dress over my head, pulling it down over my bust. "So Hudson told me you met at some college thingy," she said as she began to thread the laces.

I swallowed. I'd assumed that Hudson would have told people we met at the club, but this made more sense. It gave the fictional Alayna and Hudson time to fall in love. Still, it threw me off for a moment, and I paused before answering. "Yeah, it was a graduate symposium at Stern."

Mira tightened another lace. "I have to know, was it love at first sight for you too, or just him?"

So he'd claimed love at first sight. *Nice touch.* "Definitely for me too."

I saw Mira smile behind me in the mirror. "It's all so romantic. How he wanted to hire you and you already had a job, so he bought the club you work at to get closer to you."

I sucked in a quick breath, shocked at this new addition to the story. "He told you that?"

Mira clasped her hand to her mouth, her eyes wide. "Oh my god, did you not know?"

"No, no, I knew." I hadn't known, of course. But what really struck me was the possibility that it could be true. I'd dismissed it when it had occurred to me before. Now, I couldn't dismiss it so easily.

I also couldn't think about it right then. Not when Mira still looked frightened that she'd said something she shouldn't have. I tried to ease her. "It was crazy romantic that he bought the club. I just didn't think he'd tell anyone."

What I said worked. Mira's face relaxed. "It is surprising. He's usually so private about his emotions. You must bring out something in him." She stepped away from me. "And this dress will totally bring something out in him or else he's completely blind. You look incredible!"

She was right—I did look incredible. And when we walked out into the boutique, Hudson did more than merely smile and nod. He hung up his phone and gawked.

"Do you like?" I could already tell the answer from his hungry eyes.

That look of his, it never failed to arouse me, never failed to make my panties wet.

He nodded slowly, seemingly speechless, and I marveled that I had brought him to that state. It made me feel more attractive and more powerful than I'd ever felt.

"Wow, Huds is at a loss for words," Mira said, her hands resting on her pregnant belly. "Call Ripley's."

Ignoring his sister, Hudson walked up to me. "I'd take you in my arms," he murmured, "but I wouldn't be able to look at you anymore. You're stunning, Alayna."

"Thank you," I whispered. This moment was for us, not Mira. I was beautiful to him and that made him all the more beautiful to me. It also made my nipples stand at attention, an uncomfortable predicament when a corset already had my breasts in a vise grip.

"Okay guys, I'd tell you to get a room, but I'm afraid you'll use one of the dressing rooms." Mira threatened to break the moment, but the intensity of it lingered. "I don't have to ask if you're buying this one."

"We're taking it." Hudson didn't take his eyes off me, proving the truth in his statement since he couldn't stop looking.

A brief image flashed into my mind of him and me going at it right there on the showroom floor. But since we had spectators—and since, by my own decree it was a sex-free day—I looked away. The lapse in eye contact helped give me the strength to pull away as well. "I'll get changed."

Mira led the way, stopping at the door of the dressing room to glance at her watch. "Aw, crap, is that really the time? I'm totally late! Go on in. I'll send Stacy to help you undress." She hugged me quickly. "And it was so wonderful to finally meet you. I'll see you tomorrow at the fashion show."

I huffed at a strand of hair that had fallen over my face and entered the dressing room, not at all eager to encounter Stacy and her dagger eyes alone. While I waited for her, I reached behind my back to see if I could unlace the corset myself, snagging my fingernail on one of the threads. I was examining the nail, trying to smooth out the rough edge when I felt Stacy's hands undoing the laces. She had so much hatred for me she hadn't even offered a greeting.

I glanced up from my nail at her in the mirror. But it wasn't Stacy undoing my corset—it was Hudson.

He met my eyes, pinning my reflection with a greedy stare. Slowly, without breaking his gaze, he continued loosening the laces of my bodice. I didn't stop him. He didn't ask, and I didn't stop him.

When he'd finished loosening my gown, his hands traveled to the spaghetti straps at my shoulders. I watched as he moved the straps over the curve of my bones and down my arms. The dress fell to the floor, leaving me in nothing but black strappy heels and my red thong.

Hudson's eyes widened and my sex clenched.

I wanted him. Whatever I told myself about healthy and unhealthy relationships, it didn't matter. I was already in this with him. If there was a point of attachment that would lead me to obsession, I'd already passed it. And admitting that made me sorry I'd ever tried to be anything different with him.

Hudson's hands ran around my waist, meeting above my navel. Then while one hand traveled up to fondle my breast, the other moved under the band of my thong. I stepped my legs apart, an invitation for him to find my swollen bud. His lip twitched the slightest bit as he slid his fingers through my slick desire, parting the folds of my sex, and releasing the musky aroma of my lust. In that moment, he knew how much I longed for him, embarrassingly wet as I was.

He continued to plump my breast that was suddenly heavy and tender as he flicked his thumb across my raised nipple. The attention he gave to my bosom magnified the action below, his pad returning to tease my clit, and I let out a breathy moan. He stretched his arm over my torso, supporting me as I weakened from pleasure and I closed my eyes to relish in the nearness of climax.

"Alayna, watch." Hudson's thick voice at my ear startled my eyes open. "See how beautiful you are when you come."

My sexual history had not been comprehensive. Dark rooms with half-drunk partners and clumsy fumbling hands. Keeping my eyes open during only ever happened on accident. Mirrors and public places were never on my fantasy list. But I watched his hand moving at my core, his thumb circling my sensitive nub, his finger dipping into my wet center. He was right—it was beautiful. It was beautiful how he stroked me, how he knew what to do to make me feel the way I wanted to feel, how my skin flushed and my back arched. It was beautiful how he held me when I jolted in his arms, my orgasm moving through me in one long eruption.

"Put your palms on the mirror." His husky command and the

anticipation of knowing what he was about to do sparked a new wave of arousal, even more intense than before.

Still shaking, I reached my hands out in front of me, his arms leaving me as soon as I had managed to support myself. Behind me, I heard his zipper, the sound raising my level of excitement, knowing his cock was released and seconds away from being inside of me. The four-inch heels I still wore put me right at his level, and he pushed easily into my moist channel with a groan. "Fuck, Alayna!"

Our eyes met in the mirror, the connection between us frighteningly intense, and a panic rushed through me. He saw it, or sensed it, and he coaxed me through it, telling me he was with me, assuring me he'd take care of me, promising me he felt it too.

I bit my lip to suppress the moans that threatened to escape, aware that only a door stood between us and Stacy—Stacy who likely rehung and folded the discarded outfits I'd tried on earlier as I was gloriously fucked by the man she lusted after. But when I came this time I didn't hold back my cry, desperate to let Hudson know what he'd done to me.

I was still whimpering when his own orgasm took him, his weight heavy on my back as he leaned into his release.

And if I wondered that the whole act was a display for his sister's assistant, his whisper in my ear said otherwise. "*This*, precious. This is for real."

CHAPTER ELEVEN

Hudson let me choose the majority of clothes and shoes he purchased for me. In the end, it was a generous pile. I purposefully didn't listen to the total cost as Stacy read it off for him, afraid that I'd feel like I had a sugar daddy or, worse, that I was his whore.

We ate a nice dinner in an Italian restaurant in the Village then Hudson drove me to the club. Unusually lucky to find a curbside parking spot on the block, he took advantage and parked, letting the car idle.

"My mother's charity fashion show starts at one tomorrow. I'll need to pick you up at twelve-fifteen. I'm sorry you won't get more sleep. You're off at three this morning?"

"Yeah. I can handle it."

"Jordan will be here to pick you up. I'll make sure he has all your packages and that he helps you up to your apartment." A sly grin crept onto his face. "Unless you'd rather I picked you up."

Hudson take me home? Yes, I'd rather, but I needed to keep some boundaries. I'd already let him have me when I explicitly said I wouldn't. "I'm afraid I'd get even less sleep that way."

"Right. Probably not a good idea."

We sat for several seconds, the sexual tension sparking in the silence. Should I kiss him goodbye? Would he kiss me goodbye? Did we have time to sneak into the coatroom for a quickie? I had cleaned up as well as I could in the restroom of the restaurant, but the smell of sex still hung in the air and it had me thinking dirty thoughts. I didn't want to leave.

"Is everything okay with work?" It was an excuse to linger, but I also was genuinely interested in his series of texts and calls at the store.

"I can handle it," he said repeating my earlier words.

I'd hoped he'd tell me more, but he hadn't shared any business with me since I'd known him. There was no reason to believe he would now. I gazed at him for a bit, until it made me feel funny, my stomach flip-flopping as if I were descending on a Ferris wheel. Then I looked out the front window. Liesl strolled down the street, her purple hair making her easy to spot. It gave me an idea. Another excuse, actually. This time to get the physical contact I longed for.

"Since the ruse is on, we'd better make it official." I gestured toward Liesl, and Hudson nodded in understanding.

"Excellent idea." He paused, waiting for Liesl to get a little closer, ensuring she got a good show. Then he got out of the car and crossed to my door, opening it to let me out. He brushed his thumb down my cheek. "Ready?"

I was never ready, but I tilted my chin up so my mouth could meet his. Our lips joined, our tongues flitting around each other. My knees buckled, but his hands were around my back, supporting me. I gripped his shirt, wanting desperately to tangle my fingers in his hair, knowing that would only fuel my lust. Seriously, it had only been a couple of hours since our adventure in the dressing room, and yet it felt like I hadn't gotten any in months.

He pulled away and stole a glance at Liesl. "She saw," he said softly.

"Oh." I'd already forgotten our PDA had been meant for her. "Good." I swallowed. "Thank you," I whispered, still breathless. "For today." For buying me pretty clothes, for ignoring my request to keep the day sex-free, for taking the air out of my lungs with a kiss on Columbus Circle.

"Tomorrow, Alayna."

I managed to pull myself away from him, only looking back once as he got in the car. Liesl folded her arms across her chest, leaning against the door, holding it open for me. "Time for details," she said as I passed her.

And I delivered, telling her all about Hudson and Alayna, the happy couple, interweaving truth with fiction. I told her we'd met at Stern and that he'd bought the club to be near me, but not to tell that to David. I told her we spent all our free time together, that we couldn't keep our hands off each other, that we were madly in love.

The lies came easily and they felt good. They felt believable. Not because I knew Liesl believed them, which she did, but because I almost could too.

• • •

It was nearly four when Jordan and I had finished unloading all my packages into my apartment, but I wasn't tired yet. For a moment I had a pang of regret, wishing I'd let Hudson take me home instead. Thoughts of him had clung to me all night—I couldn't count the number of times I'd started and deleted a text to him—and my sex felt swollen and aching with want of him.

I'd been strong in the car, recognizing the unhealthiness of filling all my time with the man. Now, alone and needy, I weakened. Instead of heading straight to bed, as I should have done, I turned on my computer and allowed myself to do the one thing I'd tried so hard not to do: I cyber-stalked.

I told myself I needed to find information about Hudson so I'd be prepared. What if his mother made a comment about his college background? I'd want to know he studied at Harvard. Or what if someone asked me about my thoughts on Hudson's philanthropic investments? It benefitted me to know he was a major benefactor of the Lincoln Center and that he funded a private scholarship at Julliard.

And his exes. I needed to know about them, too. Though, I didn't find much in that department. Mostly pictures of Hudson with a variety of women. I gasped when I recognized one of the women as Stacy from Mirabelle's shop. She'd been on at least one date with Hudson. No wonder she had animosity toward me.

Not one face repeated except for Celia Werner's, the thin, pretty blonde his family wanted him to marry. They never actually appeared "together" together, but she did have a look of adoration in her eyes that caused me to doubt that she would be completely unhappy with an arranged marriage with him. But, then again, I couldn't believe anyone would be unhappy with Hudson.

I found out a great deal about my supposed boyfriend in those hours, but, truthfully, my Internet search had little to do with being prepared for Hudson's family and friends. I searched because I felt compelled to understand the man who affected me so completely. I read article after article because I wanted to know the silly little trivia that only a true fan or intimate friend knew. I sat behind my computer until my eyes were blurry, soaking up every bit of Hudson Pierce enlightenment I could find, because I couldn't *not* do it.

If I was obsessing, I didn't care. Hudson drew me to him with magnetic force. And while I knew that my behavior could only be allowed as a one-time lapse, I relished the high of fixating on the man who had already clearly stated he would never be mine.

• • •

I fiddled with the beads on the bodice of my purplish gray Valentino dress as the limousine pulled up to the Manhattan Center at a quarter to one the next day. I was nervous, yes, but also, I felt confined in the corset I wore underneath my dress as a surprise for Hudson—the one he'd chastised me for wearing in public.

"Stop fidgeting," he said. "You're beautiful."

I took a deep breath as Jordan opened the limo door. Hudson was closest to the curb, and began to step out when I stopped him. "Wait."

He raised a cautious brow. "Another request for a sex-free afternoon?"

I blushed. "No. I've given up on that."

He smirked, not at all bothering to hide his pleasure in my declaration.

"Anyway…" I peeked up at him under my heavily mascaraed lashes. "I just wanted to say…you look hot." And whoa, did he. The charity fashion show called for semi-formal attire, and Hudson rocked the look wearing a fitted John Varvatos gray suit with a muted purple dress shirt that coordinated perfectly with my outfit. He'd decided to go sans tie, leaving the top buttons undone, exposing only enough skin to drive me crazy. "Really hot."

He eyed me for a moment then shook his head before stepping out of the car. He reached back to help me out, his face still plagued with a curious expression.

"What?" I asked, wondering if I'd said something wrong.

"Alayna," he sighed. "There's so many things I want to do to you right now. But we're on-duty, and so I'll have to settle for this." He pulled me in for a kiss that, while not chaste, felt restrained, lacking the usual passion he poured into his kisses. This kiss was for the onlookers, the handful of photographers that surrounded the doors of the Hammerstein Ballroom.

When he broke our embrace, he took my hand, his fingers lightly crossing the rubber band I wore at my wrist. "What's this?" he asked as he led me inside the double doors of the venue.

"It's to remind me to buy coffee," I lied. Actually, I'd worn it to remind me to not think about him. I'd learned the technique in counseling. Whenever an unwelcome or unhealthy thought entered my head I was supposed to snap it and the sting would help curb the behavior.

Yeah, right. Like the snap of an elastic band could stop the thoughts that Hudson elicited—thoughts of us together, naked, all night long. And those weren't even the thoughts that worried me. Fantasies that we could be together beyond our little sham, beyond the bedroom—those were the ones that worried me, and I hadn't had them. Yet. But after my Internet adventure earlier that morning, I felt the need for a safety net. The elastic band was all I could come up with.

"You must really need to buy coffee."

"You haven't seen me go...." My words trailed off when I recognized more than a few of the people chatting in the lobby as celebrities. I don't know why it surprised me. The Pierce Annual Autism Awareness Fashion Show was a huge event and always drew the rich and famous. Really, I hadn't thought about it.

Hudson grinned at my stunned expression as he guided me past the ushers—the ushers who didn't even ask him for a ticket like the couple next to us who, I'm pretty sure, were the mayor and his wife. Um, yeah, Hudson was a lot cooler than I had comprehended.

We passed the bar and walked into the main doors of the ballroom. "If you'd like a drink, you can get something inside. My mother will be anxious to meet you." We stopped near the doorway, Hudson scanning the room.

I took in our surroundings. The place was extravagant—an old century opera house that had been infused with modern technology. The central focus was the runway, which extended from a low stage. A complex lighting system that seemed more appropriate for a rock concert than a fashion show hung above. Chairs lined the runway on both sides, and, beyond that, white clothed tables circled the room. Three levels of ornate balconies climbed the walls to the seventy-plus foot ceilings.

"Hudson! Laynie!" I turned to the sound of the familiar voice and saw Mira moving toward us as quickly as her round belly would allow. "Wow, you look incredible!" she said to me. "This dress looks so great paired with those shoes. And Huds matches you! How sweet!"

Hudson's arm tightened at my waist, the only indication he gave that his sister annoyed him. "You aren't the only one in the family who has fashion sense, Mirabelle."

"Of course not. Chandler's also very savvy. You, though, are generally too stiff to be considered anything at all creative."

"Ouch." But he grinned. Hudson was nothing if not proud of who he was.

Mira smiled, too. Then, her face tensed abruptly. "Excuse me, I know this is totally rude, but…" She pulled her brother's ear down to her mouth to whisper something I couldn't hear.

Hudson's jaw stiffened. He straightened, pulling away from Mira. "She knows about Alayna."

Mira nodded her head toward me. "Does she know about…?" She trailed off.

"She does." His words relaxed Mira, if only slightly.

I wanted to remain unaffected, but I knew my puzzlement read all over my face. They were talking about me and someone else, and I apparently knew about something or someone, which, of course, I doubted because Hudson never told me anything about anyone. My curiosity won out. "What?"

Mira looked to Hudson as if asking permission to fill me in. He remained expressionless. She took that as a go ahead. "Celia's here." Her mouth twitched. "I didn't know if that would be a problem."

Celia Werner. He'd said I knew about her, but I really didn't. I knew his family wanted them to marry. I knew her family owned majority stocks in television and media. I knew she was pretty. Very pretty. And she adored the man who currently rubbed his thumb back and forth across the back of my hand. The man who did not currently adore her. Or me, for that matter.

If my hand had been free, I would have snapped the elastic band. That had not been a healthy thought.

I swallowed then put on a cheerful smile. "No, Celia's no problem. Right, H?"

He grimaced at the nickname. "None at all."

"Where is she?" If the bitch was on the premises, I figured I'd better face her head on.

"There." Mira pointed discreetly.

I followed her gesture. There she was, the woman from the pictures, wearing a red, one-shoulder crinkle dress that accentuated her model thin figure.

"You look better than her," Mira said. I didn't, but I appreciated the comment. I didn't look better than her at all.

Snap. Another unhealthy thought.

"Mirabelle, must you be so catty?" Hudson squeezed my hand. "Anyway, Alayna looks better than most people."

I kissed him. Not only because it seemed a good time for a girlfriend to reward her boyfriend for a compliment, but because I wanted to. I wanted to remind myself that no matter what Hudson and I did or didn't have together, I was the one kissing him—I was the one convincing people that he shouldn't be with *her.*

He kissed me back in that reserved way of his that I had learned was for the public, his tongue sliding barely inside my lips.

"Oh, hell, no. Huds making out is not something I want to see," an unfamiliar voice interrupted our embrace. Hudson stepped aside revealing a blonde haired, blue eyed teenage boy wearing a suit jacket over a t-shirt and jeans. "But, wow." The boy scanned me up and down with a lusty stare. "Anytime you feel like moving up the social ladder, you can lay those lips on me."

"Chandler," Mira scolded. "Be polite."

Chandler. The youngest Pierce sibling. I'd read some gossip blogs that speculated the reason for the large gap between Mira and Chandler was because the three children didn't share the same father. Indeed, staring at Chandler now, I saw very little resemblance to his older siblings.

"Alayna's nine years your senior," Hudson said, a stern look on his face.

"I'll be eighteen next month." Chandler's eyes remained pinned on me.

I'd never told Hudson I was twenty-six. I shouldn't have been shocked that he knew—the man who had uncovered my restraining order had obviously done his research on me, too. Well, we were on equal ground now. As if there was equal ground with Hudson.

Hudson facilitated a half-hearted introduction. "Alayna, this is our brother, Chandler." Hudson smacked his brother on the shoulder in a gesture that almost appeared playful. "Chandler, stop undressing Alayna with your eyes. That's inappropriate."

Chandler crossed his arms with a look of challenge and superiority that could only be delivered by a teenager. "Because we're in public or because she came with you?"

"Because that's not how you treat women." Hudson's tone was clipped but even.

"And you're who's going to teach me how to treat women?" He stared at his elder brother, an unspoken conversation passing between them in those few seconds. And then Chandler dropped it. "Mom sent me to summon you. She wants to meet your arm candy." He turned on his heels, peeking once nonchalantly to see if we were following him.

Mira followed, grabbing him at the elbow to whisper in his ear. Correcting his impudence, I suspected.

Hudson sighed. "Ignore him. He's a horny teenager."

"He takes after his horny older brother," I whispered.

"Behave." He took my hand in his. I shuddered at his commanding tone and the feel of his skin against mine.

We followed the younger Pierce siblings across the ballroom, weaving around tables and the increasing crowd of people until we approached one of the tables closest to the stage.

"This is our table," Chandler said. He gestured with his chin to a group of people talking a few feet away. "Mom's over there."

I stared at the back of the woman I knew to be Sophia Walden Pierce from Internet pictures. Her dark blonde hair was swept up in a tight bun showing off her long graceful neck. Even from behind, it was evident that Hudson's mother was a beautiful, commanding woman.

As if she sensed our presence, she peered over her shoulder at us, offering a smile to her acquaintances as she did so.

A wave of unexplainable nervous energy rolled through me. What if she didn't buy our act? What if I screwed it all up?

Hudson must have sensed my anxiety because he tightened his grip on my hand and leaned in to whisper, "You're going to be great. I have no doubt." He kissed my hair.

His distraction worked. I was no longer worrying about impressing his mother, focused now on wondering whether his tender kiss had been for me or for anyone who might be watching us.

And why did it even matter? We weren't a couple, this was pretend. Tender kisses were romantic and we were not involved romantically. Sexually, yes. Romantically, no. I visualized another snap of the elastic band. Obviously I hadn't counted on holding Hudson's hand all day when I'd put the dang thing around my wrist.

By the time I'd thoroughly reminded myself that everything

Hudson did was pretend, Sophia had wrapped up her conversation and approached us. As I had suspected, she was quite beautiful. Her body was lean and trim, and her complexion perfect. She'd had Botox, her forehead smooth and unexpressive. Or else she wasn't an expressive person, which was highly possible considering she was related to Mr. Show-No-Real-Emotion at my side.

"Hudson." The slight nod of her head matched the stiffness of her greeting.

Hudson responded in kind. "Mother." Her eyes flickered to me briefly. "I'd like you to meet Alayna Withers. Alayna, this is my mother, Sophia Pierce."

"Glad to meet you, uh…" I suddenly didn't know what to call her—Sophia? Mrs. Pierce? If I had inflected my voice differently, I could have ended at "Glad to meet you" but I'd left the sentence hanging and I had to finish. I settled on the safe bet. "Mrs. Pierce." I let go of Hudson's hand and thrust mine out to shake hers, hoping my palm wasn't noticeably sweaty.

My worry was unfounded. Sophia Pierce made no effort to take my hand. Instead she scrutinized me with narrowed eyes, circling around me like a hawk. "She's pretty enough."

I lowered my hand to my side and made a conscious effort to close my jaw.

Before I could decide if I was supposed to say thank you, she'd moved on. "Where did you find her again?"

I was flabbergasted. She spoke about me like I wasn't there—like I was a puppy Hudson had found on the side of the road.

Mira tried to save me. "Mom—"

Sophia waved her away, and I caught Mira's unspoken apology in her eyes.

I looked to Hudson, but his gaze was locked on his mother's. "I told you. We met at a function at Stern."

Sophia chortled. "What the hell were you doing at NYU? Slumming?"

I flushed with anger, my hands balled into fists at my side.

Hudson stiffened as well. "Mother, don't be a bitch."

Chandler smirked openly at his brother's choice of words.

Sophia, on the other hand, made no indication that she even heard. "Tell me, Alayna—were you first attracted to my son because of his money or his name?"

Pissed didn't even begin to describe how I felt. I was seething, but still in control. Without skipping a beat, I wrapped my arm around Hudson's and answered. "Neither. I was attracted to him because he's hot. Though, I stayed with him because he's fucking awesome in bed."

Sophia's mouth fell open. I had a feeling she was a woman that was rarely thrown off guard and seeing her taken aback gave me a thrill.

Hudson raised a brow, but he didn't appear displeased. In fact, the gleam in his eyes seemed amused. It empowered me to continue. "Look, Sophia Pierce. I may not have graduated from Harvard like your son and your husband—" Admittedly, I paused to note Hudson's reaction to the fact that I knew details about his family even though he hadn't told me a single thing. Again, I saw the gleam. "But I'm proud of my NYU degree. And I didn't come here today to have my education insulted by a woman who dropped out of law school."

Sophia took a threatening step toward me. I was taller than her by a couple of inches in my heels, but she carried her stature with authority. "Why *did* you come here today?"

It occurred to me that as bitchy as Sophia Pierce was being to me, she wasn't *my* mother. And though my parents were dead, they had been kind and loving and would never have treated anyone—let alone someone I supposedly cared about—with the judgmental malice that Hudson's mother had imparted on me.

And now I understood why Hudson didn't have any qualms about lying to his mother about a relationship. If I had to deal with her, I'd do anything to get her out of my life.

So instead of backing away, I straightened, my arm still wrapped around the man at my side. "I came here because Hudson wanted me to meet his mother. He seems to care about your opinion, for some reason. And since I care about him—a great deal, I might add—I agreed to come."

Hudson wrapped his arm around my waist, drawing me in closer. I felt his grin as he kissed my temple.

Sophia's lip raised into a slight smile.

"Oh," Mira gasped. Chandler appeared to be equally shocked.

As before, Sophia ignored the reactions of her family. "We're going to our Hampton house later this week. I expect you and Hudson will join us."

I opened my mouth to say, *thanks, but no thanks*. Okay, maybe I really meant to say, *fuck off, bitch*.

But Hudson spoke before I could. "We can manage a long weekend."

Sophia appeared to want to interject, which was nothing compared to what I wanted to do.

"That's all I can promise, Mother. Some of us work for a living."

She sighed. "Fine. Now I have important people I need to speak with. Excuse me, please." She waved her hand in greeting. "Richard! Annette!"

I watched her saunter away, amazed by her suddenly pleasant and friendly tone of voice. I guessed pretending ran in the family. When I turned my attention back on the Pierce offspring, I saw they were all looking at me. "What?"

Mira and Chandler exchanged a glance and then burst out laughing.

I furrowed my brow, still confused.

Hudson pulled me into his arms, a grin playing on his lips. "Alayna. You're amazing."

I started to melt into him, but remembered he'd told his mother we'd join her in the Hamptons. I punched him lightly on the shoulder. "I'm working this weekend."

"Get out of it." It wasn't a request, it was a command.

I couldn't tell him that "getting out of work" was impossible, because, well, he owned the place. It would be awkward though. I had a meeting scheduled with David for the next day—hopefully to officially give me a promotion. What was I supposed to say? *Thanks for the raise, now I need Friday and Saturday off?* I'd have to tell him I was seeing Hudson, though the thought made me cringe.

Beyond that, I didn't want to go to the Hamptons with Sophia Pierce. I pulled back from Hudson's embrace. "H, I'm sorry to say this since she's your mother and all, but I can't handle spending time with her. She's not nice."

He laughed. Then he locked eyes with mine, sweeping his thumb down my cheek so softly it made me shudder. "We won't spend every minute with her. And, anyway, you seemed to handle her just fine."

I couldn't help it. His boyish grin and gray eyes had a power over me. And, he'd said we wouldn't spend every minute with Sophia, sending my imagination into overdrive with images of what we'd be doing instead. My nipples tightened at the thought. How could I resist him? "Okay, but I can't be responsible for my actions if she's like that again."

He leaned in to kiss me, whispering as he did. "That's what I'm counting on."

Chapter Twelve

Lunch passed quickly. Sophia was too busy greeting high-paying donors and socializing to eat with us, thank god. Adam, Mira's husband, joined us after our salads had been served. He was a surgeon and had an emergency case that morning. He looked good with her despite their differences in height—Adam tall and lanky, Mira petite and small. For half a second, I tried to picture them having sex before I realized that once I thought it, I wouldn't be able to unthink it.

Though nothing eventful happened during the course of the meal, I enjoyed myself. I watched the friendly banter between the siblings, joining in the laughter when one had a particular good burn on another. The conversation directed toward me was easy and unencumbered. I often feared it wouldn't be with new people who wanted to know all about me and my family. When something got too private, I noticed that Hudson deflected for me. Was it because he knew the sadness of my past? Or was he politely keeping my job light and carefree? Either way, the luncheon was more intimate than anything I had experienced in a long time.

When I sent a casual look toward him midway through the meal, his smile made my chest tighten. It may have been for show, but my reaction was genuine. I realized that no amount of elastic band snapping would stop whatever I was beginning to feel for him.

After dessert and coffee, the ballroom became a bustle again with people visiting with other tables and more guests arriving who'd only purchased tickets to the fashion show. Chandler found a group of younger girls to hit on, and Mira roped Adam into assisting with her backstage where she was managing the models and designers.

Though I'd liked getting to know Mira and Adam, and while Chandler never failed to entertain, I was glad to have a minute alone with my date. I trailed my hand across his shoulders and down his back, drawing his gaze to me. I saw longing, the few flecks of copper blazing in his eyes. He grabbed my thigh and leaned in, but the anticipated kiss never came.

"Oh, you don't need to be all PDA on my account," a silky voice purred behind us. "Remember, I know."

Hudson stiffened under my hand and my eyes followed his, landing on the leggy blonde taking a seat next to me. She was intimidating, not because of her attitude, but because she was drop-dead gorgeous. I tucked my hands into my lap, though Hudson's hand remained secure on my leg under the table.

"I'm Celia." She smiled, showing white perfect teeth. "I thought we should probably meet. Though, it doesn't look like Hudson's too keen on it."

I glanced at Hudson who indeed appeared uncomfortable.

"No, you're right. You should meet," he said, his hand stroking my thigh. I felt purpose behind his touching me, but wasn't sure if he meant it to claim me, calm me, or calm himself. "Now you've met."

"You aren't getting rid of me that easily, you oaf." She smirked at Hudson then delivered another smile to me. "Believe it or not, we're actually friends."

I believed it. She felt comfortable around him, and he didn't even flinch when she'd called him an oaf. It made my stomach wrench unexplainably. Then, when I wondered if they'd had sex, a sharp stabbing began in my chest. I didn't need to flick the elastic band, already associating the thought with pain, but I did anyway since my hands were finally free under the table to do so.

Hudson sighed. "What do you want, Ceeley?"

Someone Hudson actually called by a nickname? The stabbing deepened.

"I wanted to personally thank Alayna for this whole charade."

So, she really did know. Which really put me at a disadvantage since I knew almost nothing about her.

Celia leaned into me as if confiding a secret, but loud enough that Hudson could still hear her. "You can't know how dreadful the idea of marrying that pain in the ass has been." A teasing grin appeared on her lips.

"Um, I can imagine." The stabby pains in my chest made me want to stab Hudson, too. "He's not the settling down type."

Hudson removed his hand from my leg, and I instantly regretted my words, even though they hadn't been *that* mean, had they?

Celia giggled. "Wow. You already know him so well." She giggled again.

Ugh, she was a giggler. I wanted to puke. Or hate her. But something about her also drew me in. "It's nice to talk to someone else who knows."

"But isn't Hudson amazingly good at pretending?" She narrowed her eyes at him, and I caught the daggers he shot her in return.

"He is." I thought about our time together, the touches, the kisses in public. Some of them had been confusing, and I had blamed that on my own tendencies to create more when there wasn't more. But maybe it hadn't been my overactive imagination. "Quite good."

"I'd love to continue this wonderfully entertaining conversation, but I see someone I need to talk some business with." Hudson stood and reached his hand out for me. "Alayna?"

I had the strange feeling he didn't want to leave me alone with his almost-but-not-really-fiancé. The last time I'd felt that way, I'd received rather interesting tidbits of info from his little sis. "Go ahead, H. I'll hang with Celia."

"We'll be fine," Celia assured him. "And we'll end our conversation with a pretend catfight if you want to up the charade."

Hudson's jaw tightened. "No catfight. In my script, you're friendly toward each other."

"Then she and I should sit and chat, since we're supposed to be friends." Celia winked at me. "Right, Alayna?"

"Right." I winked back. I couldn't help it. She was sort of adorable. "And since we're friends, you should call me Laynie."

"Friendly, not friends." He took a deep breath, but his voice was still tight when he spoke again. "Fine. I'll be back shortly."

I watched him stroll off, the tight muscles of his butt hidden by his jacket, but his backside attractive all the same. Suddenly, I remembered I had a witness to my ogling, and I turned my attention back to Celia only to find she was ogling as well. Plus she had the adoration look that I'd spotted in the pics of her with him.

"You like him," I said before I could help it. I wasn't sure I wanted to know.

She shrugged then cocked a brow. "Seriously? I'm probably your one opportunity to get any real information about Hudson and his life and that's what you want to know?"

I laughed. "You're right, I'd like some info." The list of questions I could attack Celia with was so long I didn't know where to begin. Since I wasn't sure how much time we had, I needed to make it good. "Okay, Mira seemed to think I should be jealous of you. Should I be? I mean, should I be pretending I am?"

Celia pursed her perfectly plump lips. "Well, isn't that a clever way to ask the same question? No. Hudson and I have never been anything but friends. If he were a boyfriend who spilled his guts to his girlfriend, he'd tell you that I liked him, but that he's never felt anything for me but friendship. So unless you're the shallow type who's jealous of all girls her guy's friends with, then don't play jealous."

I was a bit shallow like that, and definitely the jealous type when in the throes of obsession. But I was playing a part, so why not make my character void of my own imperfections? "No jealousy then. What about his family? Is he close to them or is he as withdrawn with them as with everyone? I can't quite tell."

"He loves them all, deeply. As deeply as Hudson can love anyone, I mean. But it takes quite a lot of perception to get that." She leaned back in her chair and eyed me. "I think someone he was in love with would know that."

I nodded, taking it in. Then I dove into the question that had plagued me since I'd first heard about his predicament. "Why doesn't Hudson's mother believe that he'd be in love? Other than that she's a cold-hearted bitch herself." This elicited a grin from Celia. "Has he never dated anyone before?"

"Sort of. I mean, he's dated women. Not women he ever brought to meet his mother, but, yeah, he dated."

The stabbing pain returned. Simultaneously, I noted a flash of agony darken Celia's bright face. It occurred to me that this conversation must be even more difficult for her, considering she actually had feelings for the guy and I had…well, not feelings, but something.

"You know, date is not the right word. He'd sleep with them. And then he'd mess with them. It got him in all sorts of trouble. More than once."

I stilled. "What do you mean messed with them?"

"I shouldn't tell you. He doesn't want you to know. But I really think you should. Otherwise you might be caught off guard if

Sophia says something."

My voice was a whisper. "How did he mess with them?"

She sighed. "It's hard to explain. Like, he'd say he only wanted to be friends or friends with benefits, but then he'd manipulate them in that way of his, you know, how he always gets what he wants?"

Boy, did I. I could only manage to nod.

"He'd manipulate these women into falling in love with him. Which isn't really hard, I mean, he is Hudson. But he'd really play them. Lead them on, get them really hooked on him. It was like a game for him—one of the crappy things spoiled rich kids do just because they can." She paused. "I can say that because I love Hudson dearly. Also, I'm a spoiled rich kid, too."

The world felt like it had fallen out from underneath me. Was that what Hudson was doing with me? My throat felt tight. "Does he, um, still do that?"

"I honestly don't know. He's had a ton of therapy so I'd like to say he's 'better' now, but who knows? Of course, because of it, his mother got the idea that if he married someone like me, I could keep him in line. And my parents want me married to the Pierce name and bank account—they're disgustingly greedy. But I could never deal with those head trips—even though I am very fond of him. And I'd love to get in that beautiful man's pants. Can you imagine how gorgeous our children would be? Sigh."

She said the word sigh instead of actually sighing. That was what I clung to from her monologue because I didn't want to think about the rest. Therapy helped people—it did, I couldn't deny it—but I had doubts that it had fixed me. And knowing what I knew about patterns of past behavior, I recognized that Hudson should not be having just sex with anyone if he were seriously "better."

Exactly like I shouldn't be in an emotionless relationship if I were "better" since a lack of affection from a person I desired was one of my triggers.

I put a hand on my knees under the table to stop their knocking. I had to get out of there.

Celia continued, unaware of my torment. "But this plan of Hudson's is brilliant. As soon as Sophia relaxes enough to believe he's fallen for you, she's going to be ecstatic. She wants him to be normal. She wants him to be happy and in love. *I* want him to be happy and in love. Too bad it's not real."

Yeah, too bad.

She frowned, concern etched in her brow. "Are you okay? You seem really pale."

No, I wasn't fucking okay! I'd just been informed that the man I shouldn't have been fucking in the first place was probably trying to fuck with my head as well as my body. "I'm not feeling well all of a sudden." Not a lie. I seriously thought I might throw up. "Excuse me, I have to…" I couldn't think of any excuse to leave. I only knew I had to…"Go."

I snaked quickly through the crowd toward the doors, pushing my way into the packed lobby. The show was starting in fifteen minutes and I was going against traffic. I ducked and headed for a different door when I saw Sophia by the bar, hoping she didn't see me. Not because I cared anymore about Hudson's stupid scam but because I didn't want to deal with her.

Focusing on avoiding Sophia, however, made me completely miss that I was walking right past Hudson.

"Where are you going?" He reached a gentle arm out to stop me, and familiar tingles shot straight to my womb.

Accompanying the tingles, my stomach churned in disgust. I threw his arm off mine. "Don't touch me!"

Hudson's brow knit in confusion. "Whoa." He put his hands out in front of him, showing he wouldn't touch me but blocking my route of escape. "What's wrong with you?"

I scanned the lobby for a way to sneak past. "What's wrong with you would be the more appropriate question."

"Alayna." He stepped toward me, his voice low and stern. "I don't know what you're talking about, but you're making a scene. You need to calm down and save whatever this is for later."

He moved to grip my elbow, but I pulled away before he could. "There isn't going to be a later—I quit." I darted past him and out the main doors to the sidewalk.

"Alayna!" He followed me.

Anger surged through me, tears forming in my eyes. I was vulnerable and floundering and he had taken advantage. I turned on him, hot tears streaking my cheeks. "Tell me, Hudson, did you pick me because you thought my obsession issues would make your game more fun? Because really, where's the challenge in that?"

Hudson's jaw tightened, realization setting in. "Fuck Celia and her big mouth." He took a step toward me, his hand reaching for me. I stepped away. He softened, but his glare was insistent. "Let's talk about this in the limo."

"I don't want—"

He cut me off. "Alayna. It's not fair of you to listen to a stranger tell her story and not give me a chance to explain." His eye twitched, but, other than that, his features and composure were controlled. "I'm telling you we will talk about this in the limo which is parked in the lot next door. First, because my mother is watching, I'm going to bend down and kiss your forehead. Then I'm going to walk over and tell her that you aren't feeling well. I will meet you in the car."

I peeked over his shoulder and saw Sophia inside the doors, a smug grin on her face. I'd already told him I was quitting. I'd get a job at whatever loser place Brian wanted me to work at, because I obviously couldn't work anywhere that Hudson Pierce would be. But I knew he wouldn't let me walk away unless I agreed to his plan. Then, when I got to the limo, I'd tell Jordan to take off before Hudson joined us.

I gave him a tight nod. He approached cautiously and kissed me softly on the forehead. I crossed my arms over my chest to hide my nipples that had pebbled traitorously.

"The limo, Alayna. I'll meet you there."

I wiped the tears roughly from my face as I walked toward the lot he'd pointed to, picking up my pace as soon as I was out of his view. There were several limos parked, but I spotted Jordan leaning against the hood, playing with his phone. When he saw me walking toward him he opened the door without a word.

"Take me home, please, Jordan," I choked as I slipped in.

Jordan shut the door and I heard him get into the driver's seat. He hadn't said anything, hadn't agreed or disagreed to my direction, and, for a moment, I feared he'd only take his orders from Hudson.

Relief swept over me when the car started…

…and then immediately left when he pulled up next to the ballroom and Hudson climbed in, the doors automatically locking after he'd closed the door.

Shit! Hudson had probably texted Jordan that I was coming out, to pick him up after, and to not take me anywhere without him. Unreasonably, I felt betrayed by my driver.

As the car pulled into traffic, I pressed into the opposite corner, as far away as I could from the man sharing the car with me.

Hudson pressed a button and spoke. "Jordan, drive around until I say otherwise. Or find someplace to park for a while."

Normally I'd blush, afraid of what Jordan would think we were doing in the backseat. But I was too pissed and hurt to care.

We sat a few minutes, not speaking. I couldn't imagine that the always-in-control Hudson Pierce was at a loss for words, so I assumed his silence was meant to calm me down. Or unnerve me. Some sort of expert manipulative tactic.

It didn't calm me. Instead, the silence gave me time to review every moment of the past few days, allowing me to recognize his domineering hand in all of his actions. It gave me fuel to hate him for his control over me. And myself for falling in with the prick in the first place.

Finally he spoke, quietly. "What exactly did Celia tell you?"

I couldn't remain silent. "Oh, just how you fuck with vulnerable women's emotions. Is it true?"

"Alayna—" He moved across the seat, placing his hand on my knee.

"Don't touch me!" He removed his hand. "And stop saying my name. Is it true?"

"Will you calm down so I can explain?"

His soft tone felt patronizing, emboldening my fury. I needed him to admit it. I had to hear him say it. "Is. It. True?"

His answer came in a burst. "Yes, it's true!" He took a deep breath, regaining his control. "In the past, it was true."

I froze, my eyes riveted on him. I hadn't expected a confession. Hadn't expected him to tell me anything—he never did—and I feared if I moved he'd stop talking. So I remained still.

He took his time, not looking at me as he made his admission. "I did…things…that I'm not proud of. I manipulated people. I hurt them and often it was deliberate." He turned to me, piercing me with his intense gray eyes and the grit in his voice. "But not now. I don't do that now. Not with you."

His delivery affected me, but I bit past the emotion, knowing I had proof that betrayed his words. "Really? Because it seems completely obvious that you did exactly that with me. The way you picked me out at the symposium and you tracked me down and gave me a spa vacation and Jesus, you bought the club!"

He shook his head. "It's not like that. I explained the gift and I was looking at the club anyway. When I found out you worked there, yes, it helped me make my decision—"

I cut him off. "And you 'hired' me and seduced me. And when I told you I needed to not have sex with you, you somehow got me to do exactly that. You *are* manipulative. You're a bully, Hudson." I wrapped my arms around myself, hoping to stop the new onslaught of tears that threatened.

"No, Alayna. I didn't want that with you." The anguish in his tone set my tears into motion. He leaned forward and I sensed he wanted to touch me. Instead, he put his hand on the seat next to me, putting himself as close to me as I'd let him. "I don't *want* to be like that with you."

I swiped at the tears, unable to keep up with their pace. "Then what do you want to be with me, Hudson?"

"Honestly? I'm not sure." He sat back against the seat. His expression confused, torn.

Suddenly, he looked much younger than I'd ever seen him. He no longer seemed the confident, commanding alpha male that I knew him to be, but like a group member in one of my therapy sessions, exposed and accessible.

He let out a brief laugh, as if he recognized his own vulnerability and it amused him or confounded him. "I'm drawn to you, Alayna. Not because I want to hurt you or make you feel a certain way, but because you're beautiful and sexy and smart and, yes, a little crazy, maybe, but you're not broken. And that makes me hopeful. *For me.*"

I let out a shaky breath. God help me, I wanted to reach out to him. I wanted to comfort him, knowing his words about me said more about himself than any he'd ever spoken.

I didn't move, though, still not willing to break the moment. Even my tears had stilled, as if they'd interrupt.

"And maybe I've been a bully. But I'm a dominant person. I can try to change things about me, but the fundamentals of my personality are never going away." His voice lowered further. "You of all people should be able to understand that."

He had me earlier. Probably back when he'd insisted he didn't want to be whatever with me, but for sure when he'd inferred he was broken, and that I was not. And if none of that had reached me, his last statement would have. I *did* understand him. More than I had ever thought possible.

What it felt like to be a certain way and to loathe myself for it. How difficult it was to change and learn to accept the parts of me that were fundamentally never going to change. And what it did to me to believe I was incapable of falling in love the way normal people do.

I knew what it felt like to be that person.

"I'm sorry." It came out as a choked whisper so I repeated it. "I'm sorry. You didn't judge me and I judged you."

He nodded once and I knew that was his way of accepting my apology.

"And I exaggerated when I called you a bully. I haven't done anything I didn't want to. And your whole confident, domineering thing is actually kinda hot."

He almost smiled, but squeezed his eyes shut as if trying to reign in his emotions. When he opened them again, they were pleading. "Alayna, don't quit. Don't quit me."

I looked away, knowing how easy it would be to give in if I kept staring into those gray eyes. "Hudson, I have to. Not because of this, well, not only because of this, but because of my past. I'm not well enough to be with someone who has his own issues."

Truthfully, I didn't know if I was well enough to be with anyone.

"You are, Alayna. You only tell that to yourself because you're scared."

That drew me to face him. "I should be scared. It's not safe. For either of us. You should be scared, too."

He let out a heavy breath. When he spoke again, he was resigned, as if he didn't expect his words to make a difference yet he spoke them anyway. "I don't believe that. I think spending time with another person who has similar compulsive tendencies can provide insight and healing."

I leaned my head back against the seat and stared at the car's ceiling. I wanted to believe like he did—that we could make each other better. But I couldn't. All I'd witnessed and experienced in my life around addicts told me otherwise. Besides, if he'd wanted me around him to confide in and give some understanding, he should have told me his secrets from the beginning. And he hadn't.

As much as it pained me, I had to break things off. I had to do the right thing once and for all.

But there were my own financial woes. As irrelevant as money might have seemed at the moment, being able to keep my job at the club had an enormous impact on my own mental well-being.   "I   won't quit." I turned to face him. "But I can't have a relationship with you, Hudson." My throat felt tight, but I kept on. "All I can give you is the fake. I have to protect myself here." I should have ended all of it, but I didn't have the strength for that. This had to be enough.

Hudson's shoulders lowered slightly. "I understand." He nodded as if to reaffirm that he understood, making me suspect that he didn't understand at all but was accepting my decision anyway. "Thank you." He straightened, his poise returning, and I knew that he was back to his regular confident self.

I had one more thing to say, though. I leaned toward him, placing my hand firmly on his knee. "Hudson, you're not broken."

His expression faltered briefly, his eyes cast downward. When they rose again I saw them pass my exposed cleavage. His brow rose. "What are you...? Is that...?"

I looked down to see what he saw. The corset. Damn, I'd forgotten. A familiar tug of desire formed low in my belly, followed by a more painful ache in my chest. "Yes. I'd worn it for you."

He sighed. "Wow. That was...that was very thoughtful of you."

We still wanted each other, and it would be so easy to let that want rule us.

But I was stronger than that. I could be stronger than that. "I'm sorry."

"I know. I am, too." His eyes lingered on mine for a moment, before he shifted gears entirely. "This may be poor timing, but I need to get back to my mother's show."

"Sure."

"And since you're supposed to be sick, you will need to go home."

I listened as he ordered Jordan to drive toward my apartment.

"When is our next show, boss?" I asked, half praying the answer was soon, knowing that the more time before I saw him again, the better.

"I'm not sure. I have to fly to Cincinnati tonight." He pursed his lips. "And I am not your boss."

"Cincinnati? Tonight?"

"Yes, tonight. I have a meeting first thing in the morning. My jet's leaving early evening." A private jet. Of course. "I'll text you later to arrange the Hamptons. We'll leave Friday afternoon."

"So you'll be gone all week?" I don't know why I asked. It shouldn't have mattered.

"I'm not sure yet."

"Oh." He already felt distant, like he'd already gone. I turned my head to hide the tears that were filling my eyes.

The car pulled over to the side of the road. I looked out the tinted window and saw we were in front of my apartment. Jordan got out of the car, and shortly after, my door opened.

I didn't want to get out. It felt awkward and awful—my second sort-of-not-at-all break-up in a week. Why did this one hurt so dang much?

Without looking back at Hudson, I stepped out of the car.

"Alayna." He called me just as I stood fully. I pasted on a fake smile and ducked my head back in. "Thank you for today. I think you've truly made an impression on my mother. Good work."

I stayed at the curb until Jordan had shut the door and gotten back into the car. A shiver ran through me, despite the hot summer day. Wrapping my arms around myself, I headed up to the small studio apartment that felt big for all the loneliness it held.

At my door, I found a bag of gourmet coffee and I dissolved into tears, completely melted by his gesture. *My elastic band lie.* Hudson never missed a beat. I wracked my brain trying to figure out when he had arranged to have it delivered, and realized it had to be before the limo conversation. It was a sweet gesture. I wondered if he wished he hadn't done it now.

Whether he regretted it or not, it gave me an excuse to reach out to him once more. I pulled out my phone and typed a carefully thought out text. *"Thanks for the coffee. And for everything else."*

It was a goodbye to the great whatever it was we'd had, fleeting as it was. I needed the closure. Maybe he did, too.

I pushed send and had a moment of panic, wondering if I'd done the right thing by ending our relationship, wondering if I could undo it, praying that his response would show me he was having the same doubts as I was.

But Hudson didn't respond at all.

CHAPTER THIRTEEN

I stalked Hudson online again that night.

Not because I felt I needed to learn more about him, but because the distance between us felt so overwhelmingly vast. It was a familiar feeling, one I'd felt with guys I'd dated only to discover later, in therapy, that I'd been overreacting. But this was different. We were apart for real, not only in my psycho head. And I couldn't bear it. I had to get closer to him in whatever way I could, even if it was only via the Internet.

There were already new blog posts and news feeds from the fashion show. The event had great reviews, and more money had been raised than projected. I flicked through the pictures of models, a little wistful that I had missed that part of the day. And there were pictures of me with Hudson, kissing outside the limo when we were on our way in. I stared at those the longest, saving one particularly close shot as my wallpaper desktop.

Most of my stalking, however, was on Pierce Industries and its business ties in Cincinnati. I searched way longer than I should have, trying to deduce if Hudson really was going there, and finding nothing helpful. Did he really have business or did he just want distance?

It shouldn't have mattered. Our next assignment wasn't until Friday. But the need to know ate at me, consuming my mind until I'd spent hours exhausting every avenue of research I could think of.

At least I stopped myself at online stalking and checking my phone over and over for a response from him. I didn't call the airport to see if a Pierce Industries jet had taken off—that wouldn't have been healthy behavior.

Besides, I had no idea what airport.

• • •

I awoke the next afternoon with a knot in my chest. My muscles felt jittery even before I'd had any coffee. They were my usual anxiety symptoms, but I couldn't say for sure what had caused the attack. Worry about my meeting with David? Or stress about Hudson?

In an attempt to relax, I popped in a yoga DVD before I had to get ready to leave. The narrowed focus and rhythmic breathing loosened me for the most part, but the edge still lingered.

I spent longer than usual prettying up for my meeting at the club. Not for David, but for myself. Sometimes looking good made me feel good, and I was willing to try every trick in the book to get rid of the tension. But no matter what I did, the anxiety remained, buzzing through my veins with a steady electric current.

It was simply nerves about the promotion, I told myself. I'd feel better after meeting with David.

As I was on my way out the door, I got an incoming text. I checked it eagerly. But it wasn't from Hudson. It was from David.

"Something's come up," it said. *"Reschedule for Wednesday at 7."*

Then I knew. That the stressing had nothing to do with David, because moving our meeting did nothing to change the way I felt. I should have felt relief, or a spike in the tension since it would have to be dragged out two more days. Also, I should have wondered about what had come up. David and I were close enough that he'd tell me. But I had no desire to ask.

Hudson. It was Hudson that kept coming to mind. Where was he? What was he doing? Was he thinking of me?

I texted back a confirmation to David and paced my apartment, trying to decide the best way to get my ex-lover off the brain. I needed to catch a group. Checking online, I made sure there was still an Addicts Anonymous session scheduled on Monday afternoons. There was, but I had plenty of time before the session started.

I could run. With Jordan driving me around so much, a bit of aerobic activity would be good for me. I changed into shorts and a tank top, put on my running shoes and started out.

The run helped clear my head, the endorphins flowing through my body making me feel better and more confident. And invincible. Which was why when I found my route had led me to the Pierce Industries building, I convinced myself it didn't mean anything. It wasn't a big deal to be there. Especially since I only went inside to use the bathroom in the lobby before resuming my run.

I felt so good from the exercise that I decided to skip therapy all together and keep on with my run for a while longer, continuing to the Lincoln tunnel before turning around. I passed the Pierce Industries building again on my way back. And since I knew there was a drinking fountain inside, I went in again, this time lingering a bit in the lobby, scoping out the elevators looking for some sign of Hudson in the building. I managed to make myself leave before I slipped into a car and pushed the button for the top floor.

The next day I didn't possess as much strength.

Not only did I return to the building three times, but each time I rode the elevator. I told myself it couldn't be called stalking exactly, because Hudson was out of town—though I had yet to accept that as truth—and because I never actually pushed the button for Hudson's floor. Instead, I let fate take me wherever, journeying with whoever stepped on to whatever floor they were going to, then forcing myself to return back to the lobby. It felt like elevator roulette—if the car took me to the top floor, then I was meant to stop by Hudson's office. But each time, I missed the bullet, the other passengers never choosing his floor.

Until Wednesday.

Even though my shift the night before had gotten me home at almost six in the morning, I was awake and back at the Pierce building before one that afternoon. My first ride took me only to the fifth floor. When the passenger stepped out and the doors closed, I leaned against the back of the car and sighed, knowing the car would return to the lobby if I didn't push a button.

But instead of going down, the car went up. Someone must have summoned it from a floor above. I held my breath as I watched the needle rise higher and higher. Then it stopped on the top floor. Not the secret top floor that required a code and would take me to the loft, but to the floor that Hudson's office was located on. I braced myself for what I'd see when the doors opened, hoping I'd learn something by peeking around whoever stepped into the car with me.

But I wasn't prepared for the sight that met me. Three men in suits were laughing and joking as the doors parted. And with them was Hudson.

"Alayna." His voice was even as always, with only a hint of surprise in his tone.

I froze, my body unable to move, my mouth unable to speak. A wave of jumbled emotions ran through me: I was happy to see him, yet petrified. Enraged to find he was in town after all and somewhat satisfied that my suspicions had been right.

Hudson held a hand out to me. Automatically my arm moved to take it, and he pulled me out to stand next to him. He turned to the men with him. "Gentlemen, my girlfriend has decided to surprise me with a visit to my office."

I managed to smile before pinning my stare to my gray running shoes.

"That can never be good," one of the other men said and they all laughed. "Well, we'll leave you to her then. Thank you again for meeting with us."

I barely heard the goodbyes the men exchanged with Hudson before they took my place in the car, and how I made it the short distance to his office was beyond me. I was numb, my mind consumed with the fact that I was someplace that I shouldn't be.

The office doors clicked closed behind us. Hudson must have held my hand the whole way there, but I didn't notice until he dropped it and walked away from me. "What are you doing here, Alayna?"

I couldn't bring myself to look at him, but the absence of anger in his tone brought me out of my haze. I could get myself through this. I'd been good at talking my way through things in my obsessive days. I'd explain and he'd believe me and all would be fine.

But I didn't want to be that girl anymore.

It was right then that I'd realized the severity of what I'd been doing: I'd been stalking. For the first time in years. I'd fallen off the wagon with probably the worst person I could fall off the wagon with. If I'd thought restraining orders and lawsuits had been a nightmare when they were filed by Ian, my last object of obsession, imagine what it would be like with a powerful man like Hudson.

But even more than that—recovering from my addiction to Ian had been hard, but possible. Hudson, though…I couldn't even bear to think about not being around him in some way or another, no matter what the context.

Hudson was waiting for my answer. I could feel him studying me. I hugged my arms around myself and took a deep breath. "I, uh, I wanted to see if you were back."

I nearly sobbed with the honesty of my statement, but if Hudson noticed, he didn't let on. "I got back late last night. You could have called. Or texted."

My mind reached for the steps of talking through unhealthy behaviors. I'd learned them many times in therapy. *Communicate your fears openly and honestly.* Closing my eyes to stymie my tears, I said, "You don't answer my texts."

"I didn't answer one text."

I opened my eyes and found him staring at me intently as he leaned against his desk. I brushed away the one tear that had escaped down my cheek and met his gaze. "It was my only text."

I heard how it sounded. Ridiculous. An overreaction. We weren't together. Why should he answer my texts? He had to be regretting his choice for a pretend girlfriend now. Now that he saw the extent of my crazy.

Our eyes remained locked, but I could read nothing in his expression. It seemed like forever before his face softened and he said, "I didn't realize it was important to you. I'll make a better effort to respond in the future."

My mouth fell open.

He straightened to a standing position. "But you can't just come here like this. How do you think it looks to have my girlfriend wandering around the lobby, riding the elevators when I'm not even in town?"

"How did you...?"

"I pay people to know things, Alayna."

He knew. Of course, he knew. I'd decided to communicate honestly, but had hoped I didn't have to be that honest. That he knew I'd been by his office several times, that I'd roamed the building...I was humiliated.

More tears fell. "I...I'm sorry. I couldn't help myself."

"Please, don't do it again." He was stern, but did I detect a note of compassion?

His reaction was all wrong. He should have been more pissed, more freaked out. "Why are you being like this?"

His brow wrinkled. "Like what?"

"I've fucked things up, Hudson! You should be calling your security to escort me out. I'm a mess and you're taking it all in stride." The tears fell fast now. There was no stopping them.

His face eased and he stepped toward me. "No," he said softly, his tone embracing me even though his arms didn't. "That's what I meant about being around someone who understood. I know about compulsion. I know about having to do things you know you shouldn't."

He wiped a tear from my cheek with his thumb, his hand resting there longer than necessary. "When you feel you can't help yourself, talk to me first."

The anxious knot I'd felt for days dissolved under his words. Had he been right? Could we help each other through our pains? Could we fix each other?

I looked into his eyes and wanted again to believe as he did, this time much closer to saying that I did.

But before I could say anything, his secretary's voice boomed through the office. "Mr. Pierce, your one-thirty is here."

Hudson sighed, dropping his hand from my face. "I apologize for cutting this short, Alayna, but I have another meeting now. And I'm leaving again this evening."

My spirits sank. I didn't know if I believed him, but I did know I didn't want distance between us. That was what had spurred my obsessive episode this week. Well, he'd asked for me to share... "I hate that you're leaving. It makes me feel a little distraught." A lot distraught, actually.

His eyes lit up. "I'll be back tomorrow." He took my hand and squeezed. "Join me tomorrow night for the symphony."

My heart flip-flopped. "Yes."

"I'll pick you up at six. Wear the dress."

• • •

I made it to group that afternoon before meeting with David. I'd made a mistake, but Hudson was willing to look past it. More than willing. And that made it so much easier to believe that I wasn't doomed to be totally freaky with him. I had to make an effort to stay well.

Not comfortable telling my situation to everyone, not when people might know about my connection with Hudson, I was vague on my turn to share. "I'm...I've slipped a bit."

It was an accurate enough statement. My behavior hadn't been as bad as it could have been. But every journey starts with a single step—even the journeys we shouldn't be taking, and at the rate I'd been going that week, I'd be well on my way down the obsession road before I had a grip.

Lauren nodded sympathetically. "When you get home, I'd like you to write out a list of your recent negative behaviors, including behaviors you only thought about engaging in. Then come up with a list of healthy behaviors you can substitute whenever you feel compelled to engage in an unhealthy one. Do you need any help?"

"No." I'd done this before. More than once. I still had all the substitute behaviors memorized from the last time I'd gone off the wagon: *Run, do yoga, take an extra shift at work, concentrate on school, visit Brian.* Obviously my list needed updating.

"Good. You know your patterns. Are you still journaling?"

"I haven't in a while." A long while.

Lauren smiled. "I recommend you start again." She was always good for a swift kick in the butt.

"Okay." And I would. But something told me that of all the suggestions I'd received that day, the best one had been from Hudson himself: *When you can't help yourself, talk to me.*

I was quiet the rest of the session, replaying an old favorite quote over and over in my head, committing myself to modifying my actions. *If there is no struggle, there is no progress. If there is no struggle, there is no progress.*

I felt better after group, stronger and my head clear. As Jordan drove me to work later, I added to my substitute behaviors list, including making it a goal to watch every title on the AFI's 100 Greatest Movies list and continue reading the top one hundred books on GreatestBooks.org.

My good mood and healthy attitude gave me courage to send a text to Hudson before I walked into my meeting with David that evening. *"Do you really have to leave town again?"*

This time I got a response instantly. *"I'm afraid so."*

He'd listened—had adjusted his behavior knowing how it affected me to not get a response. Before I could decide how to answer, he sent another. *"But I'm glad to know you're thinking of me."*

A tingle spread through my body. *"Always,"* I told him before I could stop myself. What was I doing? What were *we* doing? We weren't lovers anymore—were we becoming something else? Something more like friends? Friends who flirted by text?

Whatever we were doing, it felt good. So good that I followed my last text with another more dangerous message. *"Are you thinking of me?"*

David opened his office door, interrupting my feel-good moment before Hudson had a chance to reply. "Laynie, come in." David was stiff and his voice tight.

His serious demeanor made me stuff my phone in my bra. "Is everything okay?" I thought back to his message from Monday. "What came up the other day?" I asked as I took a seat in front of his desk.

"This." David threw a folded newspaper down on the desk before sitting in his chair across from me.

Puzzled, I picked up the newspaper and scanned for what might have put him in such a foul mood. And there it was, in full color on the top of Monday's society section, the picture of Hudson and me kissing.

"Oh. That." David had been the one person I'd been scared of telling. I feared he'd jump to conclusions. The wrong conclusions.

And he did. "You want to explain this, Laynie?" He stood and began pacing, not pausing long enough for me to answer. "'Cause I'll tell you what it looks like. It looks like you were so eager to get your precious promotion that, when you couldn't get it by playing me, you chose to go after the next guy who could get you what you wanted."

I put a hand out in front of me as if to stop him from saying what he was saying. "It's not like that, David. It was never like that." How could he think that I'd liked him for a promotion? That I'd been insincere when I'd been with him?

"It wasn't?" He stopped pacing and leaned toward me, his palms on his desk. "Then tell me what it was like, Laynie."

"It's…I can't…" My floundering was exacerbated by the buzz of my phone against my breast. I knew it was a reply from Hudson, and I longed to read it. But there was no way I could right then. Not with David raging in front of me.

"Yeah, that's what I thought." He straightened, a look of utter disgust joining the scowl on his face. "Now I'm forced to move you up, implement your ideas, never mind that I was going to anyway, or fear for my own job." He laughed dryly. "I'm probably grooming you to take my place."

"David, no." This was worse than I had imagined. I didn't want him to think I ever wanted to take his job from him. I had imagined us running The Sky Launch together. Though the romantic part of that duo was no longer appealing to me, I still very much wanted the business duo.

"Does Pierce have any idea about me?"

"David, don't."

His eyes narrowed. "Does he know that you're The Sky Launch slut?"

That was the turning point. Instead of feeling bad, I got pissed. And when I got pissed, I used all the weapons in my arsenal. "If you really believe what you're saying, David, that I have some power over Hudson, then maybe you should be a little more careful how you talk to me."

His eyebrows lifted, surprised by my steady tone and pointed words.

"Now, sit down," I continued, "and we can talk about this in a civilized manner." I waited while he plopped down in his chair. "Good. Let me see if I have this right—you think I'm dating Hudson so that I could get a promotion at the club. A promotion that you've basically promised me because of my hard work here over the past few years. A promotion I earned before you and I even kissed."

"Why else would you be dating him?" His words were challenging, but the fight had left.

"Not that it's any of your business, but I'm dating Hudson because…" I was on-duty in that moment, but my reason was honest. "Because I like him. And he likes me. We connect. And, even before our first date, he spelled out to me that he would have nothing to do with helping me move up here. And I accepted it because I knew I could get the manager title on my merit alone. Tell me, did Hudson instruct you to promote me?"

His shoulders slumped. "No."

"And were you going to offer me the position before you saw our picture in the paper?"

"Yes."

"Then what are we even talking about?"

He shook his head and shrugged. "Laynie…I…I don't know what to say. I guess I jumped to conclusions. I said things that were uncalled for."

"I get it. I knew it would look that way." I let out a silent breath, relieved that he'd calmed so easily. "Maybe I should have said something earlier."

David shook his head. Then he met my eyes directly. "No, I was acting jealous. And I didn't have any right to. I'm the one who ended things."

"It's okay." I looked away. His jealous remark hung in the air between us. Once upon a time, I would have jumped all over it. Now, it felt weird to have him feeling things about me.

So I changed the subject. "Um, about the promotion…did you say you were giving it to me?"

He smiled. "Yes. Of course I am. Pierce didn't tell you?"

Up until recently, Hudson and I didn't talk much when we were together. But I wasn't telling that to David. "He really didn't."

"Good. I'm glad to be the first to tell you. Congratulations." He outstretched his hand to shake mine then took it back. "What am I doing? Come here." We both stood and met at the side of his desk for a hug.

I pulled away first.

He noticed, covering by jumping into work mode. "And we're taking your suggestions. We'll extend the club hours starting in August. Which means you have a lot of work to do to get the place ready. Plan on lots of marketing and promotional meetings."

I put a hand on his arm. "Thank you, David."

"You deserve it."

We spent the hours until the club opened working on a business plan. It was distracting and exhilarating and exactly what my obsessive mind needed. Work would automatically make it to my list of substitute behaviors. I now had a salaried position and many of my shifts would take place during daylight hours. Wouldn't Brian be proud?

When the club opened, I shadowed David, learning more managerial duties. By the time we closed, I was exhausted and grateful that I didn't have to walk home.

It wasn't until Jordan was helping me into the backseat of the car after my shift was over that I remembered to read my text from Hudson. *"Always,"* it said.

My heart stopped. I reread my text to him to be sure I correctly remembered what I'd sent. I did. I had asked him if he was thinking of me, and his answer was *Always*.

Chapter Fourteen

Jordan was waiting for me with the Maybach at six outside my apartment, but I saw before he even opened the door for me that the backseat was empty.

"Mr. Pierce is late getting back in town," Jordan explained. "He'll meet you at Lincoln Center. I have your ticket."

Having felt anxious all day about seeing Hudson, not sure what the context of our evening would be, I didn't want to be alone. "Do you mind if I ride up front with you?" I asked.

"I'm sure Mr. Pierce would rather you sat in the back."

I pulled the back door from Jordan's grasp and shut it without getting in. "Then we won't tell him, will we?"

Jordan shook his head at me and crossed around to the driver's seat. I opened the front door myself and climbed in next to him.

We rode in silence for a bit, and I read the ticket that Jordan had given me. The New York Philharmonic playing Brahms's Symphonies Two and Three. *Nice.* I loved the arts and it had been forever since I had treated myself to an event of any sort.

Luckily, I didn't have to be at work until one a.m. since I was staying after close to learn how to do monthly inventory. Leisl had come to my apartment that afternoon to help me tie the back of my dress and had taken some of my clothes to work with her so I could change when I got there. It meant Hudson and I had all evening for...for what? Were we on show tonight? Was this a date? Were we going out as friends? I had no idea.

Glancing over at Jordan, I felt inspired to get answers to some of my questions. "Jordan? What has Hudson told you about me?" Jordan had been in the office when we were negotiating the terms of our arrangement. What did he think about us?

Jordan didn't answer.

"You're not supposed to chat with me, are you?" His expression gave me my answer. "Oh, come on. He probably also said to keep me happy. And right now some validation is what would make me happy."

He sighed as if not believing what he was about to do. "He said you're the lady in his life."

"He did?" Of course, he would have. That was my role, after all—to play the lady in his life. But had there been others? "How many ladies has he had in his life?"

"I haven't been hired to drive any others, Ms. Withers. I've only always driven him. Occasionally he might have a date, but not very often."

I frowned, not wanting to think about Hudson on dates.

"Certainly none of them held his interest like you do."

I rolled my eyes, not wanting to be patronized. "You don't have to say that."

"I don't. But it's true."

What did that mean, exactly? That I was special to him? Or that I was the only one he'd hired to show off?

But I couldn't ask Jordan those questions. So instead I asked, "What do you think about Hudson?"

"Me?" Jordan's eyebrows rose in surprise. "Well, he's a good boss. Very clear with his expectations. He demands a lot but the benefits are proportional."

That was nice to know—that he was a decent employer. But it wasn't what I was looking for. "I mean as a person."

Jordan laughed. "I don't know him as anything but a business man." He glanced at me. "You may be one of the only people I've ever met who knows him as just a man."

"I doubt that." Not only because I didn't know him but because I suspected Hudson didn't let anyone know him.

"I wouldn't be so sure."

I wanted to continue the conversation, but we'd arrived at Lincoln Center. It felt strange to arrive by myself, but Jordan directed me to Avery Fisher Hall and gave me all the information I needed. "Tonight is a donor's event. So there's a light buffet in the lobby. Mr. Pierce insisted you enjoy yourself."

I smiled as I pictured Hudson giving the orders to Jordan. Had it been by phone? By text? Either way, I recognized that a great deal of care had gone into the evening. "Do you know when he'll be here?"

Jordan shook his head. "A late meeting of the day delayed his take-off. But he assures he'll arrive as soon as he can." He paused before stepping back behind the driver seat. "Ms. Withers? If I may say, you look quite lovely."

I blushed as I thanked him, but his compliment gave me the courage to make my way into the hall by myself. Finely dressed patrons crowded in with me, the richest in the city, the people who had money to donate to such trivial things as the arts. I'd always been into nice clothes, but had never cared about designer names until that moment when the only thing camouflaging me in the sea of expensive clothes was my own designer gown. I was out of my element. I needed a cocktail.

As Jordan had said, buffet tables lined the lobby and caterers wandered around with trays filled with delicious appetizers and glasses of champagne. I wasn't very hungry, but I grabbed a crab puff as it passed so I'd have something in my stomach when I drank the champagne that I acquired soon after. I spent the next forty-five minutes nursing my drink and nibbling on veggies, my eyes pinned on the front doors searching for my date.

When the crowd thinned, I reluctantly made my way to the seat listed on my ticket. Box seats, of course. My spirits perked up as I noticed patrons entering the box ahead of me. Perhaps Hudson had managed to sneak past me.

But when the usher showed me to my seat, I found the seats on either side of mine empty. Three other seats in our box were taken by a middle-aged couple and a woman my age—a woman I knew. It was Celia.

"Laynie!" Celia said as she sat down. "I'm so glad you came. Where's that handsome man of yours?" Her voice wasn't exactly quiet, and I realized she wanted her companions to hear.

My chest constricted. Definitely not a date, then.

"I wouldn't have missed tonight. I've been looking forward to seeing you again." I did my best to pretend I knew that Celia would be there as she had seemed to know I would be in attendance. "Hudson's late flying in. He's been out-of-town most of this week." I'll admit I hoped the mention of him being out of town would be news to Celia. I felt I needed the upper hand somehow and knowing things about my supposed love that Celia didn't was the only trick I could play.

"Oh, yes. He told me he was leaving again when I talked to him yesterday." So much for insider knowledge. "Let me introduce you to my parents, Warren and Madge Werner. This is Alayna Withers, Hudson's girlfriend."

Mr. and Mrs. Werner exchanged glances before they leaned over their seats to shake my hand.

"It's nice to finally meet you," Madge said. "Sophia has told me so much about you."

Huh, yeah. Whatever Sophia Pierce had to say to her best friend about me couldn't be anything I'd want to know. My stomach knotted at the thought. Where the hell was Hudson? How could he leave me alone with these people?

"Sophia's a delight," I said with as much pleasantry as I could muster. It actually wasn't hard to smile as I said it, as if I had told a private joke about Hudson's monster of a mother.

"Isn't she?" Celia muttered so only I could hear.

Her dig made me feel more comfortable.

Until Madge started to grill me. "Where did you meet Hudson again?"

I repeated the story, embellishing as many romantic moments as I could without going too far overboard, all the while checking over my shoulder, wishing Hudson would appear.

"Withers," Warren said when there was a lull. "Any relation to Joel and Patty?"

"No, sorry." If he was trying to discover the depths of my breeding, I'm afraid he was going to be sorely disappointed.

Relief flooded over me when the lights lowered, ending our conversation. Simultaneously, my resentment toward Hudson grew. I quickly shot him a text, something I should have done an hour earlier. *"Where are you?"*

The response to my text came as a whisper in my ear as the conductor walked on stage and the audience began clapping. "Right beside you."

Chills spread through my body and I looked up to see Hudson had slipped into the seat next to me. *He was there.* Even in the dim theater, I knew he looked gorgeous, wearing a classic tuxedo. His hair was mussed as if he'd dressed quickly, and his face scruffy, increasing the sexy factor.

He nodded to Mr. and Mrs. Werner then took my hand.

His hand in mine—the warmth of it, the strength—it didn't matter if it was for show, I had needed it, and I clung to it until intermission, only letting go so we could applaud.

While the audience was still clapping, he leaned toward me. "What did you think?"

"I loved it." I'd never heard the New York Philharmonic, and Brahms had never been my favorite composer, but the performance had been breathtaking. That I had experienced it with the hottest man on the planet sitting next to me didn't hurt.

"I knew you would." As the lights came up, he pushed a strand of hair behind my ear, and whispered, sending a fresh set of shivers down my spine. "Showtime."

He stood and took my hand to help me up, then turned to face the Werners. "Madge, Warren. I wish I'd been here to make introductions. I take it you've all met now."

"We have," Madge said. "Celia introduced us."

"Good. I wanted the most important people in my life to know each other." Then, with all eyes on us, he wrapped me in his arms, turning my knees to jelly. "I'm sorry I was late, darling. You look stunning. The most beautiful woman here tonight."

He'd said I was stunning when we'd bought the dress, and just as I'd known he'd been saying it for my benefit then, tonight I knew it was for the Werners. He'd never call me "darling" otherwise.

I stared into his eyes, not needing to fake my adoring gaze. "You don't know that. You've barely looked at anyone else."

He rubbed his nose against mine. "Because I can't take my eyes off of you."

God, we could write sappy romance novels. We were that good. *He* was that good.

"You were out of town this week?" Warren asked, not seeming to care if he interrupted fake Alayna and Hudson's moment. "Celia said you were away on business."

I hid a grimace. Celia hadn't said that. *I* had said that.

Hudson kissed my forehead lightly before letting me go and directing his attention to Warren. "Yes. A development with Plexis."

Warren shook his head. "That's been a thorn in your side for some time."

"Excuse us," Madge interrupted. "While you men talk about all your boring business, us girls will freshen up."

I wasn't sure if Madge meant to include me as one of "us girls," but I planned on staying. I wanted to hear the boring business talk. I didn't want to leave Hudson.

But Celia took my arm, obligating me to accompany them, and Hudson appeared to be waiting until we left to continue. Besides I did need to pee.

I didn't miss Hudson's warning glare to Celia. Even I, who hadn't been lifelong friends with the man, knew that look told her to be careful what she said to me.

He didn't need to worry. The conversation on the way to the restroom and while we waited in line was banal and trivial. Mostly Madge made snide comments about what other people were wearing and tried to discern what and how much Hudson had bought for me.

It was after I'd peed that the talk became interesting. Madge and Celia were powdering their noses in the side mirror, and didn't see me come out of my stall. I moved to the sink to wash my hands, and found I could hear their conversation perfectly.

"She's pretty," Madge said. "I'm sorry she's so pretty."

"Mom," Celia groaned. "Stop."

"I'm sure it's only a fling, honey. This is Hudson's first real girlfriend. You never settle down with your first."

I washed my hands for a long time, listening.

"Mother, I don't feel that way about him anymore. I've told you. He's psycho, anyway. You wouldn't want our kids to have those genes."

"He's got better genes than most. And I know you say you're over him, Ceeley, but you don't have to pretend with me. Just make sure he gets thoroughly tested when you get him back."

"Mom!"

An immense wave of rage swept through me. Not only because Madge had insinuated pretty shitty things about me and my sex life, though that did sting. But also because Celia, the woman who was probably Hudson's closest friend, had called him a psycho. No wonder Hudson kept himself so guarded and shut off from the world. Even the people who were supposed to care most for him seemed to have no understanding or empathy for the inner demons that he likely fought on a daily basis.

No wonder he'd come looking for me.

I spritzed cool water on my face, attempting to fan my fury. Then I dried my hands and rejoined the Werner women. Even though I'd just been with him, I suddenly couldn't wait to be with Hudson again. I regretted that I'd pushed him away. He needed me, I realized now, in a very profound way that I couldn't put into words. And I needed him. I practically ran to the box.

Hudson put his arm around my waist when I came to him, though he continued his banter with Mr. Werner and I melted. Wanting even more contact with him, to share physically the epiphany I'd had in the bathroom, I slid my hand under his jacket, desperate to touch him more, gliding my fingers along his lower back.

He stiffened.

I withdrew my hand and he relaxed.

I had to concentrate to not let the sting of his rejection show on my face. Maybe he didn't realize what I was trying to tell him. So I tried again in the dark when the symphony started again, placing my hand on his knee. Then I trailed it higher along his thigh.

He stopped me, taking my hand in his. He held it there for the remainder of the show, and though it still held warmth and strength, it felt like a restraint rather than a comfort.

Disappointment wrapped around me with a cold chill. I was too late. I'd pushed him away and now the invitation was gone. I was grateful for the dark. He wouldn't notice my eyes filling.

After the concert was over, we walked out with the Werners toward the parking garage rather than the pickup area.

"I drove," Hudson said, answering my brow raise.

He kept his arm around me as we walked. His touch was constant, but it was all pretend. The pressure and passion he'd shown me in private was missing.

Also gone were his eyes. Before, whenever I was with him, his eyes never left my body, my face. Now he didn't make eye contact once and he barely talked to me at all. Instead, he chatted comfortably with Celia, sharing inside jokes. With each step we took, I felt more and more distraught. Sobs built up in in my throat and I concentrated on forcing them back down, keeping them at bay.

We parted with our companions at the Mercedes. Celia gave me a quick hug while Hudson shook Warren's hand and kissed Madge on the cheek. I nodded to the Werners then Hudson held the door open for me as I climbed into the passenger seat.

Before getting in himself, Hudson said goodbye to Celia. I watched through the window, my stomach curling. He hugged her and whispered something in her ear that made her laugh. I wiped away the stray tear that slipped past my defenses.

Besides destroying me, watching them made me mad—mad as in crazy and mad as in angry as hell. Wasn't Hudson supposed to be proving that he and Celia *shouldn't* be together? And after I'd learned her true thoughts about him, I knew they shouldn't be together. She was all wrong for him.

Envy spread through my veins like liquid ice. Celia might not have romance with Hudson, but neither did I. And she had friendship with him. At the moment, it appeared I had nothing.

We didn't speak while we maneuvered through the long line out of the garage, Hudson humming fragments of the Brahms symphony as he drove. Was I the only one feeling the thick and heavy tension? A tension that seemed to grow thicker by the minute.

By the time we were on the road I couldn't hold in my feelings of frustration and heartbreak any longer. "So you knew Celia would be there tonight." It wasn't a question. I already knew the answer, but I wanted him to say it.

His eyes widened, as if surprised at my harsh tone. "I knew Celia would be there with her parents, yes." He glanced at me sideways. "Her parents, whom are friends with my parents, remember?"

Right. Fooling them was as essential as fooling Sophia Pierce.

What was my problem? I wrapped my arms around my chest and banged my head against the window once, twice, three times. I shouldn't have been angry—he'd told me he'd be fake with me. I shouldn't have been jealous—Celia had him as a friend way before I came along. And she didn't have more than that.

And neither did I. Not since I'd ended things four days before. Funny how I'd been afraid that being with Hudson would make me fall into bad patterns. Instead, not being with him had been what triggered my anxiety that week and what made me feel so rotten at the moment.

Another tear slipped down my cheek. I dabbed at it with my knuckle.

"What's wrong?" Hudson asked, concern in his voice. Or maybe it was simply puzzlement.

I considered what to say. I could keep the barrier up between us and evade the question. Or lie. Or confess my envy. Or I could be honest.

Unable to go another minute with the loneliness that had settled in my chest, honesty won over. "I want you," I whispered, my face pressed against the glass, too embarrassed to look at him.

"Alayna?" I felt his eyes on me.

"I know what I said." I wiped my eyes, determined to keep the rest of my tears in my eyes. "But maybe I was wrong. I mean, I don't know if you're right—if spending time with you can make me better. But I know that since we've been apart, I've been worse." Taking a ragged breath, I braved a look at him. "I miss you." A nervous giggle escaped from my throat. "Told you I get attached."

A trace of a smile crossed his lips. "Where do you think I'm taking you?"

I glanced out the window, having not been paying attention to our destination. Lincoln. Headed East. We were blocks away from Pierce Industries. The loft.

I straightened, a blush crawling on my cheeks. "Oh," I said, the lonely ache inside burning away with the spark of desire. Then irritation took over. "I told you no more sex, and you were taking me to the loft without asking?"

"Alayna," he sighed with frustration. "You are a bundle of mixed signals. At the symphony you seemed to indicate—"

"And you totally blew me off," I interrupted. "Don't talk to me about mixed signals!"

He put his hand on my knee. "I was trying to avoid mixing business with pleasure. A difficult task with you, precious." His voice grew low. "Especially with your wandering hands and how hot you look in that dress."

I blinked. "Oh," I said again. How did he do that? How did he compartmentalize, dividing the pretend from the real, never the two to cross while I tied myself up in knots?

"If you want me to ask, I will, though you know it's not my style." He took my silent stare as a "yes" even though it was simply me processing. "May I take you to my bed, Alayna?"

His request came out in a rumble that had my passion buttons going off like fireworks. "Yes," I half moaned as he pulled up to a red light.

His hand moved to my head, pulling me to him. His mouth was greedy and full of need, his tongue tasting of deep lust and the Amaretto coffee he'd had at intermission. My panties felt slick, and the corset binding of my dress felt tight against my breasts.

The honk of a horn pulled him back to the steering wheel. He shifted in his seat and my eyes shot to the bulge straining his pants. My mouth watered, wanting it inside me.

Hudson shifted again. "Those hungry eyes are not helping the situation."

And then we were there. Pulling in at the valet station of Pierce Industries. I was oblivious to the motions Hudson went through, greeting the valet, handing over his keys, moving to walk behind me toward the elevators, his hand firmly on my ass.

In the elevator we were alone. Hudson entered the code for the penthouse and, as soon as the doors closed, he pressed me against the sheer metal wall of the car. Pausing inches from my lips, his breath mingled with mine. "You're so beautiful, Alayna."

"Then kiss me."

One side of his mouth curled up seductively. "I think I'll take my time." Slowly, he traced his nose against my jawline, and down my neck. I moved my mouth to try to capture his, but he was quicker, always a step ahead of me. His merciless seduction turned me on to no end, creating a pool of moisture between my legs.

His slow pace was killing me. "I think I'll urge you to move faster." I slid my hand down to fondle the bulge in his pants.

"Fuck me, Alayna!" he hissed as I continued to knead his erection through the material.

"You'll get no protest from me." I felt him growing stiffer under my palm. "Actually, I'd like to fuck you with my mouth."

His eyes widened, but before I could act on my statement, the elevator stopped at the top floor. He pulled me out of the car, letting go of me to fumble for his keys. I rubbed his back while he unlocked the door, unable to stop touching him. "Get in," he growled as he held the door open for me.

We'd only made it over the threshold, the door slamming behind us before he'd pushed me to the wall. He flipped on one light, then he took my face in his hands and my mouth in his, thrusting his tongue inside to battle with mine, his stubble chaffing against my tender skin. I loved his aggressiveness, as if he couldn't get enough of my taste. I certainly couldn't get enough of his.

But I'd been serious about wanting my mouth elsewhere on his body, and though Hudson liked to dominate our time together, I wanted to please him. While he still cradled my face, controlling the intensity of our kiss, my hands unzipped his fly and slipped inside to stroke him.

Even through the material of his briefs, Hudson groaned against my lips at my caress.

His sounds ignited my desire. I pulled away from his grip and turned him to the wall. He was going to need support for what I had planned. Then I wrestled his pants and briefs down his legs enough to release his cock. "There's the big boy," I purred as I swirled my hand across his head. Catching a bead of pre-cum, I circled my fingers around his shaft and let the moisture glide my hand down his erection.

He moaned again, and I sank to my knees. Holding his cock at the base with one hand, I curled my lips around his crown, and sucked him gently. He gasped, gripping my hair in between his fingers, pulling it to the point of a delicious sting. "God, Alayna. That's so…ah…so good."

His praise encouraged me. I stroked my fist up and down his shaft, quickly developing a steady pace, while I licked and sucked his head into my hollowed cheeks. I gave him the full treatment, trailing my tongue along his thick ridge and softly grazing my teeth across his crown. He grew thicker under my attention, and my own arousal spiked.

I hadn't thought whether or not I intended to suck him to orgasm, but suddenly I was desperate for it. I needed his climax, maybe as much as he did, and my mouth greedily portrayed that need.

"Alayna, stop." Before I could react, his hands pulled my head away, his cock falling from my mouth with a pop.

Shocked and confused, I let him help me up. "Did I do something wrong?"

"No, precious. Your mouth is amazing." He reclaimed my lips for a deep kiss. "But I need to come inside your cunt. I've been thinking about it for days." He wrapped his arms around my back and began working on the ties of my corset. "And you need to be naked."

I groaned, knowing it would take forever to get me out of my dress. "That will take too long," I murmured into his neck.

"It has to be." He pulled me tighter so he could see what he was doing over my shoulder. "I have to have access to your breasts. I love your breasts."

I sighed and began working the buttons of his shirt. "Then you have to be naked, too."

He shook his head against mine. "That will take longer."

"But I love the feel of my breasts against your bare chest."

His chuckle turned into a groan of frustration. "I don't even want to know how you got into this dress. Turn around." I did so, lifting my hair so he could work better. His fingers moved deftly and soon he had loosened it enough for me to take over.

I felt his fingers leave me and heard him fumbling with his own clothing. With my back still toward him, I slipped the gown off the rest of the way, and climbed out. Then I removed my panties. I left my shoes on, knowing he liked to do me in heels. Before I turned around, I took a deep breath, knowing that when I saw him naked, he would take it away.

And, boy, was I right. I'd only really gotten to look at him naked the one time in the shower, but I hadn't forgotten how the sight affected me. His stomach was washboard tight, and his thigh muscles strong. And in between his legs, his erection stood proudly, even more virile and beautiful without his clothing to hinder the view.

Finally my gaze made it to his face, and I noticed he was leering at me with the same amount of intense desire I felt for him. Our eyes met. Then I was in his arms—his strong, beautiful arms—as he kissed me with deep hunger, my breasts smashed against his torso. Soon, he tucked his hands under my ass and lifted me. I wrapped my legs around his waist and my arms around his neck, as he adjusted my hips over his cock.

He paused at my entrance. "I haven't gotten you ready."

"I'm close enough. Come on in, Hudson."

He smirked as he rammed into me in one fierce drive. His cock burned inside my not yet fully wet pussy, but it also felt so wonderfully good. So deep and so hard.

He wasted no time establishing a steady rhythm, powering into me with each stroke. The strength it must have taken to hold me in that position and to fuck me with such force amazed me. I'd known he was fit, but hadn't realized the extent. The awareness heightened my arousal and slickened my sex, allowing him to slide in and out with ease. My breasts bounced with our movement, and shocks of delight shot through my body as my sensitive nipples brushed against his chest. "Hudson, yes. God, yes."

Our eyes remained locked and I could see the strain and the pleasure etched in his forehead as he continued to pound us toward climax. "So… damn…good," he panted. "You feel…so…damn…good."

His encouragement and the sound of our thighs slapping drove me insane, so close to orgasm. With each thrust of his hips, my sex tightened around his steel erection. He turned me to the wall for added support, adjusting his stance so he could pummel me with greater impetus. The new position freed his hand, and he rubbed my clit as his crown found a tender spot. "Come with me, Alayna," he commanded. "Come."

His authoritative tone and circling thumb were my undoing. I threw my head back into the wall, my cunt trembling as my orgasm crashed through me. He followed, groaning my name while he released into me in long, hot spurts.

I unwrapped my legs from his waist and felt numbly for the floor with my foot, knowing that he couldn't possibly continue to carry me after that violent of a release. Though he no longer held my weight, he didn't let go of me.

"Can we do that again?" I panted, before our bodies had even cooled.

His brow furrowed as he released his grasp on me to look at his watch. "You have to be to work at one? I think we can manage to do that again twice."

Chapter Fifteen

"Okay, H, we need to have a heart to heart." We'd been on the road to the Hamptons for less than ten minutes, but I was too anxious to postpone this conversation. I swiveled in the front seat of the Mercedes and pushed my sunglasses to my head so I could see Hudson clearly.

He glanced sideways at me, his own eyes hidden behind his dark Ray Bans. "Sounds intriguing."

I took a deep breath. "I have some grievances about last night."

His brow rose skeptically over his sunglasses, but he kept his eyes on the road.

"Not that part of last night." I hit his arm playfully. "The earlier part of the night. The later part was fine."

He frowned. "Only fine?"

"More than fine," I laughed. "It was spectacular. Incredibly spectacular." My thighs tensed just thinking about the sensual delight we'd experienced the night before at the loft. A kernel of insecurity crept in under my praise, causing me to wonder if he felt the same. Bracing myself, I asked, "How did you think it was?"

"Fine." His smirk let me know that he was teasing, but I lightly pinched his thigh anyway. Another excuse to touch him.

He took one hand off the wheel and grabbed the hand that had pinched him. "Careful! I'm driving." He brought my hand to his mouth and nipped at my finger before letting it go. "But you have grievances?"

I pushed away thoughts that his mouth on my skin had elicited. "Yes. I do. I was not prepared for the situation you put me in. I need to know more going forward. I knew nothing about the Werners being at the symphony last night. Couldn't you have at least given me a heads up?"

Hudson took off his sunglasses and studied me, as if trying to gauge my seriousness.

I was very serious. I was tired of always being in the dark about him and the world that he weaved me in and out of so flippantly.

He tucked his sunglasses into the compartment above his mirror, not needing them anymore with the sun setting and us directed east. "Except for your predilection for putting your hands all over me—"

"Oh, don't exaggerate."

"—you were magnificent." He was serious as well, which shocked me. I felt anything but magnificent. "How would any information I could have given you have changed how you performed?"

I opened my mouth but found I didn't have a specific answer. "I would have been more at ease because I was prepared." That was the best I could come up with. "The same goes for the day at the fashion show. I could have handled your mother, Celia—" I paused, wanting to indicate what I'd found out about his past without actually saying it. "You know, the whole day would have been better if I'd been prepared."

"Again, I thought you were brilliant."

"Not on the inside. And it's the inside stuff that makes me do crazy things. Like stalk office buildings." I winced as I mentioned the embarrassing behavior that I wished I could forget. But if I wanted to be well, I needed to address my insecurities, and not knowing much about Hudson led to many of mine. "Anyway, I have you trapped in a car for over two hours—"

"Are you sure I don't have you trapped?"

"You're driving. I'm providing the entertainment." Though, I found his uncharacteristic playfulness extremely entertaining as well.

"I like the sound of that." He grinned, sneaking a look at my bare legs.

I resisted the urge to tug at my black skort, one of my prizes from shopping at Mirabelle's. I enjoyed that he liked looking at me, but his gaze turned me on to the *n*th degree and I wanted to keep focused. "Stop interrupting. We are playing a get-to-know-each-other game." I put my hand up as if to shush him. "Don't even say whatever it is you're about to say. If we have any hope of fooling your family when we're with them twenty-four/seven then we need to know more about each other."

"I already know plenty about you." This time his gaze went to the bosom of my super tight tee.

"No, you don't." I snapped my fingers by my face to get his attention to move upward. "Have you ever gotten to know a woman—nonsexually? Besides from a background check?"

"Not on purpose."

His answer was quick and honest. And it pissed me off. "Hudson, you're kind of an asshole."

"So I've been told." He met my glowering eyes. "Fine. How do we play this game of yours?"

The triumph wiped out my irritation. "We'll take turns. On your turn you can either ask a question or tell a fact about yourself. Your choice. Nothing too heavy. Basic stuff. I'll go first. I don't like mushrooms."

His eyes widened. "You don't like mushrooms? What is wrong with you?"

"They're gross. They taste like rotten olives."

"They taste nothing like olives."

"They taste like rotten olives. I can't stand them." I made a face to show my disgust, but inside I was ecstatic that he was taking an interest in what I had shared. I hadn't been sure he would. Especially with such a benign subject as food tastes.

Hudson shook his head, seemingly bewildered by my confession. "That's a terrible inconvenience. That has to hinder your fine dining experiences."

"Tell me about it." For some reason, mushrooms seemed to be in a great deal of fancy recipes. "Imagine my horror when my senior prom date made dinner for me and it was chicken Marsala."

His eye twitched, almost unnoticeably. "Your senior prom date? Was this a serious relationship?" His voice had also tensed slightly.

I narrowed my eyes. Was he jealous? "Are you asking that question for your turn?"

"Uh, yes, I suppose I am."

He *was* jealous. Of a high school prom date. I was flattered. "It was a serious relationship for me. Not for Joe."

"Joe sounds terrible." But his smile returned.

"Thank you. He was." Hudson pulled onto the Interstate, and I put my sunglasses in my purse. "My turn." I sat back, chewing my lip. I'd eased us into the game, but now I wanted some answers. Something good. "Why do you never call people by their nicknames?"

He groaned. "Because nicknames are so gaudy. Call a person by their given name. That's why they have it."

I rolled my eyes. He was so formal. Sometimes I wasn't sure I even liked the guy. That was part of the reason I had wanted to play this game.

I had to know if my attraction went beyond the physical.

And I really wanted him to call me by my nickname. "But nicknames show a degree of familiarity."

"You tell everyone to call you Laynie. Even people you've just met."

Because answering to Alayna was weird. The only people who had really called me Alayna were my parents. "Maybe I feel familiar with everyone I meet." I made an effort to say my next words casually, as if the fact didn't really bother me. "And you call Celia by a nickname."

"Really?" He knew it bothered me. I hadn't covered well enough. "She's the only person on earth, Alayna. I've known her my whole life. I didn't even know her name was really Celia until I was almost ten."

I crossed my legs, pleased when he glanced as I did so, and swung my foot with irritation. "If you are trying to convince people you care more about me than Celia, then you should have a nickname for me. It will establish endearment." And I really wanted his endearment.

"Calling me 'H' shows endearment?"

My phone vibrated in my pocket. I lifted my hips so I could pull it out, and Hudson eyed me as I did so. "It does. I don't go for the real lovey-dovey words like sweetie and honey. But Hudson is way too formal."

"I like formal."

"I like cherry-flavored blow pops. It doesn't make them appropriate for every situation."

"Blow pops?"

"Yeah…blow pops." I planned to respond with a sexy comeback, but was distracted by reading the text on my phone. It was from Brian asking me to call him. I'd ignored all of the texts he'd sent over the last week, and wasn't about to start answering now. I threw my phone into my lap, frustrated. He didn't know I'd found a solution to my money issues and still expected me to give in to his terms. Not happening.

"You didn't like 'baby'?" Hudson's question pulled me back to the car.

My answer held the tension I meant for Brian. "Not so much." Only because it was unoriginal and insincere. It wasn't a name Hudson had picked specifically for me.

"I'm sticking with Alayna."

I turned to him and glared. "Come on. You could call me 'precious' every now and then in front of other people."

"No way," he murmured.

"Why? You call me that sometimes already."

His voice rumbled low and quiet and serious. "That's private."

I shivered. Even if his tone hadn't indicated the matter was settled, I would have dropped it. His answer was perfect—sensual and even a little romantic. Not like I was getting my hopes up romantic, just sort of sweet.

Hmm. Hudson never failed to surprise me. I shook my head. "It's your turn."

My phone buzzed again. Another text from Brian. This time saying he was coming to see me first thing the next day. And I wouldn't be there. Guess the laugh was on him. I grinned as I turned off my phone and stuffed it back into my pocket.

When my focus returned to Hudson, he was eyeing me, his brow cocked. "Who keeps texting you?"

Something about his jealousy made me want to purr. "Is that your question?"

"It is."

I considered making something up, something that would really provoke envy from the man, but the game was meant to be about honest answers. "My brother. He's an asshole."

"Like I'm an asshole?" he asked, recalling what I'd said to him minutes before.

"Worse. He's an asshole who doesn't know it."

Hudson grinned. "And you're ignoring Brian?"

He knew Brian's name. It made me realize that he already knew I had a brother. I wondered what else Hudson knew about Brian. And my parents. My whole life.

Well, if he wanted to know anything more about Brian he'd have to wait until his turn. "You already asked your question. It's my turn. I lost my virginity when I was sixteen."

I meant it to be a shocker, still irritated about Brian's constant texts and Hudson's knowledge of things he shouldn't know about me until I told him. "Sixteen? Fuck, Alayna. I don't think I want to know that."

"Sorry." I smiled.

He shook his head, his eyes narrow. "I seriously doubt this is going to come up in conversation with my family."

"You never know."

"Who was the guy?"

His jealousy was seriously hot. "Is that your turn?"

"No."

I cocked my head, questioning his sincerity.

He changed his mind. He couldn't help himself. "Yes."

I didn't even try to hide my elation. "He was a random guy I met at a party. I thought that having sex would help me forget that my parents had died. It did not."

"No, I suppose it wouldn't."

He sounded sympathetic and I was glad he didn't press. It had been an awful time in my life. My parents' fatal car accident had pushed me to behave in ways I wasn't proud. Random sex, excessive drinking, drug experimentation. And then the addiction that had stuck—obsessive love, which shouldn't be called love at all, but rather obsessive wanna-be-loved. If I was really with Hudson, I mean really his girlfriend, then he should know all the details, and I liked to think I'd tell him. But for a strange moment, I was exceptionally glad that I wasn't really with Hudson so I wouldn't have to tell him.

Whoa. Did that mean that there were other moments when I wanted to be really with him? When had that started?

I shot a glance at Hudson who seemed to be heavy in his own thoughts. What would it take to get in there? I tried to guess what he could be so absorbed with. "What were you doing in Cincinnati?"

"Business."

I pinched the bridge of my nose. It was so much easier to have sex with the man than to get him to share anything real. "That's not very much of an answer."

"I wouldn't talk to my girlfriend about business."

"You wouldn't be my boyfriend if you didn't." Despite finally believing that Hudson was indeed out-of-town that week, insecurity nagged at me still. I pushed for more information. "Didn't your mom and dad talk about business with each other?"

"My parents don't talk about anything. If Dad's at the house when we get there, he will not sleep in the same room with Mother. Loveless marriage, remember?"

"Not a good example then." I tried a different tactic. "Look. I'm a business major. I like to know about these things." I licked my lips purposefully. "Doesn't my smart mind turn you on?"

"*Your* smart mind, not mine." But he was hiding a smile.

I slipped my hand down his thigh. "Come on. I've shown you mine. Show me yours."

He couldn't resist me in full flirtation mode. He sighed. "There's been some outside interest in Plexis, one of my smaller companies. But I'm not keen to sell to this particular buyer. The other members of the board feel differently."

Hudson furrowed his brow and I thought he'd finished, but he went on. "Actually it's been quite stressful, fighting to keep Plexis together when so many are opposed. Many stand to gain a sizable profit from a sale. I know that this buyer would run the place to the ground. The company would be torn apart. People would lose their jobs."

I sat mesmerized. In his brief divulgence, I saw something besides his passion for his companies and the people that worked for them. I saw him relax and maybe even enjoy telling me about something that weighed heavily on him. Did he have anyone he shared these things with? It didn't seem likely.

He noticed me staring and he shifted.

I was sure he'd be disturbed to discover how much I'd discerned from such a brief conversation. So I deflected and lightened the mood. "Thank you! Was that really so terrible?"

His mouth tightened into a straight line, but I saw the gleam in his eyes. "I'm not answering that. It's not your turn." He only paused a second before he said, "Fine. It wasn't that terrible. That's what I'm offering for my turn."

"Hudson?" I asked softly, hoping he didn't see the full extent of my adoration in just the speaking of his name.

"Yes, precious?"

"You aren't really an asshole."

He brought one finger to his mouth. "*Shh*. You'll ruin my reputation."

We continued the game through dinner at a clam bar in Sayville, covering a variety of topics from favorite movies to worst dates to first kisses. Hudson and I had very few things in common, but that only intrigued me more, and I had the distinct impression he felt the same. Most of our differences seemed to come from our backgrounds rather than our tastes. I didn't know if I loved the opera—I'd never been. And my favorite pastime—buying one movie ticket and sneaking into several movies after—was born of a lack of funds that Hudson had never experienced.

Underneath it all, we both knew we shared one very vital commonality—our destructive pasts. Though we seldom spoke of it, it shadowed many of our confessions. But unlike with other men when I went through the routine of talking about myself, I didn't feel like I was holding back the truth. I wasn't lying, like I had to so many others. We didn't talk about it, but it didn't lie in the deep recesses of ourselves, threatening to be revealed. It made the simple exchanges between us easier and more poignant.

After dinner when we returned to the road, we played the game at a relaxed pace, letting long moments of comfortable silence fill the spaces between turns. Finally, Hudson turned off Old Montauk Highway onto a private drive. At the gate midway down the entry, he entered a code that opened the wooden doors and allowed us to continue past the high hedge to the circle driveway. He stopped the car in front of a traditional two-story estate.

"We're here," he said in a sing-song voice not typical of Hudson Pierce.

My mouth fell open as I stared up at the mansion, clearly lit with bright torchlights like the fountain in the center of the circle drive. I'd tried not to think too much about Hudson's money, not wanting that to be the focus of my attraction to him, but if there was ever a time to be appreciative of his wealth, this was it. The stone house was breathtaking and extravagant, the kind of thing I'd only seen in movies.

"It's…wow."

Hudson laughed. "Come on. You'll love the inside."

I opened the car door, immediately overwhelmed with the smell of the ocean air mingled with a variety of early summer blooming flowers. The front doors opened and an older balding man in a light gray suit approached us.

"Good evening, Martin," Hudson said, slipping his arm around my waist. "This is my girlfriend, Alayna Withers. Martin is our household assistant."

"A pleasure, Ms. Withers," Martin said, taking my hand. After he released it, he spoke to Hudson. "Mr. Pierce, I'll set your bags in the guest suite in the west wing."

Hudson frowned as he handed Martin the keys to the car. "Is everyone in the west wing?"

"Yes, sir."

"Then set us up in the master of the east wing."

With his hand still at the small of my back, Hudson escorted me through the double doors into the entryway of the house. The entry was bare except for an ornate table set into the curve of the wide staircase.

"Hudson, we're in the kitchen," Mirabelle's voice called from the back of the house.

"I know it's late," Hudson said to me, his tone full of apology, "but we should at least say hello. Do you mind?"

I wasn't tired in the least. This was my time of day. If we hadn't left town, I'd just be starting my shift at the club. "It's not late for me."

For some reason, this made Hudson smile. "Good."

The sensual promise in his tone made my thighs tense. God, with his endless flirting in the car and the intimacy of our get-to-know you game, I was more than seduced. All I needed was a bed and Hudson alone. And the bed was optional.

Hudson directed me through the back hallway of the entry toward the back of the house, his fingers at my hip not providing nearly enough contact. At the kitchen, he dropped his hand, and I sighed at the loss.

Fortunately, I was able to disguise the sigh as one of awe at the room we'd entered. The kitchen was larger than my apartment. Hell, the entryway had been larger than my apartment. The walls were a light yellow cream, and the counter tops a brown and white flecked granite. All the appliances were stainless steel, a striking comparison to the hardwood floors. Even as someone with no interest in kitchens, I admired its beauty.

We found Adam and Mira leaning over the center island, scraping out what seemed to be the final crumbs in a pie dish.

"I'm pregnant," Mira said before anyone could ask. "I don't know what Adam's excuse is."

"Was that one of Millie's pies?" Hudson asked.

Mira nodded.

"Then there's his excuse right there. No one makes better pies than Millie. I can't believe you didn't save any for us."

"There's more for tomorrow," Adam piped up. "We were strictly forbidden to touch them. Millie's our cook," he said for my benefit. "She's amazing."

"Now that the little one's been fed," Mira said, rubbing her belly, "I can give a proper greeting. Laynie!" She wrapped her arms around me.

"I'm so glad you came!"

"Thank you," I said, stunned by her exuberance.

"How was the trip? Did you get anything to eat?"

"Are you offering to fix them something?" Adam put his hand near his mouth and mock-whispered, "Mira doesn't cook."

She narrowed her eyes at him, playfully. "I know how to use the microwave, though."

"No need to prove anything. We stopped in Sayville," Hudson said.

"The clam bar? Ooh, I'm jealous." Mira moved to her brother and hugged him, giving him a light peck on the cheek. "I'm still glad you're here. It's been ages since you've come out."

Hudson slipped out of her grasp, but smiled. "I am too. Did Dad come?"

Mira took the empty pie plate to the sink and filled it with water before leaving it to soak. "Yeah, he's already gone to bed for the night. Or he's hiding from Mom. He's in the guest house."

I exchanged glances with Hudson, remembering our earlier conversation about his parents' loveless marriage.

"Where is Mother? And Chandler?"

"I'm here." I looked behind me to see Sophia Pierce leaning against the arched doorway. She wore a dressing robe and had a glass of something light brown on ice. "Chandler's out with the Gardiner girl. I don't expect him until late."

"Hello, Mother." Hudson walked over to her and kissed each of her cheeks.

"You made it." Sophia glanced at me. "Both of you."

"Alayna and I are seldom apart," Hudson lied, pulling me to him.

"Good evening, Mrs. Pierce." I had been dreading seeing her again, but I made my greeting as warm as possible. Hudson's arm around me helped. "Thank you for the invite. Your house is lovely."

She nodded. "I'm sure you want to get settled. I chose a room for you in the west wing."

Hudson straightened. "I told Martin to set up the master suite in the east wing."

Electric tingles spread from my lower belly throughout the rest of my body. Hudson and I sharing a master suite…the thought made me squirm. I'd tried not to dwell on how we'd spend our nights in the Hamptons—whether they'd be filled with sex or considered on-duty hours, I didn't know. But now that the idea had been firmly planted, I couldn't stop thinking of the carnal possibilities.

Sophia obviously didn't feel the same way about her son and me sharing a bed. "Hudson, that's so far away from the rest of us." Her ire was evident. Like Hudson, I had a feeling she rarely had anyone oppose her. I imagined the shared trait made for some pretty uncomfortable family meals.

And I was about to share several of them before the trip was over. Lucky me.

Hudson knew how to handle his mother. "We need the distance, Mother." His tone was final.

"Why? We don't bite."

"Alayna does," he grinned wickedly. "And she can be quite loud."

I turned ten shades of scarlet. Did he actually believe every pretend girlfriend wanted their sex life discussed with the mother? Though, I really could be quite loud.

It was Sophia's shocked look that Hudson responded to, her expression likely the intended outcome of his scandalous remark. "Oh, Mother, don't look at me like that. Neither Alayna and I have been virgins since we were sixteen."

Sophia pursed her lips and walked past us, finishing her beverage before placing it in the sink.

Hudson leaned into whisper in my ear, the warmth of his breath sending a shiver down my spine. "Well, what do you know? That virginity fact did come in handy."

I elbowed him in the ribs, exasperated at being the victim in his poke at his mother.

"Don't get pissy, Alayna." He pulled me in front of him and wrapped his arms around me, my backside to his chest. "Trust me—we want a room away from them."

I sighed into his touch, aware that we were on show, but enjoying the contact nonetheless.

And maybe he enjoyed the contact, too. Or he simply wanted to get away from his mother because he excused us then. "We'll see you in the morning. It's late and we'd like to get to bed."

Or maybe he really did just want to get to bed. God knew I did.

CHAPTER SIXTEEN

As we climbed the stairs and turned toward the east wing, nervousness set in. I had learned that Hudson was very intent on separating the fake from the real, and that left me to wonder what would happen between the two of us at night when we were alone. It stood to reason we'd have sex, and he had made sure our room was away from the others. But did he want privacy so we could be intimate or so that his family wouldn't know we weren't being intimate?

It was so confusing. He so easily compartmentalized, but for me it was impossible. Everything I knew and felt about him wrapped itself tightly around me at all times. There was no separation of the pretend and the real except for how he reacted to me.

Silently as I worried about the impending situation, I followed him through double doors into a beautiful master suite. The room had two ornate mahogany dressers and a matching four-poster queen bed. Our luggage sat at the foot of the bed, opposite a small sitting area with two armchairs and a mahogany table. A fireplace lined the inner wall and the floors were hardwood covered almost entirely by a plush rug. Though it was traditionally decorated, a flat screen TV centered the wall across from the bed.

As I stood taking the room in, worrying out our situation, Hudson removed his suit jacket, humming as he did, obviously unaware of my anxiety. Next he loosened his tie and flung it over one of the chairs. He turned back to me as he unbuttoned his shirt and paused, noticing I hadn't moved since entering the room.

Before he could ask, I blurted out what had me fretting. "Am I off-duty or on-duty?"

A small smile crossed his lips. "My family's not around." Yes, he'd made sure of that. "Off-duty. Besides, I told you I'd never use sex as part of the sham and I intend to have sex with you now."

The shiver that passed through me caused every hair on my body to stand on end. "Really?"

"Of course." He continued to pin me with his stare as he resumed his unbuttoning, moving slower than he had before.

I took in a shallow breath. "We've never spent the night together."

"So we haven't." He took a step toward me, his sly grin growing wider. "Are you nervous?"

Yes. "No."

His brow rose as if he sensed my lie. "You should be. You'll be within my reach all night long. I expect you'll be sore tomorrow."

My nervousness melted away, replaced by intense arousal. "Hmm. Sounds lovely."

"Good. Go get ready for bed." He nodded toward the en suite bathroom door. "Don't take too long. I'm eager to lick you senseless."

I didn't hesitate, grabbing the small bag that held my toiletries as I scurried into the bathroom. After I shut the door behind me, my finger lingered at the handle while I considered locking it. But why would I do that? Any invasion Hudson planned I would welcome.

After washing my face and brushing my teeth I paused again. What should I wear? I had packed a sexy nightie, not sure if I would use it or not. Nighties seemed to suggest a romantic tone. Didn't they? It didn't matter, because I'd left my suitcase in the bedroom. Should I go out clothed? Naked?

I decided to strip to my underwear, thankful that I'd worn a pretty black lace bra and matching lace boy shorts under my outfit. I folded my clothes and left them on the counter then stepped quietly out of the bathroom.

Hudson had turned off the overhead lights and switched on the nightstand lamps. His back was to me, and I could see he'd lost his dress shirt and belt and his feet were bare and sexy. God, feet had no right being sexy, but his were.

He turned and my breath caught. Our sexual relationship was still so new. Seeing his naked chest still thrilled me to no end. His hard angles, the way his pants hung low enunciating his hips, his abs of steel—I didn't think I could ever get tired of looking at him.

Eventually my gaze fluttered to his face where I found his dark eyes, devouring me where I stood. "Nice choice." He nodded at my attire, and my skin tingled with his approval. "Come here." His low growl pulled me to him as effectively as if he had me on a rope. I stopped within his reach, but he didn't touch me. He circled around me instead, standing so close I could feel the body heat radiating off of him, increasing my own already rising body temperature.

He stopped behind me, and I felt him at my neck, his breath grazing my skin. "So beautiful," he murmured before his lips nipped at my ear. "I need to make you come." I jumped as his hands skimmed down the length of my arms. "Over and over." He licked along my lobe. "Do you think you can handle it?"

Words failed me. I answered with an incoherent moan, leaning my body into him, letting his heat envelop me.

He let out a wicked laugh then spun me around to face him, his mouth stopping centimeters above my own. "You don't know if you can handle it, do you, precious? Let's find out."

He took me with his mouth, consuming my breath with his ravaging kiss, urging me to succumb to his control. I didn't fight it, giving myself over to him in every way he demanded. And with each demand, I lost more of myself to him as he taught my body how to be adored and worshipped. How to be taken and dominated. Like I was made simply for his pleasure, but by the same token, that he was made for mine.

He did lick me until I was senseless, and he did make me come over and over. And in several moments I feared I couldn't handle it. But he pushed me through each climax—both those that rolled slowly and those that ripped violently through me—with the experience and confidence of a lover that had known me intimately for far longer than he had.

After several orgasms passed between us, he lay heavily on the bed next to me, his shoulder touching mine, either spent for the night or taking a break, I wasn't sure. My own body was boneless, every muscle lax. Sleep threatened at the edges of my consciousness, but I pushed it away, unwilling to put our evening to bed yet.

I turned my head toward him and caught him watching me, a satisfied smile on his face. Returning his grin, I sighed. "That was…incredible."

In a flash he was on top of me, his body covering the length of mine. He laced his hands in mine and lifted them over my head. "What was your favorite part?"

All of it. Every minute of it. But that answer seemed lame and I knew he wanted something more concrete. Several amazing moments came to mind, each making me blush simply from thinking of them—like when he'd crawled up my body and straddled my neck, silently ordering me to take his cock in my mouth. That had been pretty hot.

And when he'd commanded me to play with myself while he sucked and tugged at my breast. Again, pretty hot. Also, a bit awkward. But only until I warmed up to it.

Unable to voice the memories, I turned the table on him. "What was *your* favorite part?"

He trailed his nose along my jaw. "The way you respond to anything…everything…I do to you." He licked along my lower lip and I opened to kiss him, but he pulled out of reach. "Your turn."

His mood was unusually playful and inspired me to join him. "I'll never tell." I grinned.

"Tell me." He moved my hands together and pinned them with one of his. His other hand he lowered to rest lightly at my hip.

My exposed ribcage made me feel vulnerable. He could tickle me mercilessly. I tempted him anyway. "Make me."

"I can't make you do anything." His hand flickered across my sensitive side and I flinched.

"I think you could." I braced myself for his assault. "I hear you're quite good at making women do things."

And suddenly I wasn't playing anymore, but hinting at deeper meanings. I hadn't meant to go there, but his confession of manipulating women for sport always hung right below the surface of our time together. Lying nude beneath him now, completely stripped of senses from multiple orgasms, it bubbled to the top and escaped my lips.

His eye twitched, the only indication he gave that my true implication affected him. "I *am* good at making women do things."

I couldn't help myself. I nudged the conversation on. "But not me."

"No." His voice lowered, the playfulness gone. "Not you."

"Am I not…" I searched for the question I wanted to ask, needing the answer even though I couldn't yet form the words. "…intriguing… enough to play that game with?"

My hands still pinned above me, he propped himself up with his other arm so he could glare down at me. "God, Alayna, do you want me to do that to you? Possess you? I would crush you. I would destroy you." His tone was dark, but also honestly inquisitive. "Is that what you want?"

My eyes filled. I hated the truth of my answer. "No, but a little bit yes too. That's how my stupid brain works. If you don't do with me what you normally do with other girls, there must be something wrong with me."

He laughed as he lowered himself to the bed beside me. "Oh, it's all you, huh? It's not that there's something wrong with me? How self-centered of you."

Free to move, I rolled to my side toward him. "I'm very self-centered. I want to be special. I'm afraid that I'm not."

"You are." His words were emphatic. "Even more than you could imagine you are." He turned his body so he could face me. "Because I don't want to destroy you more than I need to possess you. That's progress for me."

We were both vulnerable now. Two damaged souls spilling our brokenness in a private therapy session. Was this what he had wanted between us? Sharing like this, without judgment, without shame? It was…nice.

I stopped worrying about being exposed and spoke from the gut. "Then I'll try not to fixate on what it means that I'm different for you. That will be progress for me."

He nodded, the weight of my words sinking in. "Do you know why you do it?"

"Why I become obsessive about guys?"

"Yeah."

"My counselors have said it's probably about not feeling loved as a child. Aggravated by the early death of my parents. So I'm constantly seeking affection and doubting it when I receive it because I don't know what it really feels like."

"How did you get over that?"

It wasn't at all what I thought he'd ask, and I sensed he was asking as much for himself as he was about me. I'd gotten this far into the depths of candidness, might as well dive right in. "I haven't. It's a constant battle. Lots of self-affirmation. Lots of silly little tricks, like wearing elastic bands to remind me."

He nodded, understanding about my elastic band settling in. "You still fall into old habits."

"Yes."

"With me?"

"You know the answer to that." My voice came out a whisper. I wanted to look away, but our eyes were locked and in the softness of his gaze I found the courage to tell more. "I didn't believe you were away on business. I thought you didn't want to see me. That's why I came by your building."

His face fell, as though my honesty crushed him. He closed his eyes briefly. When he opened them, they were dark and intense. He reached his hand out to cup my nape, insuring that my face was fixed on his. "Alayna, I will never lie to you." His voice was gruff. "Not when we're off-duty. I will always tell you the truth. I swear it."

His grip loosened, and his thumb stroked across my bare cheek. "Do you understand?"

I nodded and covered his hand with mine. "Hudson, *this*," I choked, my throat tight with emotion. "*This* was my favorite part."

For a split second I worried I'd scared him with my intensity, that he'd pull away. But he didn't. Instead he put his hand on my ass and pulled me closer. He stroked down my thigh, urging it forward to rest around his waist. Then he slid inside me, my pussy already wet from earlier orgasms. He was slow and steady with his pace, less rough than he often tended to be, his usual sex talk absent. But, because of the things we'd shared, his measured thrusts felt raw, more intent on connecting than on gratifying.

Climax came quickly for both of us, mine crashing through me in waves that tightened my belly and curled my toes and caused fireworks to cross my vision, his spurting hot and prolonged as he groaned my name. His eyes never left mine, though they narrowed as he came, and it deepened the intimacy. I knew he'd told the truth, I trusted him. In his words, in his actions, I felt fixed. I'd fallen into something that had nothing to do with love. Into healing.

And it was love too. If I could stand to admit it to myself, love was exactly what it was.

CHAPTER SEVENTEEN

Streams of sunlight poured through the windows, warming and waking me up earlier than I would have on my usual sleep schedule. Before looking, I sensed I was alone. When I turned, I squinted at the clock on the nightstand next to where Hudson should have been sleeping. Nine-twenty-seven.

I blinked several times, adjusting my eyes, while I considered whether I wanted to get up and search for my lover or roll over and go back to sleep. I still hadn't made a decision when the doors opened to the bedroom and Hudson appeared wearing nothing but black silk pajama bottoms and carrying a breakfast tray.

"Good, you're awake," he said as I sat up, the smell of coffee luring me further out of sleep. "I'm showing my family what an awesome boyfriend I am by bringing you breakfast in bed. Omelets. Sans mushrooms, of course. No cherry-flavored blow pops." He winked as he set the tray on the table in the sitting area.

"This is one of those inappropriate moments for a blow pop anyway. And you should have said amazingly awesome boyfriend. Breakfast in bed is the best." Though the thing making my mouth water was the never tiresome sight of Hudson barefoot and shirtless.

"I'm not that awesome." He left the tray and untied the string of his PJs, letting them fall to the ground, exposing his beautifully erect penis. He slid under the covers and climbed over me. "I'm going to make you eat it cold."

Before his kiss prevented me from speech or thought, I mumbled, "Cold breakfast sounds perfect."

• • •

It was almost noon before we were ready to dress for the day. Hudson had offered to draw me a bath to soak my sex sore limbs, but I opted for a shared shower, wanting to extend our intimacy as long as possible before we were on-duty again.

After we'd dried and dressed—Hudson in khaki pants and polo, me in a cream sundress—he left me to take our dirty dishes down while I finished primping. I chose to sweep my hair into a ponytail, an easy and quick option, so I could follow him shortly, though the idea of hiding out in the bedroom as long as I could, had crossed my mind. Truth was, as much as I didn't want to face Sophia, I wanted to be with Hudson more.

Not knowing my way around the house yet, I headed first to the kitchen, hopeful that he'd still be there. I paused outside the swinging kitchen door when I heard voices—Hudson's and Sophia's.

"—didn't invite you so you could stay in your room all day and fuck like bunnies," Sophia was saying.

Yeah, I wasn't walking in yet. I pressed my ear to the door, listening.

"Then why did you invite us?" Hudson's voice was calm, his ability to smoothly wield his mother impressing me. Was Sophia the first woman he'd mastered? Had he practiced his skills of manipulation on her? Was our elaborate scheme to fool her now a substitute for the games he'd played on other women?

I wasn't judging him for any of it. Just curious.

"I invited you because I think she—any woman you involve yourself with, for that matter—has a right to be protected. Has a right to know."

"Her name is Alayna, Mother." He surprised me with the sharpness of his tone. "And she already knows." He laughed gruffly. "I love how you believe no one could possibly feel something for me because of who I was in the past."

My chest tightened, ached for what I knew Hudson must be feeling. Brian had held my mistakes over me as well, always doubting that I could ever be better. The lack of familial support made healing all the more difficult.

Maybe Hudson and I could be strength for each other. It was a dangerous thought, putting too much importance into our solely physical relationship, but whom was I kidding? I'd long passed the moment when my emotions had entered into the picture. What was the point of fighting it longer?

Maybe we could be…more.

I'd missed some of the conversation, lost in my own head, but Sophia's raised voice drew me back. "—can't understand how you could tell her? What if she exposes you? Exposes us? Our family doesn't need that kind of scandal."

"My life is more than a scandal waiting to happen, Mother."

"Your life is a series of scandals. Scandals that your father and I are continuously cleaning up. Your bartender whore is just the next scandal."

Even though I'd promised myself to not let her get to me, Sophia's insult was a punch in the gut. My eyes stung, but before tears could form, Hudson's defense softened the blow.

"Don't you dare talk about Alayna like that again. If you do, I—"

"Finding out anything good?"

I jumped away from the door, the unfamiliar male's voice behind me both startling and shaming me for being caught eavesdropping. I forced my eyes to his and blushed even deeper. The chiseled face was more attractive in person than in the pictures I'd seen on the Internet, and the resemblance to his son so striking it was almost eerie, as if I were viewing Hudson thirty years in the future. He looked younger than the sixty years I knew him to be, his frame trim with only a slight paunch, and his features striking against his goatee and long salt and peppered hair.

Hudson's father cocked his head and stroked his goatee, a gesture that seemed so natural I imagined he frequently employed it. "I'm judging by the look on your face that you already know who I am."

"Yes. You're Jonathan Pierce."

"And you...hmm...don't tell me..." He looked me over in such a way that I knew he appreciated what he saw, yet I didn't feel ogled. "You're a little old for Chandler, and Mira doesn't ever pick friends who are prettier than her. That leaves Hudson. I'd heard a rumor he was dating someone, but I never imagined it was true."

His tone was charming and easy, a hint of a drawl revealing his Texas roots. His manner relaxed me even though I'd been caught in an embarrassing situation. "I'm Hudson's girlfriend, Alayna Withers." I held my hand out to him. "But please call me Laynie, Mr. Pierce."

He took my hand with both of his and held it as he spoke. "My friends call me Jack, and I have a feeling we're going to be great friends." He patted my hand, the action managing to stay just on the right side of the okay/creepy line. When he let go, he nodded his head toward the kitchen. "Who's in there anyway?"

A guilty smile lined my lips. "Hudson and your wife."

Jack rolled his head dramatically. "Please refrain from reminding me I'm married to that woman." His eye twinkled mischievously. "We obviously don't want to go in there. Have you been given a tour of Mabel Shores?"

"Mabel Shores?"

"If Hudson hasn't told you the name of this house, he's certainly not given you a tour. How lucky that I'm available to do the honor." He offered me his arm. "Shall we?"

I hesitated only a second, Jack's charismatic demeanor impossible to turn down. Besides, Hudson had said our sham was meant to convince both his parents. Spending time with his father could only be beneficial to the cause. And the truth was, though I knew Hudson expected me, postponing my next face-to-face with Sophia sounded like an excellent idea.

Jack leisurely led me through the house, providing historical and architectural trivia spattered with the occasional humorous anecdote. The main floor featured a spacious living room, library, gym, and a media room as well as two guestrooms. The décor remained traditional throughout, but very up-to-date and stylish.

He ignored showing me the upstairs, stating that there wasn't much to see besides the bedrooms. We also avoided the dining room and kitchen, slipping out the French doors in the office on the opposite side of the house to explore the grounds instead.

We talked easily throughout the tour, Jack's charm never faltering. Though he was more than twice my age and the father of my lover, I adored him and his shameless flirting. He was harmless and fun and much more pleasant than I'd ever imagined a renowned businessman could be. I began to piece together the Pierce family, understanding Mira's welcoming personality now that I'd met Jack. I could even spot what Hudson had inherited, recognizing his magnetism and sexual prowess came from his father. And the playfulness that Hudson occasionally adopted—that was his dad.

When we'd circled most of the east gardens and were headed back toward the house, Jack grew somewhat serious. "So you and Hudson… that's a pleasant surprise."

"I'm not sure that I want to know what's surprising about us."

"Nothing bad. Hudson doesn't date much. I'm glad to see that the girl he finally brought home is someone as delightful as you. I hope it sticks."

I smiled. "Thank you." I savored my next words as I said them, relishing the sweetness of their honesty. "I'm quite stuck on the man. I've fallen for him pretty hard."

Jack stared at me, reading my face. "Yes, I believe you have. That's wonderful. Truly."

His sincerity was touching, and a rush of emotion surged in my chest. It felt good to have someone rooting for our fake relationship. It validated my growing belief in the possibility of more.

My confidence was short-lived, however, Jack's next words reminding me of the barriers lying between Hudson and myself. "What was Sophia saying about you? I've been dying to ask."

"When? Oh." I turned away, pretending to admire the purple grapelike flowers lining the cobblestone path.

He pushed gently, understanding lacing his words. "It had to be not very nice. You were ashen when I found you."

I sighed, thinking how best to sum up what I'd overheard and how it made me feel. "She doesn't like me."

Jack shrugged. "Sophia doesn't like anyone." He didn't bother to hide his own disdain for the woman, and I wondered how he had ended up with her in the first place. "But I imagine she especially doesn't like you. Which is why it's so delicious that I do."

Shaking my head, I ignored his teasing. "Is it because of me or because of Hudson?"

"The reasons I like you have absolutely nothing to do with Hudson."

I leveled a stern look in Jack's direction. "I was talking about Sophia—your wife. Why does she especially not like me?"

Jack stroked his goatee and resumed walking toward the house. "It isn't you."

Bartender whore. I followed him, Sophia's earlier remarks resounding again in my head. "Really? I bet she'd welcome Celia into Hudson's arms."

"Because she adores Celia. Always has."

We'd reached the veranda at the back of the house where Jack gestured to sit. I sank into a cushy loveseat and curled my feet up underneath me. "Doesn't she want Hudson to be happy?"

Jack took the chair across from me, a small wooden table separating us. It was his turn to sigh. "She doesn't want anyone to be happy.

Particularly Hudson. They've had many battles in a lifelong war, and she's not a forgiving woman."

Again I thought of my relationship with Brian. As much of a pain in the ass that he'd been lately, I couldn't say I didn't understand why. He and I had suffered our own battles and the wounds ran deep. And I wasn't Brian's child. I imagined the dynamic between us would be so much worse if I were. Also, though my brother could be domineering, neither he nor I could compare to the battle of wills demonstrated by Hudson and Sophia.

I rested my head back against the loveseat and stared at the rough textured concrete ceiling. "Then there's no way to win her over?"

"No." His answer was firm, final.

If that were true, then the job I'd been paid to do was doomed to fail from the start. "Your son seems to think there is."

Jack shook his head sadly, taking a long moment before responding. "That's too bad. I thought he was long past caring." His expression was raw, and I could see that though he hid it well, he'd been deeply affected by the bad blood between his wife and son.

Then the mask went back up, the pain on his face replaced with his earlier easy-going character. "Now, I on the other hand, am very easy to win over. I can give you some ideas if you need them." He winked.

I laughed, letting go of the serious thoughts and emotions weighing on me. "I've already won you over."

He feigned disappointment. "Damn. I've never had a good poker face."

"But I bet you still win plenty of hands."

"Shall we play later and find out?" He leaned toward me, his eyebrows raised suggestively. "Alone? In the guest house? Strip?"

I laughed again. "I'll play in the main house, you dirty old man. With others present and all our clothing on."

"You just killed all the fun."

We were both laughing when Hudson appeared in the doorway of the house, his features appearing anxious at the sight of his father. "There you are." He came behind me, and laid a firm hand on my shoulder. "I was worried and now I see I should have been."

"I'm fine." I placed my hand over his and craned my neck up to meet his eyes. "Jack's been showing me around Mabel Shores. I've had an amazing time."

Hudson's tone was skeptical. "Then he hasn't tried to come on to you?"

"No, he has." I smiled over at Jack. "But we're all good."

Hudson moved around to sit next to me on the loveseat, resting his hand possessively on my knee.

As if challenged by his son's marking of his territory, Jack said, "I'm telling you, Laynie, with age comes experience. If you really want an amazing time…"

Hudson's grip tensed. "I don't like this."

Jack laughed, confirming my suspicion that he enjoyed toying with his son. "Relax, Hudson. It's all in fun."

I uncurled my legs and leaned into Hudson's side, secretly thrilled with Hudson's jealous show. "We're fine, H. He knows I'm hopelessly devoted to you. Don't you, Jack?"

"I do." He paused, eyeing Hudson. "I wonder if my son does."

Hudson didn't respond, not with words anyway. But he gazed at me for several long seconds, perhaps attempting to discern exactly what had transpired between Jack and me. Or maybe he sensed that his father knew something he didn't—that my emotions were genuinely growing deeper. That my fondness for him was real.

Whatever he decided, he pulled me closer into him and nuzzled his cheek against my head. He'd promised his actions in public would all be for the benefit of our audience, but this one felt different. Almost like he wanted to believe our relationship was real, too.

CHAPTER EIGHTEEN

"Lunch is ready. Should I serve it out here?"

I twisted in Hudson's arms to see who had spoken and saw an older woman in the doorway of the house. Her hair was completely gray, and her face had more wrinkles than Jack or Sophia, but I suspected she was near their age. She wiped her hands on the white apron she wore over her plain navy dress.

"Millie, you're an angel," Jack said. "Out here is a terrific idea."

"I'll let Adam and Chandler know they should join you." It wasn't quite a question, but I understood her statement gave the Pierce men a chance to object, which they didn't.

A short time later, Adam and Chandler sat with us on the veranda enjoying a lunch of cold meat sandwiches, fruit salad, and lemonade. Even though it was simple, it was one of the best lunches I'd had in ages.

I waited until my curiosity couldn't be contained any longer to ask why Sophia and Mira weren't eating with us. Not that I wanted Sophia's company, but I would have loved to spend time with Hudson's sister.

"They're out shopping for baby stuff," Adam said in between bites of ham sandwich. He took a swallow of his lemonade. "Mira wanted to invite you. She looked for you before she left, but she couldn't find you."

"Darn. That must have been when we were touring the grounds. Sorry, Laynie." Jack didn't look at all remorseful.

My own response to the idea fell out unfiltered. "Fuck that. Like I'd go anywhere with Sophia, let alone shopping." I covered my mouth with my hand. "Sorry!"

Chandler was the first to burst into laughter, joined a moment later by Jack and Adam. Even Hudson let out a chuckle.

"I'm totally with you there," Adam said when he could speak.

"I think Mom feels the same way about you," Chandler said, putting his feet up on the edge of the table. "She seemed to be glad when Mira couldn't find you."

"Chandler." Hudson's tone was a warning.

"It's okay, H." I put a hand on his thigh, careful not to let everyone see how much I enjoyed feeling his tight muscles through the material of his slacks. "Your mother and I are a long way from friendly. It's not a secret."

Hudson nodded, but his brow furrowed. Did he really care that much about his mother's opinion? Jack was right—that was too bad.

After lunch, Adam and Chandler corralled me into playing X-Box 360 with them in the media room. Hudson spread out on the couch near us, his thick reports and folders taking up most of the sofa while he worked on his laptop. Eventually Jack brought out a deck of cards and we played poker using pistachios for chips. As I'd suspected, Jack won a great deal of the time, though Chandler also had a surprising knack for the game.

After losing all of my pistachios in a bluff that Chandler called me on, I stretched and looked over at Hudson. Even though he hadn't participated in our games, I never forgot he was near, his presence invading every part of my body like a constant electric pulse. Occasionally when I glanced over at him, which happened often, I saw he was already staring. It was our own game of secret foreplay—looking at each other, undressing each other with our eyes. Later, I knew, he'd make good on the promises in his sexy stare.

This time, his eyes were glued to his screen, his glasses resting low on his nose while his fingers moved on the keyboard at a pace that suggested he was thinking as he typed. I crossed behind him and leaned down to rest my chin in the crook of his neck, wrapping my arms around him.

At my touch, Hudson lifted a hand from his computer and patted my arm. "Game over?"

"For me." I pulled to a standing position and rubbed my hands along his shoulders. "Wow, H. You're tense." He sighed as I massaged my fingers into the knots of his back. "What's getting you stressed out?" I hoped it wasn't our girlfriend/boyfriend show, though his tight muscles could have been attributed to the activities of the night before. The man had performed some moves that had to have required a great deal of strength.

"This situation with Plexis." He paused and I knew he was deciding whether to say more or not. It wasn't in his nature to share, but I'd thought I convinced him that he could talk business with me. I continued working his back as I waited, giving him a chance to continue.

My patience was rewarded. "The board is moving to sell. I need to come up with an attractive proposal to convince them it's more profitable to keep the company."

Even though he couldn't see me, I nodded. I studied the screen over his head, enjoying the quiet moans that escaped from his throat as I massaged his tension away. "You're redistributing production?" I asked. But I didn't need his answer. I could see from what he'd entered that he was. "You'd make a whole lot more if you moved those North America lines to your Indonesia plant. You're far from capacity there."

"Oh, you're one of those types who resort to taking jobs away from American people to cut costs."

"Not usually," I said, balling my hand into a fist to push into the rock under Hudson's shoulder blade. "But you're going to lose all your USA jobs if you don't do something, right? Losing a few is better than losing them all."

"Yes," he admitted.

I smiled as he changed his data to implement my suggestion, giddy that I'd offered an idea that he'd accepted. Throwing a bit more back into my hands, I felt Hudson's tight muscle close to releasing. "Take a deep breath." He did and I pushed once more into his knot, feeling it loosen as I did.

"Thanks," he said, slightly awed, rolling his shoulders.

I shook my hands out. "You're welcome."

Returning my focus to Hudson's work I noticed the technical specifications sheet of a new product on the pile next to him. "Besides," I said, reaching to grab the piece of paper, "if you start producing this energy efficient bulb in the American plant in its place, you'll maintain those jobs and save money with that new tax law. Plus you'll get a tax break for employing Americans."

Hudson shook his head. "That law only benefits new companies."

"No, it benefits any product that hasn't been produced in the U.S. before, new company or not."

"I don't think that's correct."

I'd led an entire seminar on the new tax code my last semester at Stern. I knew what I was talking about. His opposition was a challenge. "Do you have a copy of the current tax code?"

"On my Kindle. Under there somewhere." Hudson nodded his head at the stacks of reports sitting next to him.

I moved around the couch and started to dig through his piles in search of the device. "Wouldn't you be more comfortable at a table?"

Without looking at me, his lips curved slightly as he said, "I wanted to be near you."

His answer surprised me. The other men in the room weren't paying attention to us. He hadn't said it for them. He'd meant it.

"I like being near you, too," I said, when I recovered enough to speak. I didn't look at him, hiding the blush from my admission while searching for the Kindle. After I found it, I quickly looked up the law I was referring to and handed the proof to Hudson.

"Well, well," he said after he read it. "Looks like you're onto something here."

He started to hand the Kindle back to me, but paused, studying me.

I couldn't interpret the meaning, but the intensity of his gaze made my chest tight and my thighs warm. "What?"

He shook his head. "Nothing." Passing the Kindle to me, he asked, "Would you mind sharing your thoughts on the rest of my proposal?"

My heart sped up, delighted at the invitation. From what I'd learned about Hudson, inviting his girlfriend—or woman he was sleeping with, anyway—to work on a business project with him was not his typical mode of operation. It was new territory for him, which made it exactly the territory I enjoyed charting most.

We spent the rest of the afternoon working together, Hudson bouncing ideas off of me as I researched further information when he needed it. While I'd always enjoyed the world of business, I hadn't thought it could be so fun, hence the reason I'd chosen to manage a nightclub rather than to pursue an office job. But now an office job seemed rather appealing. Especially if that job included working side by side with Hudson Pierce. Though, with all the accidental brushes and searing looks we exchanged, I doubted we could manage working together for a prolonged period of time without losing most of our clothing.

But, really, that only made the job sound more appealing.

The savory aroma of a roast wafting from the kitchen wing caused my stomach to growl. I stretched. "Is it close to dinnertime?"

Behind me, Mira answered. "I was just coming to tell you dinner is served."

"I didn't realize you were home. When did you get back?"

"A few minutes ago. Mom has a headache but everyone else is already waiting in the dining room."

"A headache, huh?" I eyed Hudson. I was beginning to suspect Sophia was avoiding me. How had the conversation in the kitchen ended that morning? Had Hudson won the battle, giving me reprieve of his mother's nastiness?

"She's known to get them from time to time." His expression was tight, giving nothing away. Which told me everything I needed to know. I'd have to repay him later for the kindness.

After supper, Chandler left to meet friends and the rest of us headed back to the media room. Hudson got back on his laptop and I assumed he was diving back into work. Instead he handed his laptop to me. "All right, Alayna. Tell me something you need to see off your list and we'll download it from iTunes."

Puzzled, I took his laptop and found he'd loaded up the AFI list of best movies. I tried not to grin too wide, not wanting to seem too surprised because he remembered my goal to watch all the titles on the list. He was my "boyfriend," after all. He should have remembered.

But he really wasn't my boyfriend, and I found the gesture oddly touching.

"Are you going to watch it, too?" I asked, suddenly worried he meant to keep working on his Plexis dilemma without me.

"I am." He'd already begun packing away his reports into his briefcase as he spoke.

I chose *Midnight Cowboy* after discovering Hudson hadn't seen it either. Adam took care of setting up the movie then settled into one side of the couch with Mira. After Hudson cleaned up his area, he patted the seat next to him, his arm outstretched and inviting. Gladly, I sank into the sofa next to him, cuddling into his warm embrace.

The American Film Institute named *Midnight Cowboy* as number forty-three on their Top One Hundred. But watching it snuggled with Hudson—it was my new number one.

When it was over we all went our separate ways for the night. In our bedroom, Hudson sat on the bed, fully dressed, and pulled out his laptop again.

Though he'd relinquished his computer during the movie, content to hold me and to snack on microwave popcorn, he'd worked most of the day. I studied him, his intense features appearing tired. We'd stayed up late the night before, and I didn't know what time he woke before bringing up breakfast. I wouldn't be surprised to find he'd been buried in work then too. "H, you're a workaholic. Are you going to be at it all night?"

He grinned though his eyes never left the screen. "Oh, precious, work is not what I'll be at all night. But I need a few minutes to send this new proposal to the board before I can devote my attention to you. Do you mind?"

"Take your time. I'll get ready for bed." I lowered the lights as he had the night before, then took advantage of his distraction and retrieved the sexy nightie I'd brought with me before slipping into the bathroom.

I didn't hurry as I undressed, taking the opportunity to shave and apply lotion before slipping on the red lace halter baby-doll I'd purchased on Friday afternoon. The halter-top accentuated my breasts, an area of my body that Hudson appreciated. I removed the ponytail holder from my hair and let it spill around my shoulders in a seductive mess. I brushed my teeth and applied a thin layer of strawberry lip gloss.

When I was satisfied with my appearance, I opened the door to the bedroom and posed in the doorway, waiting for Hudson's reaction.

I was met with quiet snoring.

With his hands still propped on his open laptop, Hudson had fallen asleep, fully dressed. I sighed, debating how to address the situation. Of course I wanted him awake, but he wouldn't have fallen asleep like that if he wasn't truly worn out. Plus, I had to remind myself, night was my time of day—not his.

Gently, I slipped the computer from his grasp and placed it on the nightstand. The movement didn't disturb him in the least—he was out. I decided to let him sleep, but as for myself, I wasn't in the least bit tired. I wondered if Jack was still awake—maybe we could play another round of poker, though being alone with the man wasn't entirely a great idea. I peered out the window and saw the guesthouse was dark. Probably for the best.

The pool sprawled below my window though, and suddenly a midnight swim sounded heavenly. I traded my lingerie for a string bikini, threw on my robe, and grabbed a towel. Then I slipped on my flip-flops and turned off all the lights before venturing down to the grounds.

The pool was heated and felt amazing—exactly what I'd needed.

I hadn't been for a swim in months, since I'd let my gym membership expire earlier in the year. And I had the place to myself—perfection.

I pushed myself through thirty serious laps before relaxing into a dozen or so at a leisurely pace. Then I sat on the step in the shallow end of the pool, letting my heart rate return to normal while lazing in the warm water.

"Where's Hudson?" Sophia's voice startled me from my reverie.

I shifted in my spot and found her standing behind me, dressed in the same robe she'd worn the night before, and, again, a glass of amber liquid in her hand. I wondered if she was a heavy drinker or if my being in her home brought it on.

"He's…he fell asleep." I climbed out of the pool and reached for my towel, feeling small in her presence. She had that effect on me in general, but also I hadn't asked anyone if I could use the pool and I worried I'd taken advantage of my host's hospitality. Although, Sophia hadn't been hospitable in the least, so perhaps it was a moot concern.

I faced away from her as I toweled off, but I heard her take a seat in a deck chair behind me. "He doesn't love you, you know?"

I'd heard her, but didn't trust my ears. I turned to meet her narrow eyes. "Pardon me?"

"He can't." She swirled the liquid in her glass as she spoke, her tone laced with pain. "He's incapable."

Incapable. That was exactly what Hudson had said. Had it been his mother who had forced him to embrace such an idiotic idea about himself? The earlier hostility I'd felt toward her when I'd listened at the kitchen door returned and spilled like poison from my lips. "Maybe you're projecting your own incapability of emotion."

Her voice grew colder, but remained steady, in control. "Your words can't touch me, Ms. Withers. This is *my* house, Hudson is *my* son. I'm the one in power here."

"Fuck you."

She smiled. "He's had years of therapy. Extensive therapy."

So have I. I threw my towel down and wrapped my robe around me, taking the time to make sure my tone was as level as hers when I spoke again. "He's told me."

"Has he? But he hasn't shared the details." She leaned forward, her eyes catching one of the outdoor lights, causing them to glow red. She couldn't have looked nastier if she'd tried. "If he had, you'd know he can't love anyone. He's sociopathic. Diagnosed at age twenty."

She surprised me, the lack of strength in my response telling her as much. "Hudson's not a sociopath." Was he?

"He's deceitful and manipulative, egocentric, grandiose, glib and superficial. Incapable of remorse. He engages in casual and impersonal sexual relationships." She ticked off traits easily, as if they always bubbled right there at the surface of her consciousness. "Look it up—he fits the definition to a tee. He has no concern for others' feelings. He can't love anyone."

"I don't believe that." But my voice cracked.

"You're extremely naïve."

"You're an extreme bitch." I gathered my towel in my arms and slipped on my flip-flops, needing to be away from her and her horrible accusations. But her words had already done their job. I doubted, and she knew it.

"He's only with you for the sex." She stood, blocking me from the path to the house. "You're attractive." Her eyes skidded down to my bosom. "And clearly his type. He seems to like fucking buxom brunettes the most."

I had nothing to say in my defense. He'd told me our relationship was only sex. I was aware enough of my obligations to my on-duty job, though, and I spoke as if we were a real couple. "If it was just sex, he'd never bring me to meet you."

Her smile widened. "That's an added bonus for him. He can rile me up and get his kicks with you all at once. It really has nothing to do with you. It's about me and my son." She took a step toward me, and it took all my strength not to cower. "You, Ms. Withers, are insignificant."

I wanted to believe that I would have slapped her or pushed her into the pool—she deserved either, both really. But our confrontation was interrupted by Chandler and four other teenage boys boisterously entering the pool area, dressed in swim trunks and carrying towels.

"Mom?" Chandler said upon seeing his mother's back. Sophia stepped aside and he met my eyes. "Laynie," he said, surprised to see me or perhaps recognizing the stricken look that I must have worn. "I didn't know anyone else was out here."

"Alayna and I were getting to know each other." Sophia switched gears as easily as Hudson.

Chandler cocked a brow skeptically.

I used the boys' intrusion to escape. "The pool's all yours. I'm done here." Without looking back, I hurried into the house through the kitchen and up to the east wing, not stopping until I was outside our bedroom doors.

Then the tears fell, thick and heavy. I leaned against the wall, and slid down to a sitting position, unable to stand in the weight of my grief. So many emotions and thoughts warred for top billing. Sophia's insults had hurt, but what pained me most was the possibility that she was right.

What had I seen to show me differently? We'd had instances—Hudson and I—where I believed he truly cared, that he felt more for me than physical attraction, but had I imagined them? I had my own history of making meaningless moments carry heavier weight than they were meant to.

And her description of a sociopath did fit Hudson. I didn't need to look up the definition—I'd been in enough group therapy sessions to be familiar with the signs. But I'd never associated Hudson with the definition until Sophia had pointed it out. Had I purposefully ignored the connection?

Or was Sophia wrong?

I'd had therapists misdiagnose me early on in my therapy. And Brian's understanding of my problems was way off base. What if Hudson believed the worst about himself because Sophia had believed it? Maybe he'd never had a chance to prove her wrong.

Maybe that's what I was—a chance.

The possibility calmed me, though I was smart enough to realize its improbability.

I wiped my face with my damp towel and pushed myself up from the ground. Taking a deep breath I pushed open the door as quietly as I could.

"Alayna?" I heard Hudson reach to switch on the bedside lamp. "Is that you?"

"Yeah." I turned toward the door as I closed it, giving myself a minute to compose myself. "I wasn't tired, so I went for a swim." I took a deep breath then plastered a smile on my face before facing him.

"Good, I'm glad you…" He leaned forward, his body tense. "Hey, what's wrong?"

"Nothing." Was I that transparent? I couldn't talk to him—not now.

"Your eyes are red. You've been crying."

"No, no. The chlorine. Bothers my eyes." I rubbed at my puffy eyes hoping to accentuate my point.

He tilted his head, as if deciding whether I was being honest with him.

I couldn't take his scrutiny. If he pressed, I'd break, and I needed to settle my emotions about him and his mother's claims before I spoke with him about them. What would he say anyway? He'd either deny it or he wouldn't. If he denied it, could I trust him? If he didn't deny it, could I trust that?

Searching for an escape, I said, "Um, I'm going to jump in the shower."

"I'll join you."

I didn't argue. But we didn't speak as we entered the bathroom and undressed, Hudson helping me untie the back of my bikini top before he worked to remove his own clothing. I hung my wet suit on the edge of the tub and climbed into the shower, adjusting the temperature until it was near scalding.

When Hudson joined me, his penis already semi-erect, longing overcame me. I didn't know all the truth about Hudson, and I did know many damning truths about myself. But faced with his naked hard body and the awareness that—whether or not he could love me—he could make me feel better, at least for the moment, I pulled him toward me urgently, claiming his mouth with a hunger I'd never experienced.

"Alayna?" He pulled away, his hands firmly grasped on my shoulders. "Something's wrong. Tell me."

"I'm fine. I just…" I loved him. That was why I was torn up over everything Sophia had said. I loved him and I wanted—needed—to believe Hudson could love me too.

Not able to say those words—not yet—I settled for another version of the truth. "I need you."

He knew I was hiding something, but he nodded. "I'm here, precious." Then he took over, fulfilling me in ways only he could, satisfying me as deeply as he was able.

I lost myself to it, letting myself forget that he might never be able to love me in any way but this—with his mouth and tongue and cock.

Maybe it could be enough.

CHAPTER NINETEEN

I woke early, aware of Hudson working behind me in the bed, again on his laptop. But I didn't let on that I was awake, allowing myself to process the events of the night before.

Maybe because it was a fresh day, or perhaps because I wasn't face-to-face with Sophia, the facts didn't seem as overwhelming as they had. The truth was, whatever the reality of our relationship, it didn't change the fact that I was in love with Hudson Pierce. And being in love with Hudson Pierce put me on his side, whether he was capable of returning my feelings or not. His side meant proving to Sophia that her son was not the unfeeling sociopath that she believed he was, a task that might very well be impossible, but I resolved to give it my best shot. After all, that was the job I'd been hired to do.

And, if I played it right, the work might even be enjoyable.

Determined, I stretched, sat up against the bed frame, and leaned into Hudson. I needed to get him out of his computer and on board.

"Good morning, precious." He glanced over, his eyes pausing on my bare breasts before he returned his focus to the screen, a twinkle in his eyes. "Did you get enough sleep?"

"I did." The alarm clock on the nightstand read a few minutes past eight. It was early for me, but I felt rested, adapting somewhat to his traditional sleep schedule.

Hudson still in bed at that time of morning was what was surprising, even awake and working. I'd learned during our get-to-know you game that he usually got up around six. I suspected that this morning he lingered because of my behavior the evening before. He'd sensed my distress and he cared that I felt that way. Didn't that show capability of love?

Now wasn't the time to analyze. I filed it away to ponder later.

I skimmed his shoulder with my lips, running my fingers through the soft hair at the base of his neck. "Hudson? Are you going to work all day?"

He stopped typing and rubbed his rough chin against the side of my forehead. "Does my working bother you?"

"Not really. But I was thinking…" I took a deep breath then plunged in. "I didn't really see your mother yesterday. Shouldn't we try to spend some time with her today?"

He tensed. "I don't know if that's necessary."

I had guessed he was keeping his mother and I apart on purpose, that he meant to control the animosity between us. While I appreciated the gesture, it was counterproductive. We'd come to the Hamptons because of her. "Isn't she the person we need to be impressing with our fabulous relationship sham?"

"Being here together is enough." He straightened his head and returned to his screen, the matter settled in his mind.

But it wasn't settled for me. I moved to kneel in front of him, demanding his attention. "No, it's not enough." He lifted his eyes to meet mine. "I think we should go at her gangbusters. Throw ourselves in her face. You need to ignore your work to make it really convincing, though. Show her that you're so in love you can't even concentrate on business. You can only think of me."

Hudson rubbed a hand over his stubbly face and shook his head.

"What? Not a good idea?"

He shrugged. "It could be a good idea." He closed the lid of his laptop and placed it on the nightstand. "But do you really want to spend time with my mother? She can be…"

"A total bitch?"

"I was going to say abrasive, but your words fit as well."

Of course I didn't want to spend time with Sophia. But I'd realized that she hated me even more than I hated her. Spending time with her would bring more misery to her than to me. "It's only two more days. I can handle it."

Hudson reached a hand out to cup my cheek. "You're pretty incredible, you know?" His eyes wandered down. "Actually, I'm finding it hard to concentrate on anything but your beautiful naked breasts."

He pulled me in for a kiss, licking his tongue greedily into my mouth.

When his hand circled around my breast, I pulled away. "No, no, no. We can't stay locked up in here all morning. We have to be downstairs, in the public eye. Or the Sophia eye, anyway. What time is breakfast?"

He sighed. "Eight-thirty."

"Damn, I'll have to shower afterward then." I hopped out of bed and began rummaging for clothes in my suitcase. "Hope no one minds me smelling like sweat and sex."

Hudson crossed to his own suitcase. "I'm not going to complain."

As I pulled out an outfit, I remembered the night at the symphony, how Hudson reacted to my hand on his thigh. "I'm warning you right now—I'm playing this full out." I slipped on some pink panties. "Expect lots of fondling and touching and kissing and such." A pair of tan shorts followed.

Hudson dressed quickly too, pulling on a pair of jeans, not bothering with underwear. "Thank you for the warning. Though it should probably be me that initiates most of the fondling and touching and kissing and such." He paused to pull a plain dark t-shirt over his head. "Since it's my emotions we're trying to convince her of, not yours."

I stilled. Did he know my emotions ran deeper? Was he trying to hint that he knew?

No, I was reading too much into his words. I reached behind my back to clasp my bra. "Good point." I turned to face him. "But can you bring it?"

"Are you challenging me?"

"If it helps." I pulled a blue sleeveless blouse over my head.

"I don't need a challenge. I can totally bring it."

I slipped my feet into flip-flops and swallowed back a laugh, his words sounding so out of character. When I'd composed myself, I met his eyes. "Game on, then?"

"Game on."

God, he was adorable.

Arriving to an empty dining room, we sauntered into the kitchen where Millie promptly pointed us to the veranda before hustling to get together plates and utensils for us. Hudson took my hand, lacing his fingers through mine and squeezed, a silent reassurance before we stepped onto the battlefield. Then he pulled me outside through the open French doors where we found Mira, Adam, Jack and Sophia already dining on eggs, potato casserole, ham and fruit cups. Chandler, I guessed, was sleeping in after his late night adventure. He was a teenager, hardly expected to be out of bed before noon.

Sophia noticed us first. "Well, well. They managed to leave the bedroom."

Mira's expression turned puzzled then embarrassed when she saw us. "Mom!"

Adam mumbled a half-hearted greeting, consumed with whatever he was reading on his phone. Jack nodded at us, adding a wink, then sat back in his chair as if about to watch something entertaining.

Sophia set her fork down and dabbed at her lips with a napkin. "It's a fair observation. I didn't expect them down this early." Her eyes bore into me. "Especially when Alayna was up so late swimming." It was meant to be a reminder. *I'm in control. You're insignificant.*

I fidgeted as Hudson stole a glance at me, probably piecing together that my mood the night before had been because of Sophia. She knew I hadn't told him about our conversation—if I had, Hudson and I would have likely been out the door first thing that morning. She had gambled, and had won the hand. But I still had cards to play.

I kept my features even and lifted my chin slightly. "Hudson and I wanted to make sure we got to spend some time with you." My words spread like honey, but underneath they were hot pepper. "Are you feeling up to it? I mean, you were up late, too. And you had that nasty headache."

"You'd have fewer of those if you'd lay off the sauce," Jack jabbed.

Sophia ignored her husband. "I am feeling better. Thank you." Her stiff tone belied her insincerity. "And I never turn down time with my son. Please, join us."

On cue, Millie set two more place settings and Hudson pulled two chairs closer to the table, Mira and Adam already occupying the loveseat. By the time I sat, spread a napkin on my lap, and accepted a mug of coffee from Hudson, a plate of hot breakfast had been placed in front of me.

We ate in silence for several minutes, the usual noises of dining the only sound. Hudson and I exchanged several looks, both of us eager to demonstrate our supposed romance, neither of us knowing how. Under the table, my knee bounced with anxiety until he stilled it with a firm hand. He kept his hand there, resting while we continued eating, my skin tingling under his touch.

I closed my eyes and drew in a breath. The smell of summer flowers wafted through the air, the breeze warm and pleasant. It was a gorgeous day in a beautiful setting, and the atmosphere relaxed me enough to break the quiet. "So." I waited until all eyes were on me to continue.

"What's on the agenda for the day?"

Mira beamed as if grateful for conversation. "Adam and I want to hit the beach. Don't we, sweetie?"

"Uh huh," Adam mumbled without looking up from his phone. What was with the men around here? Always sucked into their electronics.

If Mira minded Adam's distraction, she didn't show it. "It's perfect weather for it. We can relax and soak up some rays. Millie could pack us a lunch. Want to come with us?"

I'd been in the Pierce estate for more than a day and still hadn't ventured down to the ocean at the edge of the Hampton property. The beach sounded wonderful. "I'm up for it. Hudson?"

Hudson grinned a little too wide, but I was probably the only one who noticed. "Wherever you are, baby, I'm there."

I surprised myself by not cringing at his choice of endearment.

"Hudson, you'll get sand in your computer," Sophia said. "And we don't get great Wi-Fi down there. Wouldn't you rather work up here?" Her assumption that Hudson would spend the day working fit right into my scheme. Now, would he follow through with his part? He'd never quite agreed.

He set his fork down and looked directly at Sophia. "Actually, I'm not doing any work today, Mother." He moved his hand from under the table to my neck, stroking gently under my hair. "I promised Laynie I'd give her my full attention for the rest of our trip."

I would have preferred that he'd played it like he couldn't even concentrate on work because of me, but, besides his version being much more believable, his use of my nickname was perfect. Even Adam looked up long enough to exchange a surprised look with his wife.

Sophia's reaction, though, was priceless. She gaped.

As much as I would have liked to take in every second of Sophia's shock, I slid my focus to Hudson. "Thank you, H." My gratitude extended deeper than the superficial show we were performing. I appreciated that he'd listened to my suggestions, that he heard me and then acted on it.

Hudson's deep gray eyes erased our spectators from my view. "It's nothing," he murmured. "You're worth it." Was his response as genuine as my thanks? Or was he just an excellent actor?

"Mom? Join us at the beach?" Mira practically bounced in her seat, the idea of a family outing right up her alley.

Sophia's expression was unchanging, her voice level. "Sure.

Why not?"

Jack guffawed. "Sophia spending the day in the sand? This I have to see."

Again Sophia ignored her husband, but Jack seemed pleased all the same.

"Adam," Mira elbowed her husband in the ribs. "Go wake up Chandler. We can take the Jet Ski out."

"Uh, okay." Adam stuffed his phone into the pocket of his khaki carpenter pants, crumpled his napkin into a ball, and stood, appearing grateful for the excuse to leave. It occurred to me that I'd never seen him around Sophia. Perhaps he had buried himself in his phone to avoid interacting with her. Smart.

Mira turned her attention to Jack. "And Dad, if you wear a thong again, I swear to God…"

"Fine." He leaned back in his chair. "I'll dress like an old man. But only for you, ladybug."

While her family conversed around her, Sophia sat solemnly, her eyes calculating. At least, that's how I interpreted her narrow gaze, fixed at nothing in particular on the table in front of her, her hands laced together.

"Hudson," she said finally. "The Werners are arriving at their Hampton house this evening."

"That's nice." He poked at what was left of his ham with his fork, his features even. "Why are you telling me this?"

I put my hand on Hudson's knee, bracing myself for where this conversation was going.

"Celia's coming, too." And there it was—Sophia's bombshell. "I know how long it's been since you've gotten to spend time together so I invited her for brunch tomorrow."

Hudson's face was steel, his jaw tight as he set his fork down with a noisy clink.

I imagined my heart plummeting through my chest, landing in my stomach with the same clink. Celia was a weak spot for me. She fueled my jealousy in ways that were absurd and unreasonable but real nonetheless. To keep from betraying my emotions, I bit my lip. Hard.

Mira's face went red. "Mom! Why would you do that?"

Jack, who had rolled his eyes at Sophia's announcement, now leaned toward his daughter, his arm resting on his knee. "Honestly, Mira, does this type of behavior from your mother surprise you?"

Sophia's eyebrows raised in mock innocence. "What did I do?"

Mira groaned in response. Hudson remained silent, anger rolling off his body in waves.

Sophia either delighted in her son's rage or didn't recognize it. "Anyway, we've been talking about redecorating the main rooms. I figured this was a great opportunity for her to show us some ideas while catching up with her dear friend." She turned up her sickening sweet smile. "Alayna, you've met Celia. Did you know that she did all the decorating for Hudson's offices and penthouse?"

I glanced at Hudson who was barely containing his fury. "I did."

I took a sip of coffee, preparing my next words. The loft above his office wasn't where Hudson lived. I'd never been to his penthouse, but, of course, Sophia assumed I had. Anything I said I'd have to phrase carefully. "Celia's got excellent taste. I think she managed to capture Hudson's style quite well in both his living and working space." It was true of his office and the loft, anyway. Hopefully it held about his penthouse.

"Which is your favorite room?"

"Sophia." Jack's tone was a warning.

Hudson tensed beside me, and I shoveled a mouthful of eggs into my mouth to stall. He'd hinted that he never took women to his penthouse, which had seemed like a good safety net for me—I couldn't stalk a man's house if I didn't know where it was. But did Sophia know he didn't take women there? Was she trying to trap me or was I being paranoid?

And underneath the concern of responding correctly was the punch of jealousy: Celia had been in Hudson's private home. She had to have been if she had done the interior design.

I swallowed the bitter sting with my eggs and gave Sophia the only answer I could, lame as it was. "Oh, I love all of it. I could never pick one room."

Hudson took my hand that still rested on his knee and laced it in his. "Didn't you tell me you liked the library the best?"

Thank god. He'd cooled himself enough to throw me a line.

"Only because it has books." Of course I'd love the library, being an avid reader.

Sophia's smile was smug. "He barely has any books at all."

Leave it to Hudson to have a library with no books.

He cleared his throat. "Actually, we're working on improving that." I exchanged a glance with him that I hoped expressed my thanks. "Alayna loves books so I've purchased quite a few since we've met. You haven't been there in a while, Mother."

"I haven't been invited."

"Since when has that stopped you?" This time Jack's comment earned a scowl from his wife. He answered it with an innocent shrug.

Sophia turned her attention back to me. "Are you officially living together then?"

"No," I said as Hudson said, "Yes."

I met his eyes, one brow raised. Saying I lived with him was a pretty big lie not to discuss with me first. Talk about bringing it on.

His eyes pierced into mine. "But you practically are. Once your lease is up, next month. Or have you changed your mind?"

A bubble of uncontrolled excitement rose in my chest. For a moment, it felt real, like he was asking me to be that in his life.

It wasn't real, though. What it was instead was an excellent move on Hudson's part, one sure to rile up his mother. I couldn't wreck it.

I swallowed then smiled shyly. "No, I haven't changed my mind. I just didn't realize we were telling your family, yet."

"Hell, I'm telling everyone." He practically beamed. God, he was good. "It's the best thing to ever happen to me."

Jack nodded, a twinkle in his eye. "I think it's terrific."

Sophia turned to her spouse and frowned. "Why are you here anyway, Jack? You haven't vacationed with us in years."

"Mira invited me."

"Hudson was coming and it's been so long since we've had the whole family together." Mira's intentions were the best. How had she lived in this family all her life without realizing it could never be the Brady Bunch she longed for? I'd known them all for only a minute and recognized dysfunction like a big neon sign.

Then, speaking of dysfunction, Mira asked, "What's your family like, Laynie? Are you close?"

I took a deep breath. "Actually, no. My parents passed away in a drunk driving accident when I was sixteen. My brother looked after me, but now we're..." I hadn't said the word aloud to anyone yet, but it was honest and it needed to be said. "Estranged."

"Oh, no!" Mira clasped her hand to her mouth.

Hudson stayed silent, but he raised a brow as he unlaced his hand from mine and rubbed it soothingly across my back. He knew Brian had been trying to contact me, probably realized the estrangement was a recent thing.

Jack shook his head slowly and *ts*ked. "I hope that drunk was held accountable, at least." I swear he looked at Sophia when he said the word "drunk."

It was an opportunity to lie. I had before when people had asked, but I wanted to say it now, whether to shock or gain sympathy, I didn't know. "You could say so. The drunk was my father. He was a full-time alcoholic, actually."

"I'm sorry," Jack said softly. "I didn't realize."

My eyes glistened. "It was years ago. I've learned to accept it."

I couldn't look at Hudson. I hadn't told him anything about my parents, but if he had looked hard enough to find my restraining orders, he likely already knew. I couldn't bear to see him look at me with pity.

"Less than ideal pasts," Hudson said, loud enough for everyone to hear, but gentle all the same, his fingers continuing their sweeping pattern across my back. "It's something Alayna and I have in common."

I turned to him and found his gaze absent of pity. Instead it held understanding. More and more I realized that I was special to him because of this unique recognition he saw in me. Were we really that alike?

"I don't like what you're implying," Sophia snarled.

"I'm not implying anything, Mother. I'm stating an unattractive fact."

"Keep your unattractive facts to yourself for the rest of the day, will you?" The fury in her tone was unmasked. She scooted her chair out and stood from the table. "Now, if you'll excuse me, I'm going to prepare for our beach outing."

With every card we'd played throughout the meal, Hudson had wounded her with one brief comment, the evidence plain in her expression.

I snuck a victory smile at Hudson, which he returned with equal delight shining in his eyes. This round had gone to us.

CHAPTER TWENTY

Round two began almost two hours later on the sands of the private beach below Mabel Shores. It took over an hour to change and load up the beach chairs and Jet Skis from the storage shed into the back of the Ford Raptor the family used to drive the half mile down the hill to the beach. Millie also made a lunch for later and packed a cooler with beverages.

Sophia was mellow when we arrived at the beach, choosing to doze while the rest of us finished setting up our chairs and other items. By the time I was lounging next to Hudson under a big rainbow colored umbrella, I'd convinced myself that I could relax and enjoy the warm breeze and rhythmic sound of the waves rolling on the sand.

The idea of quiet serenity disappeared when Adam and Chandler suggested a game of beach volleyball.

"Alayna?" Hudson looked up from his Kindle. "We could be a team."

"You play?" I'd been about ready to move my lounge chair into the sun and try to get a cancer-causing tan, but I could be talked into some friendly competition.

He scowled at me, a challenge glinting in his eyes. "Don't act so surprised. I'm very skilled."

I could tell from his tone that he was, and as competitive as I knew a man of his success had to be, I imagined he was quite good.

"He rarely loses," Jack confirmed, returning from an ocean swim. He shook his long wet hair before taking a seat. "He takes after his old man."

Hudson shook his head almost imperceptibly, not seeming to want to credit his father with any of his ability.

"Fantastic." Sophia shifted in her seat, reminding everyone of her presence. "I'm trying to relax and you all are going to be noisy and wild and disturb the peace."

"That's what beaches are for," Jack said over his shoulder, not bothering to look directly at his wife. "You could go back to the house if you don't like it."

Sophia's opposition made my decision. "I'm in." I pulled off my cover-up and began slathering sunscreen on the newly exposed areas of my body while Adam and Chandler attached the net to the permanent poles anchored in the sand.

"That's your swimsuit?" Hudson grumbled beside me. "You're practically naked. It's going to distract the men playing."

"Think of it as your secret weapon."

"Except one of those men will be me." He casually adjusted himself in his long navy swim shorts.

I shot him a smile, my insides melting at his obvious arousal. "Later, big boy." And that was a promise. "Meanwhile, would you mind getting my back?"

I leaned forward and hugged my knees. Hudson took the lotion and sat in the space behind me, straddling me. I suppressed a moan as his hands applied the lotion, his fingers kneading longer and deeper into my skin than necessary.

"I love touching your skin," he murmured near my ear, then nipped at my lobe, soothing it afterward with a smooth swipe of his tongue. It was an awfully sexual gesture, one I didn't expect from him in the company of others. Either he'd upped his game or he was no longer finding it as easy to compartmentalize as he usually did.

I turned my head into him to see if I could read his face but stopped when I spotted his mother watching us, her eyes narrow slits of anger. So that was the reason behind his display. Satisfaction rose in my chest, but simultaneously I felt a wave of disappointment. Though I thoroughly enjoyed Sophia's misery, our job had been to sway her to acceptance, not alienation. The task was impossible, I'd embraced that. But I knew Hudson hadn't, and I hurt for the distress that his mother caused him.

"Net's ready," Adam declared, kicking a pile of sand toward us to make sure he had our attention.

Hudson stood and reached his hand out to help me up beside him. Once I was up, he didn't let go, even as I pulled at my swimsuit bottoms with my other hand, relieving myself of the wedgie I'd gotten from sitting. All the while, I felt Sophia's stare, knew I was on her radar. Soon, she'd fire. I sensed it.

"Dammit. I want to play," Mira whined. "You know I'd be MVP."

"Yes, baby, you would." Adam bent down to rub her full belly protruding over the top of her bikini bottoms. "But you play rough, and that wouldn't be good for little jellybean."

"Yeah, you gotta protect my first grandchild," Jack said proudly.

Sophia peered at her husband. "But she isn't technically having the first grandchild, Jack." She paused to ensure all ears were tuned to her. "Celia and Hudson's baby claims that title."

A whooshing sound filled my ears and I felt dizzy, as if on a tilt-o-whirl. *Celia and Hudson's baby.* Why…what…?

My shock was magnified by Hudson's reaction. He didn't deny it. Instead, he tried to pull me closer. "Alayna," he whispered.

"Sophia!" I heard Jack hiss. "How *dare* you compare that to Mira's baby?"

Vaguely I was aware of Mira saying something, but I couldn't make sense of anything except the cold disappointment that rattled in my bones. I had to get away, had to think, had to breathe. I pulled my hand from Hudson's grasp and left, walking quickly down the beach, away from the Pierce family.

"Fuck you, Mother," Hudson said behind me before I was out of earshot.

A baby. Hudson had a baby. With Celia. I couldn't even grapple with trying to figure out where the baby was or what happened to it, too pained by the conception of a baby in the first place. It was ridiculous. He wasn't mine, he never was. But a baby…merely another way he belonged to Celia. Belonged *with* Celia.

I kept walking when Hudson called after me. But I didn't run from him when he jogged to catch up.

"I'm fine," I said, forcing a smile. "I'm playing the part of a wounded girlfriend."

He matched my stride, but didn't try to touch me. "Then why are you crying?"

I'd hoped we didn't have to acknowledge the tears spilling down my cheeks. I swiped at them with my palm, still holding my smile in place. "I'm just surprised." My voice was tight despite the cheer I tried to inject in it. "I didn't know you had slept with her."

"I didn't."

"You obviously did."

"No, my mother thinks I got Celia pregnant. I did not."

His words stopped me, a bubble of hope forming inside. "And why is that?"

He ran his hand over his face before he answered. "Because when Celia got pregnant I told our parents I was the father."

I folded my arms over my chest waiting for more, but he gave nothing. "Are you going to explain?"

"No." He mirrored my stance. "It's not relevant."

I spun on my heels, walking faster this time. How did he expect me to be in this fucking fake relationship when I didn't have all the information? Maybe I was only a pawn in his mind games. It was the only thing that made sense.

"Alayna, stop."

He followed after, reaching for me. This time I pulled away.

"Stop!" He caught up to me and grabbed me firmly at the shoulders. He turned me to him. "I said, 'stop'!"

"Why can't you tell me?" My tears had turned to sobs.

"Why can't you trust me?"

I let out a single laugh, maddened by the insanity of his request. "That's funny—you asking me to trust you when you trust me with absolutely nothing." I mean, what did I know about him? Besides his expertise in bed and a few random tidbits that I'd learned in one long car ride, he'd shared nothing.

His voice tightened. "You know more about me than most people."

It felt like an accusation. That I knew that thing—the one thing he didn't want anyone to know. But he hadn't even been the one to tell me that. And it was only one detail of the complex makeup of Hudson Pierce.

"No," I said, sticking my chin out defiantly. "I know one thing about you that most people don't. It's different."

"It's the only thing that matters."

"Bullshit." If he truly believed that...how could he be so blind to think that all that mattered about him were the mistakes of his past? It broke my heart and my voice cracked as I spoke. "There's so much more to you than that."

I wanted to touch him, to caress his face, to make him see. I stretched my hand tentatively toward him, but he stepped back.

"Obviously, you do know me," he spit out, "if you feel comfortable making that kind of statement." His tone was nasty, sarcastic. He didn't believe it. He was spinning my words, my meaning.

I turned away from him, processing. I did know things about him—things I'd discovered from spending time with him. I did believe there was more to him than the guy who manipulated women for sport. I saw it in him, felt it when he kissed me, and when he lay between my legs.

And if I really believed his sincerity in those moments, then I had to say I trusted him.

Which meant he was telling the truth now—he hadn't fathered a baby with Celia. But then why would he tell his parents that he had?

The realization punched my stomach like a ton of bricks. "It's because you love her, isn't it?" Voicing it made the weight even heavier. "That's why you told your parents it was your baby."

"No!"

His defiant protest spun me back to face him. "There's no other logical reason." To assume such a huge responsibility for another person—that required an emotional connection. It was proof he wasn't a sociopath—that he could care for someone at that level—but that was hardly comfort to me in that moment.

"Stop this, Alayna." It was a command, a low even tone that I guessed few people argued with.

But I was determined to hear him confirm the truth that would kill me. "You're in love with her."

He threw his arms out emphatically. "For the love of God! If I am even capable of that emotion, Celia's not the one I'd be..." He stopped himself, his jaw snapping shut.

*Celia's not the one...*His words echoed in my ears like a song I loved to hear.

He stepped toward me. Cupping his hands at the sides of my face, he lifted my chin roughly toward him. "I'm not in love with Celia. I promised I'd be honest with you, Alayna, but it does no good if you don't trust me."

I was still reeling from his slip. Celia wasn't the one he'd...what? Be in love with? Then who—with me?

But he wasn't giving that away. For now, his almost statement was enough—it calmed my nerves and steadied my heart.

He smoothed the hair down behind my ear, and I stared into his gray eyes, noting a tenderness that I hadn't seen earlier. "I've never slept with

Celia." His tone was soft but urgent. "I'm not in love with her. I didn't get her pregnant. Trust me." Even softer, even more urgent. "Please."

"Okay."

His brow creased in surprise. "Okay?"

"Okay, I trust you."

"You do?"

I thought of how eager I'd been to have Brian's trust, how disappointed I'd been when I realized I still didn't. Hudson needed someone, needed me to believe in him. I should have been telling him every second. If I loved him, like I believed I did, then I'd have to do better at building him up.

I smiled at him. "I do."

His body relaxed like a huge weight had been removed from his shoulders. "Thank you." He kissed my forehead. "Thank you."

I was absorbed with him in that space of time, but not so much as to not observe its oddity. We were holding each other close, exchanging assurances that portrayed us as more than casual lovers. *What are we doing?* I almost asked him; I felt the shape of the words on my tongue, but couldn't locate the air to push them past my lips. Did he sense it too?

If he recognized it, he hid it from me, pulling my head down to his shoulder where I couldn't look for it in his eyes. And that was fine. I enjoyed his embrace, the warmth and security it gave me, whatever it meant for us.

After the possibility of addressing the moment had passed, he said, "Look. My mother's leaving."

I pulled away to glance at the group we'd left behind. Sure enough, Sophia with her oversized sunhat was walking alone up the pathway toward the house. With her gone, it made the idea of rejoining the group more tolerable. "We should get back."

"We should." A hint of reluctance laced his tone and his eyes shifted to my lips. "We should kiss and make up first." He'd already begun lowering his face to mine. "In case anyone's watching."

I didn't have time to agree before one hand wrapped around the back of my neck and his tongue swept into my mouth. Unlike the majority of our kisses that were generally reserved for sex, this one was sweet and easy. That didn't mean it lacked passion. Hudson sucked and licked and nibbled first at my top lip and then gave equal treatment to the bottom. Then his tongue was inside my mouth again, reaching and searching, circling mine in a lazy spiral.

He labeled it as a kiss for our distant spectators, but it was completely ours—a harmonic blending of him and me, so thoroughly fused I could no longer remember where he began, where I ended, whose taste belonged to who. And it was more—a love song without words, a promise without fear. It was a spark, a beginning of something new.

We parted hesitantly, both of us afraid to break the spell. Then, I slipped my hand in his and we returned to our roles as girlfriend and boyfriend.

Hudson changed after that, perhaps because Sophia had left, but I chose to believe it had more to do with the faith I had placed in him. He became playful and lighthearted. I witnessed it first in the volleyball match against Adam and Chandler. He skillfully dominated the game, as I was sure he dominated a boardroom. But in between plays he surprised me—giving me high fives and patting me lightly on the behind. It didn't feel like he was putting on a show—there wasn't any need to convince Adam and Chandler of our relationship.

I welcomed the development, embracing it perhaps too readily, the line between real and pretend blurring.

After we'd won two sets of volleyball, we took a spin on the Jet Skis—Hudson driving, me clutching to him tightly from behind. He rode confidently across the choppy water, and I thrilled at the speed and the closeness and how easy it was to just be with him.

And when we lost our balance and fell into the ocean, he clutched me to him and laughed then kissed me mercilessly before righting the Jet Ski and pulling me up behind him. "Again, precious?" he yelled over the motor.

"Again."

Later, after we'd packed up and returned from the beach, we changed our clothes and went down for a BBQ on the veranda that included brats and dogs cooked by Jack. Sophia claimed another insufferable headache and only showed herself momentarily to say goodnight, though I suspected she really came down to fill her glass.

We finished the evening with several rounds of poker where Jack cleaned everyone out. Then Hudson and I headed to our bedroom, our eyes wandering along the landscapes of each other's bodies as we climbed the stairs.

The door had barely shut behind us before Hudson had me caged to the wall, his body pressed against me as he took my lips in a hungry desperate kiss, probing and demanding with his tongue until I was gasping in his mouth. My head swam, my panties instantly drenched with arousal, but I summoned strength to push my palms firmly against his chest. "Hold on, Hudson," I said, breathless.

"Dammit, Alayna, I have to be inside you. I can't wait any longer."

He moved in again, but I turned my head and his mouth found my jawline instead. "Soon, H." I darted out under his arm. "Lower the lights like you did the other night." I walked backward as I spoke until I hit the closet where we'd stowed our suitcases. Hudson had hung several items of clothing and put others into the dresser drawers, but I still hadn't bothered to unpack. "Get settled in bed. Naked." I winked.

"Oh, you're taking charge," he said, leaning on the wall with an outstretched arm. "How adorable."

"Don't patronize me." I bent inside the closet to rifle for the red baby doll halter nightie he'd missed seeing me wear the night before. When I found it, I wadded it up in a tight ball so he couldn't see it yet and took off for the bathroom.

"I'm not. I'm excited." He rubbed along the crotch of his pants. "I'm already hard."

My lip curled into a wicked grin. "Good. Now do as you were told." I stopped in the doorframe of the bathroom. "And don't fall asleep!"

"Then don't take forever in the bathroom."

Grinning, I shut the door. Charged with nervous anticipation, I changed at lightning speed. The day had been beyond wonderful and real. It had been so long since I felt anything more than contentment, and with Hudson, I did. I was certain he did, too. We'd been falling together. And now I wanted to celebrate those feelings with my lover, acknowledging the depths of my emotions with my body even if I couldn't yet express them in words.

I positioned my hair to fall around my shoulders, turned off the bathroom light then opened the door. The lights were low so I took a step forward where he could see me.

Hudson sat naked on top of the bed covers. His breath caught when he saw me. "Jesus, Alayna. You're so goddamn beautiful." He moved to a kneeling position. "I might have to let you wear that while I fuck you."

I was used to his forward sex talk, but I blushed anyway.

"Come here," he growled.

I started toward him then stopped. "Wait, I'm in control, remember?" He sat back on his haunches and tilted his head. "Then take charge."

Tingles spread from my belly throughout my body, turned on by the commanding way he relinquished his authority. He'd always dominated our sex, yet he was letting me take over, a choice that might even diminish the experience for him, though I hoped not. It added an element of pressure that I hadn't expected, but also thrilled me.

"Sit back against the headboard." My demand sounded stronger than I had expected.

Hudson grinned then did as I'd ordered.

Throwing my shoulders back to assume more confidence than I had—and, also to showcase my haltered bosom—I sauntered to the foot of the bed. Facing him, I climbed up and crawled toward him.

I kept my gaze on his face watching as his eyes flitted back and forth from my eyes to my breasts as I crept toward him. My hands trailed along his calves as I moved up him then swept past his knees to his firm thighs. I stopped at the base of his rock hard penis and dipped my head down, licking along the length with one swipe of my tongue.

Hudson's pupils were hot coals of desire. "Do it again."

It would have been natural for me to give in to his command, but I wasn't ready to relinquish my dominance. "Maybe I will."

His grin widened. He had been testing the hold on my control and I'd passed.

I dipped again, this time kissing along his head, my eyes never leaving his. I licked across the crown one more time, savoring the salty taste of him before I fed his erection past my lips into the warmth of my mouth.

He let out a groan. "Oh, precious, you suck me so good."

I teased him, fondling and caressing his balls in one hand while I licked and sucked and cherished his dick with my mouth, never taking up a steady pace. Soon, he threaded his fingers through my hair and began to take over, holding my head still over his penis, as he bucked into my mouth, establishing the rhythm he craved.

I let him keep control for only a moment, treasuring the grunts and groans that accompanied his thrusts. Then I pulled at his arm to release his grip on my head, and raised my body, letting his cock fall from my mouth.

He moaned.

"You want more?" I teased. "You'll have to wait." I climbed further up his body and spread my legs to straddle his waist and felt his firm ridge knocking against my ass.

His eyes widened in curiosity.

I spread my palms across his bare torso and leaned down to take his mouth. His kiss was greedy and eager, his tongue working inside my mouth. He moved his hands to the sides of my face, holding me in our lip-locked position, but I shook my head free.

"What do you want?" he asked, breathlessly.

It put him on edge, to let me dictate. But he was willing to try, and it gratified me immensely. Though he hadn't given me his trust in other areas, he was giving it to me here. That was a big step for him and, though a huge part of me wanted to let him take me in the way he wanted, I remained committed to the role reversal because of how much it meant for both of us to try.

But in answer to his question, I was at a loss. What did I want? "Touch my breasts," I said, finally.

Hudson slipped his hands inside the silk of my halter-top. With a flick of his thumbs, my nipples became stone, my breasts heavy and sensitive as he squeezed them in his firm hands.

I bent down to lick at his lips, but he ducked his head to my bosom instead. Pulling down the material of my nightie, he took the tip of my breast into his mouth. He sucked and tugged at my nipple causing a shallow cry to escape from my throat. "Hudson, oh, god."

A hand slipped under the thin lace of my panties and grazed my clit on the way to the hot opening of my pussy. Releasing my nipple from his mouth he said, "You're already so wet, precious." He licked lightly across the tip and I shuddered. "Shall I put my fingers inside you? Tell me."

Hudson was so good at turning my mind to mush, my body pliable under his hands. I gave into the pleasure he could give me, but on my terms. "I want your cock inside me." I spoke softly, not quite at ease with saying the words.

He smiled, but didn't move to take me up on my request. Instead he suckled on my other breast eliciting an involuntary moan from me. Then he said, "But you aren't ready for me, precious."

"I'm ready enough." I was more forceful this time. "I want to ride you."

A flash of desire crossed his face. In one swift move, he ripped the sides of my panties open, pulled the torn material out from under me and threw it aside. I shivered at his primal act, lust rushing through my veins like wildfire. Desperate to have him, to possess him, I scooted back to balance myself over him. I took his gorgeous thick penis in my hand and lifted the head to my wet entrance, my arousal fueled further when his cock throbbed in my grasp.

"I can't imagine why I deserve this," Hudson said hoarsely, splaying his hands over my breasts. "I should be rewarding you for your very believable girlfriend act today."

I stilled. His comment stung, but I wasn't sure if it should. Was he reminding me the day had been pretend? Or was he trying to elicit a reaction from me? Was he putting his guard up, refusing to let any emotions into our relationship?

Or maybe he felt nothing of what I thought he felt, and his words were simply a statement of what he saw as an accurate representation of our day.

No, it wasn't true. I believed with all my heart that something more had developed between both of us. He may not be able to admit it to me, or even to himself, but I knew. I *knew*.

I slid down onto his pulsing cock, taking him in with a gasp. He was right—I wasn't fully prepared, and he felt full and big inside. I squirmed, trying to ease the bite of discomfort as I worked him in deeper. Hudson placed his hand flat along the middle of my torso and pushed me to lean back. The angle opened me and I glided down to his root.

"Fuck," he groaned. "You're so tight, Alayna. So good."

I lifted my hips, raising myself up his length before lowering again.

Hudson shifted beneath me, churning his hips, eager to direct the pace, but I kept my steady speed as I slid smoothly up and down his steely erection. His hands moved on me restlessly, wandering from my breasts to my thighs to my hips before he finally settled one flat on my stomach and circled his thumb on my clit with a delicious firm pressure.

"God, oh, god," I cried, squeezing and clenching around him. The exquisite feeling of his cock skimming against my vaginal walls combined with the expert attention he was giving my tender bud drove me mad. I was on the edge, near orgasm, though not quite able to get the release I longed for. Tears formed in my eyes and sweat beaded on my skin.

"I'm happy, Hudson. You've made me happy." I couldn't stop myself from telling him, my words mixed with throaty moans.

Under heavy lids, his eyes pierced mine, glowing with the intense need to fuck. They widened at my declaration, a new spark lighting the dark desire already held there.

"And I've made you happy too." It spilled from my mouth like I wished my elusive orgasm would. I sensed the warning in Hudson's face, but I couldn't stop myself from saying more. "We're falling in love. This is us, falling in love."

"Enough." In a flash, he flipped me underneath him, maintaining our connection at the groin. He bent my legs at the knees and pushed them back while he plunged into me, pummeling me with a drive that fought to tear me apart. In that position he struck me deep, deeper than he'd ever been. He meant to punish me for my words—for knowing he'd connected with me. But the punishment only acknowledged I was right.

And in that finding, combined with his maddening thrusts, I lost everything to him, coming so violently that my body seized, quivering uncontrollably beneath him.

Hudson continued to ram into me, hitting the very end of me with each stroke until I came again. This time he joined me, burying his cock even deeper as he released, my core milking him while he spurted long and hot.

When we'd both stilled, he rolled off of me and fell hard into the bed at my side. Without words, he pulled me into the crook of his arm, closed his eyes, and went to sleep.

I tightened into his embrace. Usually he cuddled longer, and stroked and caressed me before falling asleep. But I'd challenged him in more ways than one that night. He needed time to process. At least he was still holding me at all. That had to be a good sign.

It took longer before I was taken by sleep, but when it finally came, I slept deep and peacefully.

In the morning, I awoke alone, but despite remembering that Celia would visit today, I felt happy. Until I went to the closet to get an outfit and found my belongings the only occupants.

Hudson's clothes and suitcase were gone.

CHAPTER TWENTY-ONE

I swallowed the acid rising in my throat and dressed in a flurry, not bothering with my hair or my face or shoes. Just because his things were gone didn't mean he was, I told myself as I descended the stairs, trying to squelch the growing unease. There had to be an explanation.

I followed the sound of voices and found Mira and Sophia leaning over the dining room table, examining several large poster boards spread in front of them. Mira lifted her head as I approached and smiled. "Good mor—"

"Where's Hudson?" I cut her off, my arms folded over my chest.

Sophia glowered at me over her reading glasses. "He left with Celia." An undercurrent of pleasure laced her statement.

Mira rolled her eyes and turned her body to give me her full attention. "He had a business thing come up. Some sort of emergency. He had to fly immediately to Cincinnati."

"Celia drove him."

"Mother, honestly! Stop it!" I'd never seen Mira irritated and it looked unnatural on her usually smooth, unruffled features. It worked to silence Sophia. "Celia was already here to show us the designs when Hudson discovered he needed to leave. She offered to drive him to the airport so that he could leave the car for you to get back to the city whenever you wanted."

He was gone. He'd left. With Celia.

Suddenly, the air in the house seemed stifling and thick. Breathing became difficult. Had Hudson really had a business emergency? Or was he running from our emotional connection the day before? He'd told me he wouldn't lie to me, but this time he hadn't said anything to me at all. He'd just vanished.

And the thing that I hadn't ever wanted to face—when he said he'd always tell the truth—that could have been a lie itself.

It was too painful to address, especially in the presence of others, namely Sophia. Getting back home became priority number one. He'd left the car for me. "But I don't drive."

Mira shrugged. "Hudson said you might not want to. Martin can drive you then."

"I'm not giving up my hired help to—"

Mira threw her hands up in the air and shot a piercing glare at her mother. "Then I'll take her! Or Adam or Chandler."

"I'll drive you."

I turned to find Jack behind me. Gratitude boiled inside so intensely, tears formed in the corners of my eyes. "Thank you. Give me ten minutes to pack."

I rushed out before anyone could say another word. Taking the stairs two at a time, I sped to our bedroom. *Our* bedroom. The thought pained me in the absence of Hudson. After dragging my suitcase out of the closet, I scrambled around the room picking up random items that I'd left lying around the past few days—my swimsuit, my robe. The red nightie.

When I'd returned from the bathroom with my toothbrush and other toiletries, Mira was standing in the doorframe. "Laynie, you don't have to leave yet."

I walked past her and dropped my things into my luggage.

"Stay until tomorrow. We can go do something girly, get mani-pedis if you want."

There really were great people in the Pierce household. I adored Mirabelle. And Jack had become a fast friend. Even Chandler and Adam for all their boyish personality had taken a piece of my affection.

But the goodness of all of them was outweighed by the horror of Sophia.

And no one meant anything to me in comparison to what I felt for her son. "Thank you, Mira, sincerely. But I can't stay here without Hudson."

"I understand."

I zipped up my bag and stood to face Mira, searching to see if she really did understand. From the softness in her eyes, I believed she did.

Maybe she understood more than I knew. I took a deep breath and asked, "Did he say…anything about me?" I bit my lip, embarrassed to let her see my insecurity. "Or leave any message for me?"

She seemed unsurprised by my question. "I think he was going to call you or something. Have you checked your phone?"

My phone—I hadn't looked at it since I stuffed it in my purse on the drive up. I returned to the closet and found the purse hanging on a hook inside the door. Rifling around inside, I quickly located the phone. "It's dead," I said. "I forgot to bring a charger."

"Is it a standard USB? You can take my car charger."

I wanted to hug her. "Thank you, Mira."

"No problem." She watched while I set my suitcase in the rolling position. "Martin can get that."

"I got it." I didn't want to wait to call someone up to carry a suitcase I could manage myself. I scanned the room one more time then started toward the door.

"Laynie." Mira stopped me before I'd crossed the threshold.

It was difficult to give her my attention when every fiber of my body wanted to go. I fidgeted as I met her eyes.

She took a step toward me, her face soft and compassionate. "I know he loves you," she said firmly. "I know he does. But he's been through… things…that's made it hard for him to open up, so please don't take that as, well, as evidence of anything if he can't tell you how he feels."

My eyes felt misty. Maybe Mira was as snowed as I was, but it felt good to hear. I swallowed hard. "I know."

"Good."

"But…" I might never get the chance to have this conversation again. "Why do you believe that? I mean, what makes you think that he loves me, or that he even can?"

Surely Mira knew the things Sophia claimed about her brother. That he was a sociopath, that he couldn't feel anything for others. Unless all of that had been her mother's way of riling me up. But I suspected there was more to her claims than that—they were rooted in truth somewhere, a therapist's opinion, a doctor's diagnosis.

Mira closed her eyes briefly and blew out a steady stream of air. "I don't know, Laynie. He's different around you. I've never seen him like he is with you."

"Maybe you see what you want to believe."

"Maybe." She stuck her chin out. "But I'm not giving up on him. I hope you don't either."

"I won't." But Hudson might have already given up on me.

And, if not me, himself.

Back downstairs, Mira left me in the foyer to grab her phone charger from her car. Jack had gone to the garage to bring the Mercedes up to the circle drive. I paced, waiting for him to pull up.

I sensed Sophia behind me without seeing her. Hoping she'd go away if I didn't acknowledge her, I kept my eyes focused on the front driveway. I was wrong.

"You shouldn't be surprised that he left you."

I still didn't look at her, but I pictured the satisfied grin she likely wore, imagined myself slapping it off her face. Violence never hurt as much as a good verbal argument, though. Problem was, if I reacted to her bait, she could very well win. Again.

"I told you he doesn't feel anything." She was a warrior. Good at the game. I had no doubt she'd been the one who taught Hudson to be so good at his own games. "For anyone," she added.

"That's a lie." I had no chance against her. She drew the reaction she desired. But if I had to spar, I'd put my best fight into it. "I've seen proof to the contrary."

"Because of how he seems to love you? He's a good actor."

I spun to face her. "No, because of how he seems to love *you*." I spit the words like venom. "When there's no reason he should. When you've alienated him and betrayed him and destroyed him and made him the confused man he is by your lack of affection and support and faith. If he can continue to care about a piece of shit like you, after all you've done to him, then I have no doubt of his capability of love." *You fucking bitch.*

And then I opened the front door and walked out, rolling my suitcase behind me, relieved to see Jack pulling up as I did. Sophia didn't follow.

Mira had given Jack the charger in the garage. He handed it to me in exchange for my luggage. While he stowed my suitcase in the trunk of the running car, I climbed in the front passenger seat and plugged in the charger and my phone before securing my seatbelt.

We were on the road before my phone had enough charge to turn on. I had twelve texts and four voice messages. I opened the texts and skipped the eleven from Brian, going immediately to the one from Hudson. "Plexis crisis. I'll call as soon as I can."

My heart sunk. I should have been grateful that he'd left a message at all, but didn't I deserve more? He had led me to believe that I did.

I accessed my voicemail with only faint hope. He'd never called me, and I doubted any of the messages were from him. I listened long enough to the first one to hear Brian's voice then immediately deleted it and skipped to the next one. All were from my brother. All were deleted without a full listen.

Jack was more considerate company than I could possibly ask for. After asking me to enter my address into the GPS, he offered enough small talk for me to understand he was there if I needed him. Then he allowed me to wallow in silence.

For the better part of an hour, I flipped my phone around in my hands, opening the text slider and closing it again without using it. The old me—the crazy, obsessed me—would have already sent a series of messages to Hudson, each heightening in tone and accusations. It took everything in me not to physically do so, but in my head I let myself compose them.

"Why did you go? Are you really on a business trip?"

"I can't do the on-duty anymore. I quit."

"Why won't you let me in?"

"I love you."

Finally I dropped my phone in my purse, leaned my head against the window of the car, and closed my eyes. I'd allow myself one well thought-out text when I got home. Then I'd go to a group meeting. I just had to make it until then without doing anything stupid.

I must have fallen asleep because when I opened my eyes again, we were outside my apartment building. There were no spots available along the street, so Jack had turned on the emergency blinkers and pulled up next to the line of parked cars.

Standing at the driver's door, Jack leaned across the top of the car. "If you wait here, I can find a spot somewhere and help you up to your apartment."

As harmless as Jack was, having him in my apartment did not sound like a good idea. And I didn't need the help or the company. "I can get it. Thanks, though." Standing on the curb with my bag, I felt moved to say more, to express my overwhelming gratitude. "And thank you for driving me here and for…well, for…" *For not treating me like Sophia treats me.* "For being so kind."

Dammit. I was choking up again.

He chuckled. "I'm not really that kind. I just appear so in comparison."

I didn't have to ask whom he meant to compare himself with.

"Jack." I shouldn't keep him when he was parked illegally, but suddenly I had to know. "Why are you still married to her?"

"I wish I could say it's because I remember the sweet woman she once was, but she was never a sweet woman." He looked off at the traffic behind him, not seeming to be bothered by the cars honking as they passed in the next lane. "Sophia came to the marriage with a couple of businesses given to us by her father. I took control when her father retired and have spent my life making them successful. Now Hudson runs them. If I divorced Sophia, the controlling interest would go to her. As long as we're married, she doesn't care what we do with them. And she'd never ask for a divorce—it would be too embarrassing."

He turned back to face me. "I wonder sometimes—if I'd let go of the businesses, divorced her when the kids were still young, could I have changed how they are now? But she would have gotten joint custody at the very least. And she may have messed them up even more, retaliating against me. It's not an ideal situation, but it is what it is."

Not an ideal situation—it was similar to what Hudson had said. No, it wasn't ideal, but it was life.

In my small studio apartment, I left my suitcase standing by the door and collapsed on my bed. Tears came, long and steady. I couldn't even say what I was crying for exactly. All I knew was that I hurt. I hurt from Hudson's departure, for his unwillingness to open up to me. I hurt because the lines of our pretend and real relationship had become so blurred that I couldn't tell the difference anymore. I hurt from Sophia's words and hatred. I hurt for the mother she'd been to her son and for the brother Brian had been to me. I hurt for the things I'd done to Brian, for the things Hudson had probably done to his family.

Most of all I hurt because I was alone and in love. And that was the worst combination of things to be.

An hour had passed before I'd calmed enough to send the one text I'd promised myself I could. It was as harmless as I could come up with—a message that said all I dared to say, afraid more would scare him further away. *I'll be here when you return.*

Not even thirty seconds had gone by after I pushed "SEND" when there was a knock on my door. We had a doorman in the lobby—only building occupants were allowed in without prior approval. But Hudson could pull strings, couldn't he? He was the only person I knew with such power.

The hope that it was him, as weak of a hope that it was, propelled me to my feet and to the peephole.

The man in the hall wore a crisp black suit with a yellow tie. But the face didn't belong to Hudson—it belonged to Brian.

I should have known it was Brian. His name was on the lease, he'd be allowed up. I pressed my face against the door and debated whether or not to let him in.

"Open up, Laynie." Heavy banging on the other side of the door jolted my face from its resting position. "I know you're in there. The doorman told me you came up."

Fuck. He must have been staying in town—at the Waldorf, most likely. What the fuck was so important that he had to see me? Maybe I should have listened to his messages.

Reluctantly, I opened the door partway.

He pushed past me forcefully. He was angry. Probably because I'd been ignoring him.

"What are you doing here, Brian? Are you stalking me?" The joke made me smile even though Brian's eyes only glowed hotter.

"You haven't returned any of my calls." I watched as Brian's fists clenched and unclenched at his sides. I knew he'd never hit me—at least, I hoped he'd never hit me—but I'd seen him rage enough to punch holes in walls. Maybe it was a good thing his name was the primary on the lease instead of mine. He'd have to pay for any damage.

I shut the door and turned to face Brian with a fake smile. "Oh, did you call?" Innocent wasn't usually the best tactic with Brian, but I was too exhausted for anything else. "My phone's been dead and I've been out of town."

"Yeah, I got that from your boss at the club."

God, he'd even called David. What the fuck?

Brian ran a hand through his hair then took a step toward me. "You were with him, weren't you?"

"Him, who?" But I knew he must have been referring to Hudson. That was the who I'd been with after all, and David had known that. But why Brian cared was beyond me.

Brian slammed his fist down on the top of my dresser. "Dammit, Laynie, don't play games. This is serious." He took a step toward me, his eyes narrow slits. "Hudson Pierce. Were you with Hudson Pierce?"

"Yes." I crossed my hands over my chest. "And Jonathon Pierce, for that matter. And Sophia Pierce and Mirabelle Pierce and Chandler Pierce. At their Hampton house. Brian, what is your problem?"

His brows rose almost as high as his voice. "What is my problem? *You* are my problem. Always. Alayna, I saw you in the society pages—you're dating him?"

Well, no. But I kept that to myself.

"You can't date Hudson fucking Pierce. Do you know who he is? Do you know *what* he is?"

For the briefest of moments, my chest felt like it might burst. I had no idea how, but Brian knew about Hudson's games with women somehow and was worried about me. I hadn't felt concern from him in years. I didn't realize how much I'd craved it.

Brian continued. "He's a goddamn giant, is what he is, Alayna. If you fuck with him—*when* you fuck with him—I won't be able to get you out of it. The Pierces are so big, they'll squash you like a bug."

"Wait a minute, wait a minute." I swallowed, processing what Brian had said. "You're not concerned for me, you're worried about …Hudson?"

"Why should I be concerned for you?" He pointed his index finger toward me. "You're the one with the history of going mental over guys."

"Get out." I could only manage a whisper.

"Harassment, drive-bys, breaking and entering, stalking—" He held up a finger for each item he ticked off.

"Get out," I said, stronger. There were no words for the depths of betrayal I felt, no reason to even defend myself against his accusations because he'd already marked me as guilty without even giving me a trial.

"Were you even *invited* to the Hamptons?"

"Get the fuck out!" I screamed. "Get out! Get out! Get. Out."

He didn't move. "My name's on the lease, not yours."

"Then I'll get the lease changed. Or I'll move." I crossed to the door and opened it for him. "But now I'm telling you, so help me god, if you don't leave I'll call the cops and, even if it gets me nowhere, it will at least occupy your life with yet another embarrassing sister incident. So I'm telling you, get the fuck out, now."

"I'm done, Alayna." He raised his hands up in a surrender position. Still he didn't move.

"Get out!"

This time he stepped toward the door. "I'm leaving, but I'm telling you, I'm done. Do not even think about coming crawling back to me." He turned back to face me after crossing the threshold. "You're on your own with this mess."

I slammed the door in his face.

Brian was out of my life. Out of my life for good.

Maybe because I'd already cried all those tears earlier, or maybe because I'd simply had enough of family members who constantly kept their loved ones down when they needed compassion and support most, but the sigh I let out wasn't in frustration—it was in relief.

Chapter Twenty-Two

David leaned against his desk and stared at the new brown leather sofa across the room. "Should we move it to the other wall?" It was the fourth time he'd asked since I'd arrived.

Truthfully, I couldn't care less where the sofa was. The only reason I'd come into the club so early was to have something to occupy my mind. It had been thirty-three hours since I'd left the Hamptons, longer since I'd seen Hudson, and all I wanted to do was buy a plane ticket to Cincinnati and find him, whatever it took.

But another part of me—a very small, but surprisingly solid bud of calm at the center of my being—believed that Hudson would be back. That he'd be back for me. He felt something for me. I knew he did. And maybe that emotion, even if he couldn't acknowledge it, would be enough to bring him to me. Eventually.

Hopefully.

If I didn't cling on to that small sliver of hope, I'd fall apart. It was the only thing keeping me from giving into the crazy. That and trying to concentrate on my job.

"It's fine, David. Leave it."

"Are you sure? This is your vision, Laynie. Make it work."

"It works perfectly as is."

I suspected David's anxiousness had more to do with me and my mood than couch placement. He crossed to the sofa and sat down. "It's pretty comfy, too. Check it out."

Sighing, I tossed my inventory report on the desk and joined him. "Hmm," I said, settling into the corner. "Not bad."

But really I was thinking about how the new couch reminded me of the one at the apartment above Hudson's office. It had been my initial attraction to it when I'd seen it in the catalog. I loved the way it felt masculine with its rich dark color, yet also warm and soft with its curved back and arms.

Now I wondered if every glance at the piece of furniture would bring to mind thoughts of the man who hadn't called or texted me since his vanishing act.

My thoughts traveled to the email I'd received that morning from his bank—the one that owned my student loans—stating my debt had been adjusted off in full. And the credit card that I'd kept secret from him had also shown up with a zero balance. Having them both paid for made the whole deal feel done.

And I wanted so much not to be done with Hudson Pierce.

"So what's going on in your pretty little head, Laynie?"

I'd gotten lost in my mind again. Boy, was I bad company.

"Stuff," I said, feeling bad about the brush off, but not bad enough to expound upon my answer.

He nodded and rested his ankle on his other leg. "Pierce okay with that Plexis deal?"

I twisted my head toward him. "What do you mean?"

David's brows rose. "I figured you knew. It was in the paper this morning." He stood and moved toward his desk.

I hadn't looked at the news that morning. Knowing I'd be tempted to stalk Hudson online, I hadn't even gotten on my computer except to check my email after Brian had left the day before. It had been hard to fight the compulsion, but after kicking my brother out, I'd felt a renewed sense of self-strength. So I turned off my computer and spent the night watching some of the movies from the AFI list that I hadn't seen yet while I ate a pint of mint chocolate chip ice cream. And I cried some more. Overall, a very productive evening.

David rifled through some papers in the recycling bin. "Here it is."

He returned to the couch and handed me a folded section of the newspaper. I scanned my eyes over the article he'd pointed to. The headline read *Plexis sold to DWO*. Skimming, I quickly got the gist of the story. DWO, a rival corporation of Pierce Industries, had convinced the other shareholders to sell, even though management, and lone hold-out shareholder Hudson Pierce, fought to prevent the acquisition.

My stomach sank. Hudson had really cared about Plexis and the people that worked there. He had to be devastated over the loss. No wonder he'd run off to Cincinnati the day before—he must have been making one last ditch effort to save his company.

Which also meant he'd been telling me the truth. He hadn't run from me. Why was I so self-centered to believe everything had to do with me?

I closed my eyes and felt the couch sink next to me as David sat back down.

"You like him more than you let on."

"I do. I love him." I peeked over at him, remembering how David had reacted the last time we'd talked about Hudson and me. "I didn't mean to fall in love. I just did."

David smiled but kept his eyes downcast. "That's how it usually occurs."

I threw the newspaper on the ground, put my elbows on my knees and covered my hands with my face. Awkward—that's what this was. Totally awkward.

David leaned back on the couch. "And he feels…?"

I peeked over my shoulder toward him. Did he really want to talk about this? Well, he was there, and he did ask. "I'm not sure."

"That's a real bummer." David leaned forward. He was so close to me I could smell the faint aroma of his body wash and feel the warmth of his breath. "For what it's worth, I'll tell you how I feel: Stupid."

"Stupid?" I folded my arms across my chest, feeling strangely vulnerable so near to a guy I'd once been gaga over.

"Yeah." He lowered his voice. "How did I let you slip through my fingers?"

"David…" I didn't want that, not now. My heart, my mind, my body had tuned to Hudson. He was the only guy I could think of anymore. It scared me a bit. Singular thoughts of someone—that could be the beginnings of an obsession.

But also, and I wasn't sure because I didn't know from experience, but couldn't those kind of thoughts be attributed to being in love? Lauren had said as much. As long as I remained in control of my behavior, as long as my affection was welcomed, then wasn't it perfectly okay to think of Hudson, to *choose* him over anyone else? I thought maybe so. I *hoped* so.

I opened my mouth to speak, to tell David that there was no chance for us, but he seemed to understand without me having to say anything.

He sighed and nodded. Then he shrugged. "I just thought you should know."

"Thank you," I said, because I didn't know what else to say. And because I was grateful that he'd taken my rejection so well.

He stood up and held his hand out to me. "Back to work."

I took his hand and let him help me to my feet.

David held onto my hand after I stood. "But if you ever find yourself on the market again…"

Even without Hudson, David and I couldn't be together. He'd been a safe option, someone who wouldn't drive me to obsessive behaviors. But safety had come at the price of no sincere emotional investment. Maybe I risked more with Hudson, but there was also something real to be gained.

But I smiled and said, "I'll keep you in mind. For sure."

"Can we hug it out?"

I nodded and David pulled me into his arms. His embrace felt… good. Stronger than I'd remembered, but it didn't make my heart beat faster. And it comforted me, but didn't warm me to the bone the way Hudson's arms did. Still, it was nice, and I let myself relax into its goodness.

David broke away first. Abruptly. Bringing his closed fist to his mouth, he coughed, his eyes darting from me to a spot behind me.

I furrowed my brow, confused by his strange actions then twisted to see what was behind me.

"Hey, Pierce," David said as I came eye-to-eye with Hudson.

The blood drained from my face. The hug had been innocent, but I knew what it must have looked like. And it didn't feel exactly innocent, not when David wanted more, and not when we'd sort of been together in the past. Especially since I'd never told Hudson about it.

Hudson's expression was stoic, his eyes piercing into mine. He gave nothing away and that terrified me. Not only because I couldn't read his reaction to what he'd witnessed, but because it meant he'd withdrawn further. With the way he'd left me, the circumstances of the last time we saw each other, he may have had the same blank expression if he hadn't just walked in on me hugging my boss.

"I'll, uh, let you guys have some privacy." Out of the corner of my eye, I saw David leave the office, shutting the door behind him. My focus never left the man in front of me.

Alone with Hudson, the tension became thicker. He looked as painfully beautiful as ever in a dark gray suit and a solid blue tie that made his eyes seem more blue than gray. He didn't speak, didn't move.

Just stared into me. Stared through me.

I swallowed hard, afraid I might cry. For more than a day I had longed to see him, had ached for him. Now that he was here, everything was all wrong.

"Hudson," I began, not knowing what to say next. Then I remembered the article. "I read about Plexis." I reached my hand out and took a step toward him. "I'm so sor—"

He cut me off. "What's going on with you and him?" His tone was even, controlled, but his right eye twitched.

"Nothing," I said on a heavy exhale. "David was, um,…" Yeah, where was I going with that? David was trying to get with me and I turned him down so we were hugging it out? "It was a friendly hug, that's all."

Hudson's jaw tensed. "The expression on his face was much more than friendly." He took a measured step toward me. "Have you fucked him?"

"No!"

His eyes narrowed, studying me. "But almost."

"No." Except that wasn't quite true. We had come pretty close to screwing in the past. Right there in that office, in fact. It didn't seem like a good time to bring that up, though. And all of that had been before Hudson.

"Why don't I believe you?"

"Because you have some serious trust issues." I felt a twinge of guilt knowing that his distrust might very well be because he sensed I was holding something back. Still, I didn't appreciate being drilled. And Hudson did have trust issues. "What is your fucking deal, anyway?"

He stepped toward me again. "I told you before," he growled. "I don't share."

A surge of euphoria pulsed through me. He still thought of me as his. I remembered when he'd said those words to me the first time, how it had turned me on to no end. The rawness of it, the primitive way he claimed me as his own.

Now, though, despite that it indicated I still had something to fight for with Hudson, the statement struck a nerve. "But I have to share you with Celia?"

"Goddammit, Alayna. How many times do I have to say it? There is nothing going on with me and Celia."

I felt uneasy about insinuating otherwise. I'd accused past lovers of cheating on me—many times—but it had always been paranoia on my part, doubtful that anyone could ever really love me. My accusations had ended relationships, and my stomach lurched at that possibility with Hudson.

Yet, he had secrets where Celia was concerned. That wasn't my mind playing tricks on me, he'd confirmed that much. He'd asked me to believe that those secrets weren't relevant to us, but if he wanted my trust, he had to give me his. "And there's nothing going on with me and David."

"Really?" His tone was icy. "That's not how it looked when I walked in here."

My vision blurred with tears. "Just like that's not how it looked when you left with Celia while I was still naked in your bed?"

Anger flashed in Hudson's eyes. He grabbed my upper arms and yanked me toward him until my face was only inches from his. "Leaving you that morning was the hardest fucking thing I've done in a long time," he hissed. "Don't treat it lightly."

Then his mouth crushed mine, before I could digest what he'd said, before I could let the sweetness of his words sink in. He nipped and tore at the tender skin of my lips with his teeth, his kiss abrasive and impatient.

My body begged to give into his demanding passion, his mouth and tongue coaxing me to bend to him, but my brain still held onto our disagreement and our whereabouts. Jesus, we were in the goddamn office of the nightclub!

I broke away from his lips. "Hudson, stop."

But he didn't stop. He continued kissing down my neck and his hand found my breast, which he squeezed and fondled roughly over the fabric of my dress. His cock pressed into me at my thigh, and I felt it stiffen.

"Stop!" I said again, pushing at his chest with both my hands.

"No," he rumbled in my ear. "I have to fuck you. Now."

"Why? Are you marking your territory?" I'd only been half serious with the comment, but he pulled back and the look in his eyes said that was exactly what he was doing.

I wriggled out of his grip, the nausea returning in painful waves. "You don't own me, Hudson! Stop messing with me like I'm one of your other women. *Not with me*, remember?"

"Don't you think I know that? Every minute of every day I remind myself that I can't conquer you. That I can't do that to you." His jaw twitched. "But it doesn't mean that I don't want to."

He might as well have struck me. Even though I'd told myself that it was possible that I was merely another on his list of women he'd played, I'd truly believed that I was different. The tears that had threatened earlier spilled freely. "So I am just like the others."

"No. You're not." His voice tightened. "I told you before. I don't want to hurt you more than I need to win you."

Sobbing now, I choked out, "You've already done both."

"Fuck!" His features were overcome with horror, as if I'd told him I'd killed his mother. Or maybe not his mother, but someone he was fond of.

He took a step backward, away from me. It was devastating, to be hurting so deeply, to see my pain echoed on his face through the torrents of my tears. I couldn't stand to feel like that, like I was losing him. I needed his comfort and to comfort him the only way I was sure that he would let me—I lunged for him, seizing his lips with mine.

It took only seconds for him to give in to me, and then he was the way I liked him most, dominating and in command. And I took the reverse role and gave myself over to him.

"Alayna," he growled. His hand found my breast again, and he kneaded the ache away as he devoured my mouth. He wrapped his other arm around me, drawing me to him so tightly I felt consumed from all sides. Even inside, the flames of lust licked intensely, my arousal immediately kindled by the welcome assault on my body.

"Hudson," I cried against his lips, not caring this time that we were in the middle of a fight or that the office door might not be locked. "I need you, too."

He'd known we'd needed this before when I'd pushed him away. He was such a perfect lover, understanding my body and its demands even better than I did. Submitting to him, everything became easy. I could forget for a moment what barriers lay in between us while he took me in the way where no barriers separated us at all.

Hudson moved my body backward until the couch bumped against the back of my calf, and a fleeting thought of, "Oh, yay; we're going to christen the couch!" passed through my mind when he let go of me to reach under my short A-line dress and pull my panties down below my knees. He pushed me back on the couch, spread my legs open and gathered the material of my dress up around my stomach, completely exposing my most private parts for him.

I felt beautiful like that—lying in wait for my lover who I knew would give and take as he pleased.

He gazed down at me, desire clouding his eyes as he undid his belt and lowered his pants only far enough to release his bulging cock from its prison. As fast as he moved, it seemed forever before he lowered himself on top of me, urging my legs further apart with his knees. Then he shoved into me with such force I gasped.

He pounded into me with driving thrusts, focused on his own need, his own desire for orgasm. But even through the fog of his own lust, he attended to me, his thumb pressing expertly on my clit, massaging me toward my own climax.

The act may have been primarily physical, but a deeper connection resulted from the joining of our bodies. Each stroke eased the sting of his earlier words, and I was certain that the motivation behind each deep lunge was to chase away his own torment, to release himself from the guilt of wounding me.

He didn't shower me with his usual sex words, but we were hardly quiet as I whimpered under him and he repeated my name over and over like a mantra, like a prayer. And then the sound turned guttural as he flexed into me, coming in me with such violent eruption that it spurred me to release with him on my own shaky cry, "Hudson!"

He collapsed onto me, his head buried in my neck where his warm breath against my skin felt soothing. I loved it there, buried beneath him, his cock still buried inside me, our precious bond so fragile it required this carnal connection. Hudson's breathing becoming even, and his body became lax until his weight pressed into me with sweet agony.

Just as I began to wonder if he'd fallen asleep he whispered, "I wanted to win you. But I didn't want to hurt you." His arm tightened around me. "That's the last thing I wanted."

I understood him completely. After destroying so many people, after ruining my relationship with my only living relative, it was hell to imagine hurting even one more person. It had kept me from becoming close to anyone for so long. But now, I was ready to move past that fear so that I could earn the reward of intimacy.

I stroked Hudson's hair. "That's part of relationships, H. People get hurt." I kissed his head. "But you can make it better, too."

He lifted his head to meet my eyes. "Tell me how."

Cupping his face in my hands, I rubbed my thumbs across his skin, rough from five o'clock shadow. "Let me in," I pleaded.

"Don't you see I already have?"

I closed my eyes, hoping to stop a fresh stream of tears. He had opened up, but only enough for me to slip the tip of my toes past the threshold of the door he kept so tightly closed. It was a big step for him. But it wasn't really letting me in. Everything he shared with me I had to pry from his lips. He hadn't given me his trust. It wasn't enough to build upon and if that was as far as the door was opening, we had no hope for a future.

I swallowed hard and opened my eyes, letting one teardrop escape. Wiping it away, I rolled out from underneath him and pulled my panties up as I stood.

Hudson sighed. Then I heard the sound of his zipper and, to my ears, it was a metaphor—putting himself away, shutting himself off. Again.

But when he stood, he wrapped his arms around me from behind. His voice rasped in my ear. "Why do you act like I'm running?"

"Because you shut me out. Isn't that the same as running?"

"What about you? What about how you showed up in our bedroom crying and couldn't even tell me why?"

"That was different." But maybe it wasn't. I hadn't told him what his mother said because it hurt too much. Because I was embarrassed.

He spun me around to look at him. "What did she say to you, Alayna?"

He'd thrown down the gauntlet. If I wanted him to be open, I'd have to be too. "That I was insignificant. She called me a whore." I looked at a chip of paint on the wall, not able to meet his eyes.

He cursed under his breath. "My mother's heartless and cruel." Putting two fingers under my chin, he turned my face to him. "You're not a whore, Alayna. Not even close. And the magnitude of your importance in my life can't be put into words."

"She also said that you can't ever love me."

He froze. Then his hand dropped from my face. "I've told you that before."

The pain of his statement hit me hard in the gut. I pulled out of his arms. "Well, she told me again." I swung back toward him. "So there, I opened up. Are you happy?"

"Alayna..."

I ached in the center of my being. This was why I hadn't told him—because despite what he and Sophia had said, I'd believed that he could love. That he could love me.

Tears flooded my eyes and splashed down my face. "How could you not think I'd fall in love with you, Hudson? Even if you didn't mean for it to happen, how could I not?" I wiped at my damp cheek with the back of my hand. "Does that mean anything to you at all?"

He drew back as if I'd slapped him. "How can you ask that? Of course, it does. But, Alayna, you don't know that you'd still say that if you knew me."

"I *do* know you."

"Not everything."

"Only because you haven't let me in!" We were spinning in circles, getting nowhere.

He spread his arms out to the sides. "What is it you want to know? About what I did to other women? About Celia? I'm the reason she got pregnant, Alayna. Because I spent an entire summer making her fall in love with me when I felt nothing for her. For fun. For something to do. And then, when I'd completely broken her, she became destructive—sleeping around, partying, drugs. You name it, she did it. She didn't even know who the father was."

I heaved a breath, wiping the lingering tears from my face. "So you claimed it was yours."

"Yes."

"Because you felt responsible."

"Yes. She lost the baby at three months. Likely from the drinking and drugs she'd consumed early on. She was devastated."

"That's awful." I could sense he felt as responsible for the death of Celia's unborn baby as for its conception in the first place. It was a lot of weight to carry, a lot of blame.

But even though I could concede Hudson had a role in the situation, it didn't scare me away. "It's awful," I repeated, "but I don't understand. You thought this would make me not love you…why?"

He perched on the arm of the sofa and pierced me with an incredulous stare. "Because it changes everything. I did that. That's who I am. It's my past and it's very ugly."

A sob threatened, but I choked it back with a hard swallow. The ugly things—there were so many ugly things about myself that always lay beneath the surface of every conversation, every moment. They poisoned and destroyed. I was well versed in the ugly.

It broke my heart that the same darkness haunted Hudson. That he believed his history to be so horrible that it could change things between us. It couldn't. It didn't.

I moved in front of him and rested my hands on his shoulders. "Do you think your ugly is any different than mine?"

"This isn't like following someone around or calling too many times, Alayna."

"It was an unforeseen tragedy, Hudson. A game that got out of hand. You didn't set out for Celia to get pregnant and have a miscarriage. And you can't diminish the things I've done to a simple statement like that either. I hurt people. Deeply. But that was before. Less than ideal pasts, remember? It doesn't mean it defines our future. Or even our now."

He blew out a warm breath as his thumb brushed at a lingering tear in the corner of my eye. "When I'm with you, I almost believe that."

"That just means you need to spend more time with me."

He chuckled softly. "Is that what that means?" He trailed his thumb down my face to caress my cheek. "Yesterday morning, when I got the phone call that required me to be in Cincinnati—I couldn't even let myself look at you, sleeping in that bed. If I did, I wouldn't have been able to leave."

My chest swelled with his confession. "I thought you left because you were freaking out." His puzzled look drove me to clarify. "Because of the love stuff."

"I wasn't freaking out. I was surprised, that's all."

"Surprised?"

"That that's what we were feeling." His gaze was soft. "That it was love."

I could barely breathe, afraid that if I did I'd disturb the path of our conversation. "It was." I swallowed. "It is."

"Hmm." He smiled. "I never felt this before. I didn't know." He swept his hands down the sides of my torso. "But, Alayna, I've never had a healthy romantic relationship. Every woman who's loved me…" His voice tightened. "I don't want to break you, too."

"You're not going to break me, Hudson. I thought you might, at first. Turns out you make me better. And I think I do the same for you."

"You do."

"If you decide to not…" I searched for how to say what I meant. "Follow through…with whatever this is that we have, it will hurt. But I won't be broken."

"But it would hurt?"

"Like a motherfucker."

"Then we better follow through." He drew me closer, wrapping his arms around my waist. "Alayna, you're fired. You can't be my pretend girlfriend anymore." His face grew serious. "Be my real girlfriend instead."

Joy swept through me in a dizzying rush. "I kind of think I already am."

"You are."

"Can I still call you H?"

"Absolutely not." He turned his mouth to meet mine and kissed me with lips sweet and tender, but passionate all the same.

I don't know how long we stayed there like that—on the arm of the chair, his body wrapped around me, kissing and cuddling. Time was irrelevant in that moment we were sharing.

Finally though, when I remembered that the club would be opening soon and that I still had a shift to work, I pulled my lips from his and asked the question that I knew was burning in both our minds. "What now?"

One side of Hudson's mouth curled up in a sexy smile. "Come to my place after you finish here."

Yes. Of course, yes! "I'm not off until three."

"I don't care. I want you in my bed."

"Then, yes."

With great reluctance, I pulled myself away. I offered my hand to help him up, and he took it, rising in the graceful way of his. He let go of my hand and tugged the back of his jacket down and adjusted his tie, transforming back into the man most people knew: Hudson Pierce, ruler of the business world.

I watched, mesmerized, still in shock that this man was mine. *Mine.* It was the first time I'd said it to myself, and it sounded so wonderful I thought I could never get tired of saying it—*mine, mine, mine.*

His eyes swept behind him as he buttoned his jacket. "Nice couch," he said, as if noticing it for the first time.

"Thanks," I laughed.

He studied me with amusement before fixing my hair and straightening the collar of my dress. Then he took my hands in his. "Tell

Jordan to take you to the Bowery. He knows where it is."

"Not the fuck pad?" My voice seemed unusually high, laced with surprise and excitement.

"No. My home. I'll leave a key with the doorman."

I hadn't been anywhere but the loft with him and didn't even know where he lived. I'd thought it was a good thing before. But now that he'd invited me, there was no other place I'd rather be.

And, besides, I was ready—ready to stop being afraid of making mistakes, ready to let myself be truly healed of my past, ready to start again without fear of regret.

Lacing my fingers through his, I giggled. Since when did I giggle? "We're really doing this, aren't we? Moving forward."

"We are."

He pulled me in for another embrace, seemingly as unable to let go of me as I was unable to let go of him. As fixed on me as I was on him.

"I'm going to rock your world," I said at his ear before sucking on the lobe.

He nipped at my neck, kindling my desire yet again. "I can't wait," he said.

"Neither can I."

HUDSON AND ALAYNA'S STORY CONTINUES IN THE SENSUAL SEQUEL

FOUND IN YOU

FIXED TRILOGY #2

AVAILABLE NOW!

Alayna Withers has only had one kind of relationship: the kind that makes her obsessive and stalker-crazy. Now that Hudson Pierce has let her into his heart, she's determined to break down the remaining walls between them so they can build a foundation that's based on more than just amazing sex. Except Hudson's not the only one with secrets.

With their pasts pulling them into a web of unfounded mistrust, Alayna turns to the one person who knows Hudson the best—Celia, the woman he almost married. Hoping for insight from someone who understands all sides of the story, Alayna forms a bond with Celia that goes too far—revealing things about Hudson that could end their love for good.

This is the first relationship where Alayna hasn't spiraled out of control. And she might lose Hudson anyway…

ACKNOWLEDGEMENTS

For as many times as I've composed these in my head, this task should be easy. Yet, as I sit here preparing to acknowledge the people who helped make *Fixed on You* a reality, I'm overwhelmed.

Deep breath and start somewhere.

First, a deep well of gratitude to my husband, who let me take the time to write and always missed me when I was in my book world, but never pressured me to return (almost never.) No matter who the main guy is, honey, it's always you.

To my children, who somehow managed to grow and thrive despite my frequent lack of attention. You are the lights of my life; thank you for letting Mommy be a person too.

To my mother, who has always encouraged me and is still proud despite the subject matter of my books.

To Bethany for the copyedits—you are truly a lifesaver—and for telling me, "That's not where this story begins." Also, for your editorial letters (I treasure them) and being an endless cheerleader, while still giving meaningful advice that always rang true. I'm glad I could bring some magic to your bath time.

To Sophia for my cover—it's exactly what I wanted. But also for much more. The motivation, the heart, the strength. You've taught me more about the publishing/writing world than anyone, and I can't begin to express my thanks. And yet I try: thank you, thank you, thank you.

To Robyn, for being the idea person in my life. Even though I often didn't take it, I always treasured your advice. You are brilliant. I mean, blow pops? GENIUS!

To Tristina: You are a surrogate parent to all my romances—none of them would ever be ready to send into the world without your wise input and dedication in reading each and every version. If anyone asks, Hudson is yours.

To Robyn, Jackie, and Lisa. Each of you added very different but beloved layers to this book. Thank you for giving my words the time.

To Alessa—your transparency and answering of my endless questions has been more than anyone could ever ask from another person. You are a goddess in my book.

To the WrAHM society—an adequate thank you to all of you amazing women would result in another book. And lots of alcohol. And dirty pictures. You girls are the support and friendship I've been looking for. Gen, thanks for creating this group—it's changed my life.

To Bob Diforio, my agent. Not many agents are on board with self-publishing. Thanks for being open-minded and supporting me in this decision.

To Julie and AToMR tours. You are worth so much more than you're paid. Thank you for helping get this book out there.

To Joe, my bestie. You lived through all the ups and downs and wallowing and celebrating and always had good advice and never let on how annoying I was. I owe you a drink. Or seven.

To my readers—though I don't know who you are as I'm writing this, I do know that *Fixed on You* is now in your hands and anything great that happens from here on out is all due to you.

To my Creator for the talent and the gifts that have been given to me. I am truly, truly blessed.

About the Author

With over 1.7 million books sold, Laurelin Paige is the NY Times, Wall Street Journal, and USA Today Bestselling Author of the Fixed Trilogy. She's a sucker for a good romance and gets giddy anytime there's kissing, much to the embarrassment of her three daughters. Her husband doesn't seem to complain, however. When she isn't reading or writing sexy stories, she's probably singing, watching Game of Thrones and the Walking Dead, or dreaming of Michael Fassbender. She's also a proud member of Mensa International though she doesn't do anything with the organization except use it as material for her bio.

The Fixed Universe
Fixed Series: *Fixed on You | Found in You | Forever with You | Hudson Fixed Forever*
Found Duet: *Free Me | Find Me*
Chandler (a spinoff novel)
Falling Under You (a spinoff novella)
Dirty Filthy Fix (a spinoff novella)
Slay Trilogy: *Slay One | Slay Two (fall 2019) | Slay Three (winter 2019)*

The Dirty Universe
Dirty Duet: *Dirty Filthy Rich Men | Dirty Filthy Rich Love*
Dirty Games Duet: *Dirty Sexy Player | Dirty Sexy Games*
Dirty Sweet Duet: *Sweet Liar | Sweet Fate (early 2019)*
Dirty Filthy Fix (a spinoff novella)

First and Last
First Touch | Last Kiss

Spark - short, steamy sparks of romance
One More Time
Ryder Brothers: *Close*
Want by Kayti McGee | More by JD Hawkins

Hollywood Heat
Sex Symbol | Star Struck

Written with Sierra Simone
Porn Star | Hot Cop

Written with Kayti McGee under the name Laurelin McGee
Miss Match | Love Struck | MisTaken | Holiday for Hire

CPSIA information can be obtained
at www.ICGtesting.com
Printed in the USA
BVHW070926040222
627991BV00004B/88